by
Nicholas
Roland

WHO
CAME
BY
NIGHT

New York
Chicago
San Francisco

HOLT,
RINEHART
and WINSTON

TO THE MEMORY OF
Grace de Mouilpied
WHO DWELT IN LOVE

ISBN: 0-03-091389-6
Library of Congress Catalog Card Number: 77-182751

First published in the United States, 1972
First Edition

PRINTED IN THE UNITED STATES OF AMERICA

FOREWORD

This is a work of fiction about a real person, 'a man of the Pharisees, named Nicodemus, a ruler of the Jews', who 'came to Jesus by night'. It is not intended to be a reconstruction of Gospel events. However, it is impossible to write such a book without making assumptions, and some explanation to the reader is therefore due.

Since any worthwhile explanation would be far too long for any Foreword, one has been placed at the end of this book.

Pharisaism will never be understood without a sense of humour.

I. ABRAHAMS *Studies in Pharisaism and the Gospels*

Many Pharisees served God faithfully, in genuine devotion, even with a gentle spirit. When the Gospels charge Pharisees with hypocrisy, this must be taken as prophetic speech, not as a scholarly appraisal of the entire movement, much less of every individual.

NEW CATHOLIC ENCYCLOPAEDIA

Jesus showed extreme reserve towards the title *Messiah. He actually considered the specific ideas connected with the title as Satanic temptations.*

O. CULLMANN *Christology of the New Testament*

What shall we say then? Is there injustice on God's part? By no means! . . , I ask then, has God rejected his people? By no means! . . . O the depth of the riches and wisdom and knowledge of God! How unsearchable are his judgments and how inscrutable his ways!

ST PAUL *Epistle to the Romans*

WHO CAME BY NIGHT

Part I

APRIL, AD 28

CHAPTER 1

'As you know, I do not take much interest in religion for its own sake,' said the High Priest. 'But, we have a law, and by that law she ought to die.'

'But it is abominable,' said his friend.

'But it is the Law.' Annas turned from the window. 'After all, it is not as if she was still a child. She was a woman, you say.'

'Yes, she was already past fourteen, and married twice.'

'One of these brother-in-law marriages, perhaps.'

'Yes, the first husband died soon after the wedding.'

'They always give trouble,' said Annas. 'It's bad luck on the husband's brother to have to do it, if he wants to marry someone else.'

'It is the Law,' said Nicodemus grimly.

'Yes, it is a pity, but it is the Law.'

*

The two friends stood by the upper window, whose outer wooden shutters and inner frame of some translucent material were opened wide. They might have been brothers, though not twins for Annas at fifty was eight years the older, and somewhere not far back they were related. The blood-aristocracy of Israel was small and mingled very readily with the other aristocracy, that of learning, especially when this, like the family of Nicodemus, had acquired another qualification, that of wealth.

Their resemblances were obvious: nose hooked, though with less than the fish-hook bend of the Syro-Phoenicians, rather prominent cheekbones, and under heavy eyebrows and long sloping forehead dark deep-set eyes with that settled look of utter self-confidence which—like many other things—helped to nourish enmities towards their race.

Nicodemus, following the fashion he had learned in Alexandria, was clean-shaven, apart from the curling side-locks. Annas would have liked to follow the modern civilised custom, but dared not, and preserved the full beard expected of a High Priest. Incongruously, Temple fashion imposed on him also the short-cropped Julian hairstyle of the Romans. In dress the two men were almost identical. Annas in private, and Nicodemus for all but ceremonial or religious purposes, shed the ankle-length gown and the fringed coat of the devout Hebrew. Fashion and comfort in dress had long ago triumphed in Jerusalem, first Greek and then Roman, and it was a short-sleeved white cotton tunic, knee-length, with sandals, which Annas and Nicodemus wore. Only their girdles differed. That of Nicodemus was white and unadorned, with a silver buckle. Annas, by an odd fancy, had his belt embroidered with flowers in the Temple colours, the colours of the rare and marvellous garments which the High Priest sometimes wore, blue and scarlet, purple and golden, on white.

They stood by the window in the tower of Annas' palace, taking in the view, most of the city and the whole of the Temple. They sniffed the air, and Annas congratulated himself, not for the first time and not silently. It was for this that he had transferred his residence to the extreme south-west corner of the city, away from the site opposite the western wall of the Temple exposed to the sickening stench of burning flesh from the Altar: transferred it too at vast personal expense not yet wholly recouped out of surcharges on the cost of sheep and bullocks sold for immolation on the same Altar of Burnt Sacrifice.

All the same, however pure, the east wind today was searing, unseasonably early this April, so soon after Passover. This was the wind before which the grass withered, the flower faded: it was the hot breath of the desert unloosed on the Land of

Israel a dozen times a year, recalling the dwellers in that land of milk and honey to their sense of the absolute.

This was also the wind, Annas reflected, which destroyed men's power of judgment, allowing common sense to be overcome by irritation, and brought the best of men to actions which they would afterwards regret.

'Your friends,' he said, 'have worked out all kinds of rules about the Sanhedrin meeting, such as not after the Evening Sacrifice, but it would be more sensible to forbid the passing of judgment whenever the wind is in the east.'

Nicodemus wondered whether to take this up. His friends: who were they? He knew what Annas meant, Annas the prince of the princes of Israel, elder of elders of the House of Zadok, Annas the arch-Sadducee, poking sly fun at those earnest and blinkered, learned and humble but proud of their learning, honourable, good and humourless creatures who called themselves the Separated, the Neighbours, Pharisees.

He decided to pass it over. 'Whether or not they ought, they haven't, and judgment has been passed. This morning they have condemned a young woman to death.'

'It is not the first time it has happened,' said Annas. 'The usual grounds, I suppose?'

'Yes.'

Annas was undisturbed. 'Death by stoning is not so bad as it sounds. Let us keep a sense of proportion. If it is properly carried out, the end is very quick.'

'But all the same, it is abominable,' repeated Nicodemus, raising his voice.

Annas was surprised. Nicodemus was showing himself emotional. After their years of friendship he would have expected something more rational. As it happens, I agree, thought Annas, but he did not say so. 'What matters,' he said, 'is that it was *necessary*. Have you any reason to suppose that the verdict was mistaken?'

'I was not sitting in this case,' said Nicodemus, 'but Samuel told me all about it. He was extremely distressed.'

'Then I suppose he voted in her favour,' said Annas.

'As a matter of fact he found her guilty,' said Nicodemus reluctantly. 'He broke down when he told me. It might have been one of his own daughters, he said.'

Samuel had come hastening and stumbling to the house of Nicodemus, a few minutes across the bridge, straight from the Sanhedrin Council House built into the western wall of the Temple overhanging the valley which divided it from the town. Rabbi Samuel had rushed to his friend Nicodemus, agonised in soul, late for the opening of his shoemaker's shop.

'Then, if Samuel voted against her, I suppose that all the other Pharisees did the same,' said Annas casually, beginning to smell a rat. He had the highest respect for the learning of the Pharisees and their motives, but none at all for their common sense.

'Yes, mostly,' said Nicodemus. 'Gamaliel however would have set her free.'

'Oh indeed!' said Annas, his interest now awakened. Gamaliel was about the only one he would have entrusted with a sum of money, knowing that he would neither lose it nor forget whose it was. The rest, good souls . . . He decided to probe further, not that it really mattered since the affair was either over or very soon would be, now.

'Who presided?'

'Caiaphas.'

Annas' son-in-law Joseph Caiaphas was not renowned for his character or his intelligence: if he had been, Annas would not have manoeuvred him into position as his titular successor, holder of the empty title of Israel's current 'High Priest'—a title empty so long as Annas himself stood in the background and all Israel looked to Annas still as *the* High Priest.

'Caiaphas no doubt had the best of reasons,' said Annas. 'He must have been supported by the Court.'

'Eighteen to five voted against her,' said Nicodemus. 'Only Gamaliel, two other Pharisees and two of your people would have set her free.' Far more than the necessary number against

14

her, thought Annas. Perhaps the verdict was right, after all. 'But what about the prisoner? Did she say nothing?'

Nicodemus explained. The proceedings were perfectly regular, and after the witnesses had spoken the woman confessed. Only, she said she thought it was her husband. It was dark, and her husband had been with her: he left the room because a neighbour kept knocking, and then—she supposed—came back.

'The man, she said, whoever it was, handled her just as *he* did, until it was too late to stop. That was her story, but it only counted against her. Even if the Court had believed her, Samuel said, no judge could accept a plea of *too late to stop*.'

But that is exactly what the Doctors of the Law will do, thought Annas, when they have sorted the matter out. It is just the sort of intellectual exercise which they delight in, all tied up with the inexhaustible subject of sin by inadvertence. Sin was sin, an offence against the Law of the Almighty, no matter whether the sinner knew he was sinning or not. Sinning deliberately, with a high hand, was the worst kind of sin, sin by presumption, and in grave matters it must be punished by death. The same sins, however, if committed in ignorance, also merited punishment, but the penalty was less.

Annas disliked the ingenuity of the Doctors, drawing fine distinctions of this sort. Yet, he must admit that it was necessary, for such was the nature of law. Also, he could understand the intellectual fascination: not purely intellectual either, in this particular field, mixed carnality and religion. Mentally, Annas could hear the Doctors already at work.

'If a woman is found with a man who is not her husband'—so it would one day be said—'there is no stage at which she is free, even if she acted in the first stage in error or under compulsion. If she sinned presumptuously at the first stage, Rabbi So-and-So teaches that she sinned presumptuously at all following stages. If she acted in error in the first stage, but her error then became known to her and she continued nevertheless in the following stage, does she incur the penalty for sin by presumption as Rabbi Such-and-Such maintains? Rabbi The-Other teaches that if she mistook the man for her husband in the first stage and did not discover the truth until the second stage, if she was unable to prevent the completion she is considered to have cohabited in error and neither under compulsion nor in presumption, and this is the opinion which the learned prefer.'

If Rabbi The-Other prevailed, as he no doubt would, being on the side of lenience, the penalty for such a woman taken in adultery would be to bring a lamb without blemish as a burnt-offering and not to have her breast split open with a heavy boulder dropped from a height.

But this lay far in the future. The Doctors would not deal with the problem of the Woman before they had finished with the difficulties of the Man, defining to a finger's breadth—a hair's breadth almost—the various stages and the length—if any—to which a man could go with a woman before incurring sanctions of the Law. All this, assuming the man was conscious and responsible for his actions, but sometimes—though conscious—he might not be fully responsible, for circumstances were conceivable in which he could act by compulsion or—perhaps more likely—by mistake. Or he might be partly asleep—half, or three-quarters? that was the question. In short, among frail masculine creatures, as the Doctors had reason to be aware, the threshold of responsibility often lay a good deal further back from the action than Father Moses had seemed to suppose, and all this required most detailed definition, after most careful thought.

Only then would come the turn of the Woman. Annas felt sure that in fifty or a hundred years' time this particular woman would have been let off. The Rabbis and the Doctors were not only indefatigable but generally trying to be kind, and to lighten some of the impracticable burdens imposed by Father Moses in his natural unawareness of the complexities of modern life.

Indeed, Annas himself owed to the greatest of the Doctors the foundation of his own substantial wealth. No Israelite, until quite recently, could safely lend money to another, since debts were cancelled every seventh year. Only a generation ago, however, Hillel, the greatest, mildest and most humble of moralists and teachers, had hit upon another part of Moses' Law to circumvent this Law of Moses, and now Annas like any other banker could invest his money safely without fear of the Sabbatical year.

Meanwhile he had to live in the present, unaided by the Doctors' future ingenuity and skill. And for the present, and possibly even in future, the important thing was not that the Doctors should be ingenious, or even charitable, but that they should recognise the facts.

Annas was beginning to think that they had not done so. He continued to question his friend. 'And what about the witnesses? What did they allege?'

'It was all in proper form. Two of them, friends of the husband, burst into the room. The man himself escaped, unfortunately.'

'It was indeed unfortunate. A most peculiar event. And the eye-witnesses, were they cross-examined?'

'So Samuel said. Their stories agreed in every detail.'

Annas stopped pacing, and drooped his head. 'It was conclusive,' said Nicodemus, 'but it is abominable.'

There was silence for a moment, and the two men stood together looking out of the window, half a mile across the roofs of the houses to the lofty gold-crowned sanctuary within the limestone wall.

Annas said slowly: 'It is abominable, because it is *not* conclusive. But now it is necessary, all the same.'

Nicodemus turned in amazement. 'Not conclusive? How can you say that?'

Annas said: 'It is only conjecture, but I am certain. Never repeat this, it is too late now, after the judgment. But two eye-

17

witnesses *never* agree in every detail, if they are genuine. Nor, in such a case, could there possibly be two eye-witnesses unless it had all been pre-arranged. And the woman could easily have been mistaken, if she had been misled.'

Nicodemus bowed his shoulders and turned away, concealing his shock and grief. If Annas was right, the husband had conspired with his family against his innocent wife, who had no-one else to protect her, for all the men of her family, according to Samuel, were dead. Worse, this had been done for no better reason than to save him from public reproach, the shame which fell on a son of the Law for refusing to marry his dead brother's childless wife.

Nicodemus had seen horrors enough in Alexandria, among the Gentiles, and heard of them in Rome: innocent maids ravished by the executioner and strangled to avenge the crime of their fathers, male infants stifled lest they should one day claim their father's throne. But this, in the heart of Israel, was even more sickening. For such deeds as this, the prophets had called down vengeance: thank Heaven, there were no more prophets, and Israel would be spared.

He straightened and turned vehemently to Annas: 'But if you are right the girl was innocent, and you stand there, High Priest of Israel, and say that nothing could be done.'

'I do not say it,' said Annas sadly, 'but it is the truth. It is the Law, and justice must be done.'

'Justice!' cried Nicodemus bitterly. 'What of justice for the murderers?'

'Do you mean the Court, or do you mean the false witnesses?'

'Never mind which: the point is that the girl was innocent.'

'Maybe, but this is not the first time that an innocent person has suffered. In this case, comfort yourself, her death is a worthy one, for she perishes for the nation. She dies to uphold the Law.'

Very soon, thought Annas to himself, it will be happening. Somewhere, on the edge of one of the low cliffs outside the city, the accusers will strip her and push her backwards, hoping she may break her neck, but if not they will lift a heavy boulder and drop it on her upturned bosom, and if that does not finish her . . . Oh, Lord!

'Well, it's a bad business,' said Annas, more cheerfully, 'but it will soon be over now. Unless they have to wait a long time for the agreement of the Romans.'

'According to Samuel,' said Nicodemus, 'they had no intention of waiting for any formality like that.'

Before he had finished speaking Annas was striking a gong, blow after blow till the captain of his guard stood there panting, two flights of stairs above the courtyard below.

'Take ten men,' said Annas rapidly, 'and intercept an execution party outside the Shushan Gate. Remove the prisoner, a woman, and bring her here. Inform the officers of the Court that it is an order from the Romans.'

He stopped and calculated rapidly. No doubt the Shushan Gate was the one to go for: the other execution points were under the eyes of the Romans, Golgotha visible from the Western Palace, the northern hill from the Antonia Fortress. But which route should the party take? If they went the most direct way through the city they must run for over half a mile northwards, parallel to the wall of the Western Palace, then another quarter-mile eastwards and over the bridge to the Royal Porch of the Temple, leave their belts and their weapons outside, and march decorously in a diagonal direction for almost another quarter-mile across the vast Outer Court, till they reached the Shushan Gate. Running was not a quick form of progress in the city, even for nimble Idumean mercenaries in the short Roman kilt, and leather soles were slippery on the steep steps of the streets. If however the party started in the opposite direction they would be outside the city walls in a few minutes, and from there they could drop down through the rubbish dumps and smouldering rubble in the Valley of Gehenna, and turn north up the Cedron Valley: it would be a little further in distance, and a steep descent and a steep climb after, but they could do it on horseback.

'Take horses,' he said, 'and go through the Gate of the Essenes, and round the walls.'

CHAPTER 2

The tension relaxed: the man of action had acted, rapidly and decisively. They could only await the result. There had been no chance to tell him, and Nicodemus decided it was now too late: all this military operation was unnecessary, because the prisoner had escaped.

Nicodemus had seen it happen. After his friend Samuel's emotional visit, and feeling sick at heart, he had wandered over to the Temple, across the broad viaduct. The Outer Court, the Mountain of the House as the Hebrews called it, was a world of its own, insulated by deep colonnades inside the gigantic surrounding walls. Nothing unusual was going forward. There was no sign, nor did Nicodemus expect one, of the trial's aftermath. Normally he made his way diagonally across the open courtyard to his usual place under the eastern colonnade, but today the hot east wind coupled with the sun was too much for him and he took advantage of the deep shadow under the triple-aisled southern colonnade. The Temple police and the stall-holders greeted him with their usual respect: on all such visits Nicodemus was the Rabbi Nakdemon, suitably dressed for the part. Here and there he stopped and listened: even the price of doves was going up again.

At the far end he turned left and continued in the shadow, for some two hundred yards. Then he sat on the stone bench built into the outer wall, his usual station and one much envied by the other Rabbis who wondered, as charitably as possible, why one of the best places in Solomon's Portico should be retained by a colleague whose activity, however charitably regarded, was rather less than full-time.

Nicodemus no longer gave regular instruction, but here from

time to time he would bring the son of some friend or acquaintance, visiting Jerusalem from Alexandria or Tarsus, Ephesus, Smyrna or Rome, distrustful of strange teachers and glad to be guided by someone with a reputation in the world of the Dispersion outside.

Here Nicodemus, on this occasion, intended only to sit. Tourists or pilgrims, Hebrew or Gentile, would not be many, for the Passover rush was over, and they would not disturb him, a middle-aged Rabbi absorbed apparently in contemplation of the sanctuary, the Temple proper, vast edifice within its own high-walled enclosure, set in the middle of the even vaster Court.

Then Nicodemus saw them: they must have been delayed. They had come out of a door on the other side of the courtyard, one of the access ports to the Sanhedrin's Council House. They were skirting the breast-high curtain-wall which fended Gentiles off, on pain of death, from the Temple proper. The girl was in the black mourning robes of any prisoner, her face unveiled, uncomprehending, disbelieving, despairing, the face of one abandoned by her God.

There were a dozen figures around her, two of them Levite police and another an officer of the Court, present only to ensure the observation of the rules. The expressions of the others were appalling. These were no instruments of a divine justice, sorrowful, pitying, they were as if possessed by demons, looking forward to a treat. Nicodemus had seen men turned into beasts at the amphitheatre which—once only—he had visited in Rome, and now he was seeing the same thing happening, under the walls of the Temple, the abode of the Living God.

They were making for the eastern, the Shushan Gate, outside which was a place of stoning. There, he knew, the wretched girl would first be stripped, and the rules of decency would not be regarded. Then, no matter whether she survived the ten-foot fall off the cliff-top, there she would lie exposed face upwards while the executioners dropped boulder after boulder upon her. Oh God of Israel, thought Nicodemus, who of Thy people is fit to be an executioner? Difficult enough to be a judge, but how impossible to be an executioner without meriting execution oneself. To stone, to burn alive, to strangle slowly—to be able to inflict these tortures on a human creature, one must enjoy it.

Then the thing happened. A figure detached itself from a group in the recess next to him, some fifty feet to the right, moved slowly across the limestone flags and out between the pillars, out across the broad band of shadow in the open court-yard, out into the sun. Nicodemus did not know him, but he knew of him: certainly there was something different about his dress, perhaps just the shade of blue in the tassels on his long outer coat, and an unusual pattern of the sandals.

He barred the way, it seemed, and the execution party halted. One of the officers came forward, the sun was full in his face and Nicodemus recognised him, a certain Isaac, Clerk of the Court, a decent enough man. Nicodemus heard too what Isaac was saying, but because the other's back was towards him he was not sure what the answer was. Isaac said '. . . and condemned according to the Law of Moses. Is it not lawful to do what the Law of Moses says?'

Some time after the half-heard answer, the man with his back to Nicodemus was bending down and tracing letters in the dust deposited by the desert wind in the stone-flagged court-yard, and the members of the execution party were walking slowly away. When only the girl was left, the figure straightened, and this time Nicodemus heard everything. Then, without turning round, the man moved off diagonally towards the main gateway, followed at a distance by some of his group. As for the girl, an extraordinary thing had happened. She had begun to run, not as if she was merely hurrying, but gliding, swerving and dipping, her arms outstretched in her black robes. She reminded Nicodemus of something: the victim in a Greek drama, doomed to flee but never to escape her doom. Then she had plunged down the ramp which led underground from the heart of the courtyard towards the lower city, southward, and Nicodemus had wondered, why the fear and despair?

Now, if Annas was right, Nicodemus thought he knew the answer: the girl was returning to the unspeakable vileness of her family, or rather her husband's, since none of her own family were left. Perhaps, after all, it would have been kinder to let them kill her.

There was none of this that he could now disclose to Annas, who had yet to arrive at the facts.

They sat while they were waiting. It was insufferably hot. The wind sucked shut the inner frame of the window and Nicodemus rose to open it. The window pane caught his attention, for it let light in although you could not see through it. The greenish material, streaked and pitted, was not unfamiliar, but he had never seen it used for this purpose. 'That is not a bad idea,' he said, admiring. 'Using glass!'

Complacently Annas said: 'I knew you would see the point immediately. There is a fortune, for both of us, in this.'

The mind of Nicodemus no longer ran on money, for he had long ago made enough, not in his lean homeland but in the huge fat emporium of Alexandria, where a huge fat Israelite community waxed ever fatter and more blooming, to the advantage not only of themselves but also of Egyptian, Greek and Roman. He had spent fifteen years there, in the papyrus business founded by his uncles: the Roman book-publishers, booming, had swallowed all they could produce. Then, leaving one-third of his fortune in the family business and another third invested in the profitable trade of Alexandrian shipping, Nicodemus had retired to Jerusalem with the remainder, now safely if unexcitingly lodged in a deposit account at the Temple Bank.

Nicodemus, thus, had enough to keep him in simple comfort in his simple palace, and he could afford to let his mind run on things that he enjoyed. Nevertheless, the smell of blood would not fail to attract the retired hunter, Annas knew. Annas was impatient, sometimes, with his friend for mixing up his priorities: everyone, in Annas' opinion, should stick to what he did best, and Nicodemus' strong point, Annas considered, was in

23

making money. It was a waste of talent for Nicodemus to potter about in Greek philosophy or the Hebrew religion. Although he did quite well, by all accounts, being well spoken of by good judges, and even qualifying quite creditably if surprisingly as a Teacher of the Law, Nicodemus, a first-rate business-man, was only a second-rate Rabbi.

Annas, therefore, explained his idea with hope and confidence. The pane of glass in front of them was Roman, a present from young Herod Antipas, a fanatic for anything new. For Antipas it had been only a curiosity: not so for Annas. As it stood, the thing was nothing. 'But,' said Annas, with his eyes shining, 'suppose you could see through it!' The thing was possible, though hard to imagine. Already, at the glassworks in Sidon, they were turning out clear bowls and vases, glass not murky but transparent, pale green, almost pure. 'They are Lebanese, thank God, those people,' said Annas. 'They will do anything for money.' Nicodemus, he reckoned, should go there and talk to them, make them experiment till they found out how to do it, produce a thin piece of glass, transparent, not curved but *flat*. Then, a monopoly trading arrangement. Expanded production facilities and sales network. Openings for investment of the Temple Treasure, and some personal funds of Annas, also of Nicodemus if he wished.

Israel, Nicodemus sometimes thought, was insufficiently appreciative of its High Priest's financial skill. The Temple Treasure had doubled in the twenty-odd years since Annas' first appointment, even allowing for the depredations of the Romans. Now, Annas had given fresh proof that his powers were unfaded. He had hit upon the ideal article of commerce, something which—when once it existed—would not only make everything else obsolete but create its own market. Talc and alabaster were too costly for any but rich men's houses. Lattices were a halfway measure. Wooden shutters covered the poor man's windows, but they were dark. Window-glass would naturally be sold at monopoly prices, but low enough for the mass-market: this was the beauty of the operation as Annas conceived it, for people would not simply put glass in their windows, they would make more windows in order to fill them with glass.

Annas led his friend to the window. The view was splendid but Annas, in his vision, saw it more splendid still.

From the tower which Annas had built especially for this purpose, the view was finer than from any other spot in Jerusalem save two: the foursquare Antonia Fortress towering north of the temple, and the less massive but far wider-spreading Palace on the city's western limit, both of them now in the hands of the occupying Power. The High Priest's palace, where Annas had rebuilt it, lay at the south-west corner and almost the highest point of the walled city, overtopped only by the Palace close by.

Nicodemus looked, and forgot why he was looking, breath taken as usual by the beauty of what he saw.

Jerusalem was built as a city that is compact together, built out of the rock on which it stood: stone rosy, cream and golden, melting into a tawny blur which changed colour with the movement of sun and shadow, season, cloud or rain. The least beautiful was the even light-coloured stone of the new Temple, conspicuous, gigantic, filling the view, but even this was weathering quickly and you could see the difference between the forty-year-old walls of the sanctuary and the barely finished upper courses of some of the outer walls.

Jerusalem was built in valleys and on slopes and hillocks. Hardly two buildings together stood on the same level, apart from the enormous artificial platform of the Temple, occupying the entire north-eastern quarter of the city. Dull, buildings of Jerusalem stone could never be, but the variations of level lent to the city a jewelled appearance, chunks of pale amber and rose-quartz strung on the narrow street-shadows, spread on the hills. Chunks they were, the houses, variations on the cube and the rectangle, turning for the most part blind faces to the street. Some were plain cubes and nothing else except for door and window, flat-roofed with wattle and mud, but most of these were in the lowest portion of the city, to the right of where Annas and Nicodemus stood.

Elsewhere the pattern was different, narrow blocks arranged around one or more courtyards, some red-tiled and sloping, some stone or mud-roofed and flat. The most substantial of these was Nicodemus' own dwelling, a large two-storied construction with many courtyards, about a third of a mile down the slope from the High Priest's palace. The rooms, as everywhere on the Greek or Roman pattern, faced inward to a portico or courtyard, and took their light only from a door, or a door and a small window. Nicodemus saw how his library could be transformed by window-glass. The vision of Annas was wider: he saw the whole city, with the Temple and the horrible dark rooms behind the Holy of Holies, including his own office, shimmering and glorious with glass.

'You will do it, then,' said Annas with satisfaction. 'And on the way to Sidon, will you take in Caesarea and see Pilate? I have a message.' He went to a chest in the corner, unlocked it with a small iron key from a pocket in his girdle, and took out a beaten silver model of the Antonia Fortress, a table ornament, inscribed at the base. It looked hollow, but Nicodemus almost dropped it. Annas laughed. 'The join is almost invisible, Alexandrian workmanship. The hinge is in the base.'

Nicodemus unfolded the outer shell cautiously. The hollow silver exterior was inscribed to the Praefect of Judaea, but the replica inside, solid gold, was evidently something personal to the holder of that office.

'Pilate was not due to leave till tomorrow,' said Annas, 'after his abominable Games, but he left yesterday in a hurry. Both he and his wife had fallen sick, according to a message from Festus.'

'What do you make of that young man?' Nicodemus asked curiously. 'Is he a friend?'

'No Roman is a friend, but the *Tribune* Festus might be useful.'

Annas underlined the title of the Roman garrison commander, because the Roman custom seemed to him faintly ridiculous, a mere youth, no matter how patrician, doing his turn of military service as commander of a thousand fighting troops on duty in one of the most turbulent, and certainly the most important, places in the world.

*

There were footsteps on the wooden stair. Annas turned eagerly, for he was worried, but these were soft, not made by hard military leather. The slave, the water-clock attendant, brought no message. He had only his duty to perform, reporting at regular intervals the time. Two hours before noon. Only half an hour to the meal: Nicodemus must stay, Annas said. There should be news by then.

They waited. Annas was anxious, Nicodemus not, for he already knew the result. Nicodemus was worried by another question. 'You would have let the woman die,' he said, 'provided that it did not annoy the Romans. Is it nothing to the High Priest that the prisoner is innocent?'

'Is it nothing to the priest at the Altar, that the lamb is unblemished?'

'You are answering one question with another,' said Nicodemus, smiling, 'as if you were a Rabbi yourself. Besides, you are evading the point.'

'As a member of the Sanhedrin yourself, you must know the answer,' said Annas. 'There is nothing that I could have done. I have no power to cancel or suspend the sentence of the Court properly constituted and conducted. I could not even ask for a postponement, for there is no new evidence, only my own conjecture based on your second-hand report.'

'I know the law,' said Nicodemus, 'but that is not the answer. You, in your position, could always impose delay. You could send for the officers of the execution party to see you immediately, naturally about something else.'

'Very well,' said Annas. 'What then? Re-open the enquiry, on

27

what ground?' Nicodemus did not answer, and he continued, 'On the ground that the rulers of Israel cannot be trusted to behave with common sense? Should I discredit the highest Court and Council of our nation in the eyes of the Romans? Should I discredit the Law?'

'And in the eyes of the Almighty? There is a law too for false witnesses: they shall receive the punishment in the place of the accused.'

'These witnesses have been found trustworthy, and sentence has been passed, according to the law. As for the truth, that is a different matter.' Annas had dropped his light manner and spoke slowly, seriously.

'Yet I cannot believe you are serious,' said Nicodemus. 'How can the truth discredit the Law?'

'I said *in the eyes of the Romans*,' said Annas. 'That is why I said before that if the woman dies she perishes for the nation, she dies to uphold the Law. Yes, if you like, I am in a sense guilty of the blood of the innocent, but that is a cross which rulers have to bear.'

He continued: 'Even you, my friend, do not understand the Romans. For twenty-two years I have fought them, and they can only be fought my way. Stand up for yourself, but give them no excuses. They have taken all we have except some of our jurisdiction, and they are looking for excuses to take more of that away.'

'And, to avoid giving excuses to the oppressors of Israel, you would sacrifice innocent blood?'

Annas answered, deliberately: 'I would.'

'Thank Heaven that it is not I who have to say it,' said Nicodemus.

'Pray God you never have to make these decisions. The business of a ruler is not agreeable.' Annas lightened his tone and smiled.

Nicodemus fell in with the change of mood. He looked at Annas admiringly. '*Thou* art the King of Israel,' he said.

Annas laughed with delight and clasped Nicodemus round the shoulders. 'Blessed be the Lord God of Israel who has brought Nicodemus back from exile to be a comfort to Israel's old High Priest.'

Not another soul in Jerusalem would have dared to say it or known how to say it: the hallowed phrase *King of Israel* with its overtones and undertones of salvation, used without irreverence although irreverently.

'And *you?*' Annas said. 'What are you, my friend?' He knew part of the answer. A highly civilised and educated man, Hebrew first but Greek only a short way after. What else? Blind spots, perhaps, slow and uncertain in matters requiring political judgment. Surely not a Pharisee, though on a minor point unsound. The resurrection! A foolish fancy excusable only on the score of inability to count. The simplest calculation would show it. Supposing the Kingdom of God—another recent invention—should ever really come about, and every son and daughter of Israel who had ever existed should rise up again, *where would they go?* The Land of Israel was the stock answer: stuff it with three hundred generations of Hebrews beginning with Adam, or, in case not all of them should qualify as righteous, say one hundred and fifty only, to be on the safe side. But this was absurd. The food and water problems would be insuperable, let alone housing, and the presence of the King himself would make it worse, raising and training large armies for the subjection of the Gentiles.—No, Nicodemus could never have thought this through to its logical conclusion. But that did not answer Annas' question: 'What are you, my friend?'

A retired man of business, more wealthy than most. Also a Rabbi, well-born unlike most. Age forty-two. Married, one son and four daughters. Nicodemus considered. He did not know the answer himself. Certainly not a Sadducee, one of Annas' party, the high-born worldly-wise.

'My friends,' he said, 'are of all parties, but mostly Pharisees, except yourself. My mother was one of you, and my father was a Pharisee. My wife's family is Pharisee of Pharisee. Myself, I have never been called upon to declare it, but in the last resort I suppose I should count as a Pharisee myself.'

Annas laughed. 'No, no, Nicodemus. If you have to declare yourself it will be something different. You are too civilised, you are one of us.'

Annas became dispirited. 'It looks as if we have failed. The Romans will take it very badly, much worse this time than the last.'

A year ago, only just after the Roman order, the Sanhedrin had condemned a man for sodomy, and stoned him the same morning without a word to the Romans. What made it worse, the man's partner had been a Roman. Then the Romans had hit where it hurt, in the pocket. They took money from the Temple and then, with unexpected cunning, used part of it to benefit the Temple, building an aqueduct for the water-supply, a reform long overdue. The infuriated beneficiaries had rioted, but the Romans only sent their own men disguised among the crowds, and armed them only with cudgels. The Romans, that time, had been very clever, and there had not been many deaths.

'But next time,' said Annas, 'the Romans will hit us harder, and that means that some of our people will hit them back.'

Annas broke off, his face compressed with painful recollection. 'You have not seen it, my friend; you were too young at the time to remember, but I was already eighteen. It was the end of the uprising, and I saw how Varus dealt with the sons of Israel who hit back. I counted them, all around the city, close up against the walls and clustered round the gates, so that you could not go in or out without threading your way between them, seeing them, hearing them, only a few feet from each. There was not enough wood, so the poor wretches had to wait their turn, several lots of them, a day or two for each, five hundred at a time.'

Nicodemus was silent. His life in Alexandria had been sheltered, but now he was back in the land of knives and cruci-fixion, where oppression fed on revolt, and revolt on oppression. What a land to have to rule!

'To save our people from the Romans I must save the Romans from our people,' said Annas. 'Do you envy me the task?'

CHAPTER 3

At last it was the answer. Annas could not wait: he moved to the door and flung it open at the sound of footsteps on the stair. 'Have you brought the prisoner?' he asked sharply, without waiting for the captain to enter and salute.

'No, Sir,' said the captain, puffing slightly to show that he had run. 'We were too late, because . . .' Annas interrupted him. 'Never mind the reason. You were too late. No fault of yours, Captain. How much too late?'

'Less than an hour, Sir, but no-one could tell me exactly.'

'Only an hour!' said Annas bitterly. 'Did you see any officers of the Court?'

'They had left with all the rest,' said the captain.

'That would be irregular,' said Annas. 'Who told you? They should wait to certify the end of the proceedings.'

'The proceedings themselves appear to have been irregular,' said the captain, answering point by point. 'They were not completed. I was told by two of the Temple police in the Court of the Temple. I entered through the Shushan Gate in search of information when I found no trace of the prisoner at the place of execution.'

'Then what has happened to the prisoner?' asked Annas.

'Nobody knows, Sir. I interrogated all the police on duty and the stall-holders. They all agreed that she had gone down in the direction of the lower city. Then I took a patrol down there and went all round Siloam. It would be only a lucky chance if we managed to arrest her, but you said it was an order from the Romans. That is why I am so late in returning.'

'Then she escaped?' asked Annas, unbelieving.

'She was released.'

'Who released her? Report everything which the eye-witnesses told you.'

'They said it happened like this, Sir. The execution party was advancing on a course parallel to the south wall of the Temple at a distance of about twenty-five paces from it, when it encountered an individual dressed in the usual costume of a Rabbi who had walked out from under Solomon's Porch. There was a conversation which none of my informants was able to catch. Then this person dressed as a Rabbi bent down as if to look for something he had dropped, and the members of the party all except the prisoner dispersed. Subsequently there was a short exchange of words between this person and the prisoner, who thereupon proceeded at the double towards the lower city.'

'Is that all?'

'That is all, Sir.'

'No information about this individual dressed as a Rabbi?'

'No, Sir, only that he does not come regularly, and is some-one new.'

*

'Never,' said Annas, 'have I said that with greater thankfulness over a cup of wine.' Normally, perhaps, he would not have bothered to say the Blessing at all, but in the presence of Nicodemus he would not wish to give offence.

'If I believed in the intervention of the Almighty in our affairs in particular, as opposed to the general,' Annas said, 'I would be tempted to see in this girl's escape the hand of Providence.'

'It sounds more like the hand of an individual dressed as a Rabbi,' said Nicodemus cautiously.

'Who could it be?' asked Annas.

'I think I know,' said Nicodemus. 'Gamaliel told me. He had been consulted by the Temple Administrator about a new applicant. Rabbi Jochanan died last month, and his seat in the colonnade was vacant.'

'But was the new man qualified?'

'Gamaliel thought he had better see him. He told me afterwards, a few minutes' talk was quite enough.'

'Rather short for an oral test, but anyone passed by Gamaliel is sure to be all right.'

'So,' said Nicodemus, 'Gamaliel recommended the Administrator to agree. If he is worth his place, Gamaliel said, he will keep it, and if he is not, he will not last.'

The new man, according to Gamaliel, had come from Galilee. Annas doubted it. 'There are no means of study there.'

'Not much, but a little,' said Nicodemus. 'Rabbi Eliezer in Cana takes classes. His name was given as a reference.'

'The reference,' said Annas, 'should be taken up.'

Annas considered that the new man had been sensible. 'He must have spoken pretty strongly to the execution party to get them to stop. I suppose he pointed out that we should get a tremendous crack from the Romans. There is nothing else he could have said.'

Nicodemus said nothing, and Annas continued, with growing admiration for the reconstructed conduct of today's saviour of Israel. 'Could you manage to make his acquaintance, find out more about him, his background, and his views? Galilean or not, he sounds interesting.'

Nicodemus promised.

'And have one thing in mind,' said Annas, 'while you are about it. Today's performance by the Court does not do us any credit. We need new blood. This man—what is his name?—'

'Jesus.'

'. . . seems to have character as well as common sense. Let me know if you think he would be worth grooming, for a seat in the Sanhedrin.'

*

33

Before Nicodemus took his leave he thought of another danger. 'People,' he said, 'will talk. If the girl had been killed, that would have been the end of it, but now she is free. People are going to discuss the rights and wrongs of it, and what if they hit upon the truth?'

'Oh, never worry about a thing of that sort,' said Annas cheerfully. 'I have often seen it happen, people lose interest almost at once. No,' he added with complete confidence, 'if one thing is certain it is that the whole thing will soon be forgotten. The story of the woman taken in adultery will never be heard of again.'

CHAPTER 4

'I am the Governor,' he thought. 'No, I am Caesar,' and then again: 'That is not all, I am deified.'

For one in such a special position it should have been easy, but he did not find it so. The power did not sit lightly on him, despite his rank, his fortune. He took it seriously, the word of life or death.

Pilate, he thought, had not behaved with credit: it was his wife, not he, who had fallen ill, and for her sake he had left the city abruptly, on the eve of the Games over which he would have presided, leaving the Commanding Officer, the Tribune Festus, to represent Rome instead.

'Yet who am I,' he thought, 'though I must do it, in the few moments before this rabble on the benches becomes impatient, while they still think that I am masterfully considering, who am I to decide whether the fallen vanquished is worthy of life or of death?'

Not much longer could the scene stay frozen, the prostrate figure with his left arm raised in plea for mercy, his small round buckler and his scimitar lying on the sand far from him, the victor raising his stumpy bloodstained sword and shaking his long shield at the baying benches, savouring their cheers and joining in their laughter.

'How do you think they split?' asked Festus.

'They are evenly divided, Sir,' said his adjutant, a veteran twice as old as himself. 'The ones with the sun in their eyes are mostly against him.'

'Ah!' said Festus, relieved, for now he had got what he wanted, the clue he so much needed because he had not been watching or, at least, had been thinking of something else. 'I am generally on the side of the Thracians, the shield is really too small to give them a proper chance.'

'Agreed, Sir,' said his companion.

Festus lifted his thumb.

*

The fallen gladiator had departed, on his own feet, saved by his own courage and the absent-mindedness of the Tribune.

The adjutant was becoming accustomed to the ways of his Commanding Officer, and wise enough to make the best of them. In almost twenty years of his line service, a Roman among the native auxiliaries of the east, many young patricians had been put over him for their six-month spell of service, but never for more than one tour. This one looked like staying longer: his appointment had already been extended twice, and the Governor seemed to think he was something special, moving him into the great Palace and out of the uncomfortable Fortress, setting him up as a sort of understudy of Pilate himself. So, since the Tribune was here to stay, his military education could not be neglected, and the adjutant felt that it lay within his line of duty to attend to this.

'I see you've paraded three-quarters of the garrison,' said Festus, wearily surveying the half-empty benches. 'A good move, that.'

'Thank you, Sir. Yes, it's a good lesson for the men,' said the adjutant. 'One show like this is worth a hundred hours of battle-practice. No matter how much you tell them they won't believe it till they see it done, one thrust in the right place with a short strong point is all that's wanted, take no notice of these wild chaps slashing at you with a fancy weapon, just take it on the shield, that's what it's for, get close in when he tires and that's the end of it.'

'Yes,' said Festus, 'luckily for the Roman army it's nearly always the right side who wins in the Games.' The adjutant, he thought, had missed the point. Parading the garrison was the only way to fill the seats. Herod must have been out of his mind to build a great amphitheatre in a place like this. How could a full house be expected? The natives boycotted shows of this sort, about the only thing in which they showed some sense. Then, except for other Jews, Jerusalem was right off the tourist track, too far from either Greece or Egypt.

A *bad* idea, these Games, thought Festus irritably, and especially in this heat. He could not have escaped them altogether, but if Pilate had been here he could have worn a cool military uniform: now, presiding, he must sweat inside fold on fold of a thick white woollen toga, in the furnace-like wind from the desert, suffering tortures more horrible than any awaiting the future items on the agenda. Festus called for the programme, to see how much longer he must endure.

The wind, strong enough to break the lashings of the canvas awnings, had overturned the white-painted signboard in front of the ground-floor presidential box, and they brought him a hastily written papyrus copy, two breadths only on its wooden roll but the wind was already tearing at its edges.

It was already half over, thank the gods, two pairs of mock-fights between Idumean lancers, and eight pairs with sharp weapons, presented by the world-famous gladiatorial troupe— so the legend ran—of Cassius Celsus, purveyor of combats between Samnites, Thracians, net-fighters, fish-helmets and pursuers, with their own kind or with each other, by appointment to the Praefect of Egypt, the Proconsul of Asia, the Legate of Syria, the Praefect of Judaea . . .

The last of the eight was over, and the garrison band was at work. Festus noticed something missing. 'What has happened to the trumpets?' he asked. 'I saw three men carried off, Sir,' the adjutant replied. 'One corner of the awning had got loose, and they were in the sun. Blowing is bad, in this heat.'

'If it is too late to get substitutes, see if the bandmaster can switch. Let them all have a blow in turn. We must have noise from the brass.'

This was a serious matter. Festus relied on the trumpets for the next part of the programme, they generally drowned the screams. He was all right as regards vision: he had long ago perfected the technique of not seeing while he seemed to be watching: you focused on something in front of your nose. The sounds however were more difficult, you could not unfocus your ears. It was a misfortune, this sensitivity, for it hampered him in his hobby: studying the natural world. You could learn a lot more from the behaviour of wild beasts than of men in the arena, for at least it was in *their* nature to conduct themselves like beasts.

Another half-hour, and the discomfort was increasing. It was only tolerable thanks to Paula: it was her foresight this morning, cotton is far too soft in this heat, she had said in the Palace, and sent a slave to stuff the seat-cushions with straw. The beast fighters had also been far from pleasing: the second to fight a lion had attempted a thoroughly shabby trick, pretending to be dead, and Festus was pleased when the lion tore off his head. Not a normal move by a lion, he reflected, but this one had been provoked considerably: they are magnanimous by nature, they normally just cuff you dead, and indeed if you are known to them, or a maiden and virtuous and ask them for mercy, they will sometimes let you off. Not so the leopard, though, this was where Festus had the horrors and where he needed the trumpets, the next item on the programme, execution by the beasts:

Twelve male and six female criminals, natives of the Praefec-ture of Judaea, together with twenty-four males and six females provided by kind permission of His Excellency the Legate of Syria. Despatch in twelve parties of four each by the celebrated troupe of

African leopards specially trained by Cadmus of Alexandria for all modes of work . . .

Among other things, thought Festus gloomily, that means we shall have to repay the loan from the Legate before the autumn Games in Beirut, and as he has certainly asked for repayment with interest we may have to collect an extra thirty-six evildoers in Judaea. It's no way to run a country: we shall have to divert our resources to bring in the small fry, non-politicals, or incorrigible slaves, instead of dealing with the ones who really matter, terrorists and brigands they may be but they're highly organised.

Let them get it over quickly! he thought, trumpets or no trumpets. But an air of disorganisation had descended on the arena: small terrified groups appeared from underground, wandered a little and then vanished. 'What is happening?' he asked irritably. 'Send for the Master of the Games.'

'It is the heat, Sir,' said the Master, miserably. 'It is quite wrong, so early in the year.'

'Can't you drive them on?' said Festus. 'Things will get worse, not better, and it doesn't help them if they have to wait.'

'It's not the prisoners, Sir, it's the animals. They are valuable, they have to be humoured. They get confused and do a mischief to each other if you bring them on in the wrong frame of mind.'

'Extraordinary!' said Festus. 'These are *African* leopards, I see. Surely they are used to the heat.'

'Apparently it's only a trade description, like British hunting-dogs. The best workers are bred for it specially, or else they are captured as cubs.'

'Convey my displeasure to the contractor, and inform him that until further notice he may not advertise his troupe as having performed before the Praefect of Judaea. In any case, they should have been billed to come on at the usual time, early in the morning, when it is cooler. And now, what do you propose?'

'I suggest a change in the programme. Instead of Despatch

38

by Wild Beasts we could have a show of Rolling Despatch without Mercy.'

In one way this was an attractive suggestion. Despatch of the prisoners by each other, in rotation, would be quicker, quieter and less messy than an operation by the beasts. However, Festus had already seen the course of greater advantage and determined on his action. The mental confusion of the beasts had already furnished him with a precious item for his notes on animal behaviour, but in addition to conferring this personal favour the defaulting leopards could be exploited to the benefit of the Government of Judaea. Reprieve of the prisoners would entail cancellation of Pilate's debt to the Legate: in consequence, the security forces of Judaea could get on with their proper job of dealing with the Zealots instead of picking up small fry offenders for the autumn Games in Beirut.

'No,' said Festus firmly, 'it would be improper to substitute such an item. I have no power to vary the sentence imposed on the prisoners by the Court. Since the sentence cannot be carried out at the present moment it must be postponed to a future occasion. Make an announcement: the Games are ended.'

✻

They were near the end of the two-mile journey back to the city. The chair, carried by eight Nubian bearers, was slow and jolting, but Festus would not spare the time to ride. It looked bad if he read in a carriage, let alone on horseback. In the shelter of the sedan-chair, curtained if necessary, you could do anything, even on occasion slip out of the stifling toga, but above all you could read. The leather pocket on the left below the window served as a travelling library, stuffed with papyrus rolls, works mostly on his special interest but more and more of late writings on the eastern provinces, Syria and Judaea, for this was going to be wanted if he fell in with Pilate's wishes.

On this occasion, however, he could not do much reading. The air was much too hot. Also, the pace was too brisk for his comfort, for this was a formal procession back to barracks, with his cavalry escort behind and ahead. At least, it was a better road back to the city, to the Antonia Fortress and the northern gate, more built up with all the new suburbs than the direct road to the Palace on the western outskirts. We must have this properly measured and charted, he thought, looking at the threads of new roads spreading outward like a fungus among the half-raised walls of newly enclosed gardens, there may not be much chance of regular siege-warfare but the ranges from Antonia must be accurately known.

It was not yet noon, and the shadow of the Fortress reached out to meet them, cliff and towers of stone. The round-arched gates were open and Festus entered the hollow square of the courtyard briefly, to drop all but a small party of his escort, then out again and round the outside of the walls for he would never show himself unnecessarily in the narrow and crowded streets of the walled city. That was one of the changes that Pilate had accepted. Treat them like bees, Festus had recommended, do not annoy them except for their honey, and except when taking it keep right out.

So Festus in his eight-man chair turned left outside the Fortress, and through the garden-suburb springing up outside the walls, through the arcaded streets that were the new markets, fish—from both Joppa and Galilee, he noted, at this season of the year, fruit—but there was nothing yet except from the hot and forward gardens at Jericho, vegetables, meat, spices and the rest, and in a side-street off the pottery market he noticed a familiar carriage. What is Paula doing at the slave-dealers', he wondered, she said nothing about it before I left.

CHAPTER 5

The air was still stifling but at least he did not have to wear a toga. He wore only a loin-cloth, and he need not wear even that. The night was advanced, and it was hours since Paula had left him. He could not sleep.

The flames of the lamp were steady: he tilted the sheet of papyrus towards the three-branched bronze lampstand on the wall above his desk.

'*Caius Porcius Festus,*' he read out softly, '*consul: augur: praefect of Egypt: praetorian commissioner with full consular power for the province of Asia: priest of the deified Emperor* ——' —the name had to be left blank for the present, for obvious reasons—'*curator of the bed and banks of the Tiber and the sewers of Rome: official of the Treasury of Saturn: praetor: tribune of the people: quaestor of the Emperor: military tribune in Judaea: author of works without number on the animal, vegetable and mineral species, also*'—why not?—'*the laws and wars of the Roman people: made gifts of two million sesterces for the foundation of a library, one million sesterces for the building of a school and five hundred thousand sesterces for the repair of the Temple of Jupiter: dedicated by the grateful citizens of his native city . . .*'

It sounded well, the inscription which he had just drafted, to be placed on the walls of his simple but impressive mausoleum, some forty or fifty years hence. It was subject to modification in detail, but the general outline was satisfactory.

The only problem was the beginning. Already he had wasted a year. By now, if he had done the normal thing and ended his short-service commission, he would have been back in Rome and on the threshold of a Senatorial career. His wealth was more than adequate, his connections were assured. Perhaps this was what made Pilate so anxious to keep him, apart from a certain flair which—without immodesty—he felt that on occasion he had shown. Pilate's own position was somewhat precarious: a country gentleman with barely the paltry financial qualification needed for the knightly class, unable even remotely to dream of a seat in the Senate, nobody's client but equally not protected by any great family, appointed only by favour of the Emperor's hated favourite. For such a man as Pilate, Festus reflected, a subordinate like Festus could be—if loyal—quite a catch.

But should he do it? Accept the position which Pilate seemed to have marked out for him, Pilate's eyes and ears in Jerusalem, adviser on native affairs, political counsellor in chief. Never mind about your so-called military duties, said Pilate, the second-in-command will take care of that: what I want is someone who knows about the people; I have to live down here on the coast in Caesarea and all I see is Greeks, Phoenicians, Romans, and I almost never even meet a Jew. It is quite true, thought Festus: if Pilate had known anything at all he would not have started off with that frightful blunder over the legionary standards, bringing them up here with what the Jews called their images, a frontal attack on the Jewish superstition, with no way out in the end except ignominious retreat.

Yet, if I accept, thought Festus, when does my life begin? If I stay here long enough I shall be fitted for nothing, except perhaps in thirty years to return here as Praefect of Judaea myself. Perhaps not even that, and nothing will be left of my funeral inscription except *Military Tribune in Judaea*. Perhaps, to fill up space, they would add *under Pontius Pilate*! What an epitaph! Nothing could be obscurer. Judaea is not much, but it is something, but *Pontius Pilate*! The day he leaves here he will be forgotten. No one will know his name.

He took a small sponge and wiped the lettering of his obituary: it left a smear. First-quality papyrus, he reflected, should not behave like that.

Now that his mind was off his future he returned to the present: perhaps he would once more try to sleep. He extinguished two of the three small bronze lamps and returned to the low bed at the far end of the long narrow chamber. There was no current of air, despite the open door. Herod's magnificence had not always extended to detail: a ventilation shaft in the bed-alcove would have been worth more than the roof mosaic. The sound-proofing is also defective, he thought, as the scream of a woman and a man's growling hit his ear. In fact, such a thing is intolerable in a Palace, long after midnight. He decided, something must be done.

Without rising, he struck a gong by the bedside. 'Shut the door,' he said to the attendant on duty. Perhaps that would be enough.

But it was no good. There was a long shallow slit in the wall towards the courtyard, just under the ceiling, and the sounds were coming through this. Festus rose angrily, slipped on a pair of sandals, put on his tunic over the loincloth and fastened the girdle while moving out to the ante-room. 'Fetch two of the guards and follow after me with torches,' he told the attendant. He waited until he saw them coming down the porticoes of the courtyard, and then turned left. There was no moon, nor any stars for the dust-laden east wind was still blowing, but there was light enough from the small squat oil-lamps placed in niches, shielded by plates of mica from the fountain-spray driven by the wind.

The source of the commotion could not be in this, one of the main private courtyards, but must lie in a small adjacent one reserved in Herod's time for guests of the second grade of importance, now used by only domestic staff.

They stepped out of the connecting tunnel and turned right towards a group of women under the arches, carelessly robed and screaming with ineffectual rage and anger, beating on a door. From inside there was a different kind of female screaming, and the roaring of a man become beast.

'Break it down,' Festus ordered. It was barred, but they did so, and Festus stepped inside.

It was a narrow room, not much broader than the length of the bed at one end, the only piece of furniture. The clay lamp from a niche in the wall opposite the door had just been broken: the wick still oil-soaked was giving up its last despairing flickers of light from the floor.

Festus paid little attention to a small black-robed figure reeling to the left of him, but he noticed a knife in her hand and she held it like a professional killer. He turned to the other actor, an almost naked Nubian, the colour of the darkness save that his arms were red. The man seemed almost demented, howling with rage and pain.

'Stop that noise,' said Festus, 'go back to your quarters and wait for the doctor. You will be informed of your punishment in the morning.'

What punishment would be appropriate? he wondered, the wretch has already had almost everything, a pity because he was one of the strongest bearers. Making unseemly noises at night, and exposing himself to injuries which might endanger his performance, this was less serious than other crimes for which he had already suffered, but he had been warned on the previous occasion that the next time would be the last.

This question, however, was quickly overtaken by another: the creature, out of its mind or not, turned wildly on Festus and hit him on the chest.

No harm was done, for Festus gave easily, and the swords of the guards were soon at the fellow's throat. But what to do with him? It looked as if there was nothing for it. He had already had the treadmill, the yoke, the branding, the lesser and the greater scourgings—what was there left?

There was no Court to throw the responsibility on to: the master must deal with the slave. For such an offence, after so many others, there was only one sentence, and although Festus was sorry to lose a good bearer he spoke it.

'Bind him, and in the morning he is to be scourged and afterwards led away.'

CHAPTER 6

'You are early, Paula,' he said, surprised even though he himself was late and the sun had already risen.

She only smiled, and agreed, evading the unspoken question, and this also surprised him, for her compliance was always her strength, her adjustment to every anticipated move of the other. Also, it seemed to him that there was strain in her features: last night as always she had seemed to him ageless but now there were lines in her olive, faintly pock-marked complexion. Paula was showing her age.

Also she was a little breathless, for she had followed Festus up the stairs. They were near the top of the tallest tower of the Palace, the highest spot in the city. Here Festus began his mornings, alone with his books and his secretaries, secure before descending at daybreak to his public offices a hundred feet below.

She sat down without asking, another sign of strain, for she was trespassing. The last time she had done this, he remembered, was at the same time in the morning, five years ago at the season of the grape-harvest, at his country house in the Tuscan mountains: she had looked at him in the same meditative way, as if she had overcome her own suffering and could bear anyone else's, not at all what one would expect from a woman in her position who obviously gave and derived such enjoyment. That time, it had been to inform him his father was dead, and before she left the room Festus had known that it was for this he had been waiting, and Paula had stepped without pausing into his own from his father's bed.

He pushed over to her, without speaking, his own untouched breakfast: she drank the milk but left the bread and honey, and he waited for her to speak.

'The girl,' she said. 'I am at fault and I had not told you. I was keeping it for this morning. She was a find, and very cheap.'

'You mean the one who has cost me an excellent bearer? Perhaps not so cheap. The fellow must have had his nose very close to the ground,' said Festus admiringly. 'He tracked her down at once.'

'These Nubians are like dogs with bitches,' said Paula, 'but this time he made a mistake.'

Festus sat invariably in front of the window which faced eastward. He liked the view over the Temple and clear to the Mount of Olives beyond. As a work of art the Temple was not in the same class as the Parthenon, nor even the Temple of Diana at Ephesus, but it was many times the size—an astonishing piece of Jewish presumption since they did not even have an image to put inside: however, Herod had had the good sense to copy Grecian models, so the whole thing looked all right.

Also, Festus did not like the view out of the other window, northwards, over a hillock outside the city walls.

'It should all have been over by now,' he said sombrely, 'but I see it is not.'

'No,' said Paula. 'He collapsed under the scourging, so the next thing had to be put off.'

Festus said nothing. He took no pleasure in conversation of this sort.

Paula continued. 'The culprit has asked if she may see you. Now, at once.'

Festus was astounded. A slave-girl whom he had never heard of. But, since it was Paula asking, he agreed.

*

Festus glanced at her only briefly, a half-sized black-clad shape, black eyes, black hair black-hooded, a fold of the cloak held across the lower part of her face. She pressed her back into a corner of the room and stood waiting. Paula, having fetched her up the stairs, also remained standing. Festus waited, looking at Paula, while they recovered their breath. Paula interpreted, for the dialect ran all the way up into Paula's home-country in the southern Lebanese mountains.

'She wishes first of all to thank you for having saved her.'

'There is nothing to thank me for,' said Festus. 'It was not on her account that I did it. The rules had been broken. Also, I wanted to sleep.'

'Let her go on thinking you did it to save her,' said Paula. 'Also, let us talk Latin. The natives know some Greek.'

'Well, it shows a good spirit on her part to be grateful,' said Festus, almost touched. 'She has made a good start.'

He made as if to dismiss her, but Paula stopped him. There was something else.

The creature, to the astonishment of Festus, had the audacity to plead for mercy, not for herself. Her attacker had already been scourged almost to extinction: let Festus remit the rest.

'Why should he not die?' asked Festus, reasonably. He was arguing with Paula, not the girl.

'She does not wish anyone to die on her account by cruci-fixion,' said Paula. 'Her father and all her brothers died like that.'

There was only one possible meaning: they were Zealots. Festus started in his chair. 'In the name of the gods, Paula,' he said vehemently, 'what nest of poison have you been delv-ing into? You must get rid of this she-scorpion at once.' He remembered a thing he had noticed, when he saw her last night, the knife expertly held and most expertly wielded. The dagger-men had evidently trained their sister, and done it very well.

'Oh no,' said Paula equably, smiling. 'This one will not sting, she is different. She has lost her own and she has been cast out by those who were left to her. She is something rare.'

'All right, Paula, keep her for the moment. But this request. Explain that the sentence cannot be commuted because the

Games are now over, and it would be too long to wait for the next, for death by the beasts.'

Paula said: 'The man deserves death, but you will lose nothing if you show mercy. Your household will respect you: they will see it as strength and not weakness.'

'Are you sure of that?' said Festus, doubting.

'I know how slaves feel in these matters,' said Paula. 'After all, I have been one myself.'

Festus saw her glance at the girl in the corner, solicitously, as she sometimes looked at him. I wonder if that is it, he thought sadly and with insight, the daughter that has always been denied her. Perhaps she does not know it herself.

'But what else is there for it, Paula? I will not send anyone to the mines, on principle. That is not mercy, only a slower death.'

'I do not know,' she answered submissively. 'If you cannot think of anything, then there is nothing to be done.'

Am I then to be considered lacking in imagination? thought Festus. Is there no safe way of showing mercy, to punish but allow escape from death?

'The time is running out,' said Paula sadly. 'I will explain to the girl that there is no other way.'

'No,' said Festus, finding the answer suddenly. 'There is another way. The man shall go to the beasts, but not for execution. He shall be sold to fight them. After this morning's Games the contractor has a vacancy in his troupe. He should pay a good price for a strong Nubian.'

He struck a gong; his Greek secretary entered and Festus dictated a message. Another thought, and he said to the secretary: 'Bring me the notes I extracted on leopards the other day.'

'I thought so,' he said, reading. 'Many kinds of leopard are repelled by spicy odours, and the inhabitants of countries infested with these animals are said to protect their children by rubbing them all over with garlic.' Still only doubtful, he thought, and confirmation is needed.

'Convey a message also to the contractor. A five per cent discount will be granted if he undertakes to apply this precautionary treatment before any future contest with a leopard, and to *report the result.*'

*

They were alone again. 'What is she, then?' he said to Paula, curious.

Paula was sitting again, by the northern window: nothing would now be happening on Golgotha today. Festus looked at her: outwardly nothing was different. The white cotton robe, long, shapeless, tucked and folded, bound with a gold-clasped girdle, was her usual morning wear, and her dark hair was dressed as always in the morning with a double tier and a back-binding. The lines of strain in her features had vanished, and she looked at him as always, mother and lover in one. Nothing had changed in their relationship, but something now was new. It did not occur to Festus to be jealous, and he thought it strange to be so curious about an inconsiderable being whom, till twenty-four hours earlier, neither of them knew.

Paula told him of the message from the merchant: an exceptional subject for disposal, and for very special reasons very cheap. The family had a reason for getting rid of her in a hurry, disgracing them by adultery, they said. Only, they had made it a condition that she should be sold secretly, and not to a Jew. The sale, by the Jewish Law, was illegal, though the title of the buyer would be sound.

Festus was unwelcoming. 'Just the thing to set the Jews a-buzz. I'd rather turn her loose in the street again.'

'She has nowhere to go,' said Paula, 'and her own people might kill her.'

'A pity,' said Festus, 'but not our affair.'

'As a matter of fact,' said Paula, 'I had thought of her for Pilate. His wife has always wanted one, ever since they stayed with the Legate of Syria in Antioch, *his* wife had such a good and clever Jewish serving-maid. And they are almost impossible

49

to come by, because the Jews are very strict, they'll almost never sell a girl-child even, and never when she's passed a maiden's age.'

As a presentation-piece for Pilate, the proposition looked different. Festus cared little for Pilate, but much for his good-will, and here was a cheap and easy way of putting Pilate in his debt. Paula had not, as he feared, been thoughtless. On the contrary, he told her, she had been very astute: only, the girl must be got off to Caesarea as fast as possible, before the Jews found out.

'She is quite untrained at present,' said Paula. 'Could we risk keeping her here a bit, to polish?'

'Well, yes, if it's only a week or two. Yes, that's a good idea. Pilate's wife will be much more grateful. Take her away and clean her and dress her properly, and teach her to speak.'

'They are very clean, this sort, and she can more or less speak already.'

'Oh yes, you said so, though how they know Greek I can't imagine.'

'They are quite intelligent,' said Paula, 'except in matters of religion.'

'Ah!' said Festus, as another advantage of keeping her struck him. 'They are very superstitious, these people, but what *is* their superstition? We don't know enough about it. Perhaps the girl could help.'

CHAPTER 7

They will not like that, thought Nicodemus, as the raven settled in a gap among the gilded spikes. If only they would allow skilled workmen, up on the roof of the Sanctuary, but they will not, and the priests must do it themselves, and of course they do not know how to, and the spikes are always coming loose.

Nicodemus sat in his usual place in the outer Court of the Temple, under the eastern colonnade, with the block of the Temple in front of him, in the midst of the wide and crowded space. The sixty-foot walls cut off the whole interior from the eye at ground-level, save for the topmost portion of the flat façade of the Sanctuary, more than double their height. Smoke, rising from the Altar far below in the inmost court, scattered in the east wind as it rose out of shelter, dimmed the glitter of the golden vine above the porch of the Sanctuary, hid the black intruder on the spike-studded roof. This was the slack midmorning time between the dawn and the afternoon sacrifices, and the smoke was only that of private offerings: priests were fewer in number in the courtyard round the Altar, and this was a favourable moment for raids on the offal.

They must do something soon, or the bird will foul the porch, perhaps even the Altar, thought Nicodemus, and as he watched a white-capped figure appeared above the rear edge of the flat roof, scaring the raven and tripping among the spikes in his long white garment, a hundred and fifty feet above the ground, replacing the fallen spike in its socket: no good at all, thought Nicodemus watching, they need fire up there, and pitch, and someone who knows how to use it. He wondered, should he raise it in the Sanhedrin? He could quote Solomon, whose own people were glad to be apprenticed to the Phoenician builders of his Temple. Also, Annas' people, impatient of fine religious scruples, would probably vote on his side. But he was not optimistic, the Pharisees would be against him. Allow some impure foot to tread above the Temple! The next thing is, he'll be bringing in a Gentile!

Nicodemus, from where he sat, could see the slabs set at intervals all round the curtain-wall of the Temple, rectangular inscriptions, some in Latin characters and some in Greek: no Gentile is to approach within this place, and whoever does so will be guilty of his own death which will follow.

There is no place for the Gentile near the Only God.

I suppose that is right, thought Nicodemus: at any rate, no-one can alter it.

His attention moved to the group which had been forming, down the line of the pillars, in the place adjoining his own. They were for the most part the usual young followers of a Rabbi, earnest beyond the point of seriousness, their beards half-grown. Mostly they squatted on the ground some distance in front of their teacher, and their brown coats made a pattern like rocks on the pale limestone flagging. A few stood further back, mingled with stragglers from the public curious to know what was happening or perhaps only cooling themselves in the shadow, away from the sun in the Court.

The question was coming from one of those standing, whom Nicodemus recognised, some sort of relation and a friend of his son Gorion. The Rabbi had evidently spoken before Nicodemus began attending, and now his audience was free to take him up.

The young man spoke: 'Rabbi, we know the heaviest of the heavy commandments, but what is the second?'

The Rabbi, it seemed, was not to be put on trial by a student, especially by one who did not belong to his own flock but was a stray, apparently, from that of his colleague Gamaliel. 'How many are the commandments of the Law?' the Rabbi asked.

'Six hundred and thirteen,' the youth replied correctly.

'And of these, how many are heavy ones?' the Rabbi pursued.

'The Masters differ.'

'And with which of the Masters do you agree, my son?'

Nothing that the Rabbi said could be unkind in intention, thought Nicodemus, but this might be considered a little unfair. The young man however parried, and Nicodemus recognised in him the true Rabbinical ore: another ten years and he might be up there teaching. 'I am a follower of Gamaliel, Rabbi, and shall I differ from my own Master?'

The Rabbi approved. 'Well said!' he exclaimed, and continued. 'And the heaviest of the heavy commandments, let me hear it from your lips.'

Without hesitation the young man intoned the opening words of Israel's prayer, said by every dutiful son of Israel twice each day: *Hear, O Israel, the Lord our God is one God, and thou shalt love the Lord thy God with all thine heart and with all thy soul and with all thy might.*

The Rabbi listened, as if with all his heart and with all his soul and with all his might, rapt but intent, as if looking for a new point of departure in himself. He took up where the young man left off, in an even reverent voice: *And the second commandment is like unto it: Thou shalt love thy neighbour as thyself.*

The sins of Israel must have been washed away, Nicodemus thought, for surely the Holy Spirit is speaking to us once more, through this man: nothing like this has been heard since the days of the prophets.

There was a murmur from the crowd. Something extraordinary had been said. A neglected word of Moses had been lifted out of its obscurity and placed side by side with the greatest of all commandments. The great Hillel, a generation ago, had fumbled after it but not quite got there. Now that it had been said it seemed eternal. A new jewel had been added— no, revealed, for the Law had been there from the beginning, before all worlds were created—in Israel's crown that day.

Only someone as bold as Nicodemus' young relative would have dared to continue: 'Rabbi, is there a third of the great commandments?'

For the space of a dozen breaths there was silence, and then, with a smile, the crushing answer: *The third of the great commandments is this: Thou shalt not take the mother-bird from her nest with her eggs or the nestlings.*

There was a longer pause, while the audience digested this even more extraordinary piece of teaching. The Rabbi had quoted what every schoolboy knew to be the lightest of the light commandments: how so could it be the third greatest of the great? Nicodemus saw it at once, professionally admiring the depth and the wit of the scholar, but surely the Rabbi would not leave the lesson unspoken, and nor he did.

'The least of the commandments is like the greatest, for if you do our Father's will in the least of all matters as in the greatest because you love to do his will, you will do his will also in all the rest.'

'Well said, friend Samuel!' Nicodemus cried aloud. 'Yours is the crown of the Law!' Then, glancing to his other side, down the long outer wall of the Temple colonnade to the seat of his other neighbour, just now vacant, Nicodemus added softly: 'Match that, if you can, Rabbi Jesus!'

'Rabbi,' the persistent young man was saying, 'is every Pharisee my neighbour?'

Nicodemus admired the skill but not the intellectual conceit of the question: the Pharisees called themselves 'the Neighbours'.

Samuel avoided the question. 'There are seven kinds of Pharisee, and six of them shall have no place in the Kingdom of Heaven.' Samuel took them one by one. 'Not the Pharisee who is a Pharisee for the pride of being a Pharisee. To what is the matter like? It is like water in a jug, for just as water does not keep fresh in vessels of gold or silver but only in earthenware, so does the Law keep only with a person who makes himself humble like an earthenware pot.'

Relentlessly, Samuel listed and dismissed them, all those who called themselves Pharisee out of love for the regard of man, or the regard of themselves, or anything but the pure and selfless love of God.

Passers-by in the Court, between the colonnade and the Temple, turned their steps: if a crowd was already listening, this was something not to be missed. Samuel stopped on the words '. . . do their works secretly for love of His Name.'

He had been speaking for nearly an hour now, Nicodemus reckoned, and would soon dismiss his class, for Samuel was punctilious in his working hours and always put in another couple of hours after noon, in his shoemaker's shop, before going to the bath.

The young questioner however continued. 'Rabbi, if there is no place in the Kingdom of Heaven for six kinds of Pharisee, to what place shall they go?'

Samuel once more gave an indirect answer.

'The ways of our Father in Heaven are more merciful than man's ways, for a man would seek the life of one who offended against him as man offends against God, but God provides food for even the serpent which he has cursed, and although he cursed the woman he lets all men run after her.'

Not a flicker of a smile! thought Nicodemus, only just able to keep his own features grave. These young prigs, the rising hope of Israel, that is their strength. Let them once start laughing at themselves as I sometimes do, the Rabbi Nakdemon, infected by the spirit of Greek and Roman, and the fanatic unwavering will of Jewry will be weakened. Smile, and perish! These were disagreeable thoughts, which he pushed from him.

'For to what is the matter like?' Samuel was again saying. 'It is like to the son of a king who said to his father: Give me my portion that I may go into a far country and make for myself a kingdom, for if I stay here it will be long before I enter into my own. And the king gave him his portion, and he went into a far country, but there he did not make himself a kingdom but wasted all his substance in riotous living, until he was forced to hire himself out as a labourer and ate the fodder of the cattle which he tended and slept with them in their stall. Then when the king heard of this he sent his steward with a new robe and servants to bring back his son, but the son sent back the steward saying: How can I return to my father, for I have brought dishonour on him and I am ashamed? Then the king sent once again, saying: My son, how can you be ashamed of returning when it is your father who asks you to return, and your father to whom you will be returning?'

Glorious, thought Nicodemus, truly this man is inspired.

Some of the hangers-on, also, were not without their comments. 'What king does he mean?' some woman was saying. 'Not one of those bad Herods, dearie,' another replied: 'the young ones wouldn't have listened, they'd know the old man only wanted them back again to chop off their heads.'

'Not a real king, then,' said the first, disappointed. 'Why does the Rabbi talk like that?'

'They all do,' said the other, 'I've often heard worse than that. The other Rabbi down there . . .' she pointed '. . . not him,' she said, passing over Nicodemus, 'but further where it's empty now, he's another of the same sort. Quite a crowd he has, the Rabbi Jesus. Try it one morning.'

'Not if it's just another Rabbi.'

'This one,' said the other, 'is different. He talks to women. You should see them in the crowd.'

*

Now, surely, Samuel would come down from the heights of Sinai, and make full speed for his shop. To give the impression that things were over, Nicodemus rose and made his way across the breadth of the colonnade and out into the Court. The hangers-on at the fringe of the audience began to follow his example, and fell to drifting off. No good: another questioner had started, and on Samuel's special subject, alas. Nicodemus sighed, retreating: no doubt all this was true and maybe some of it was necessary, but the time of men like Samuel could be better spent than that.

Samuel's thin voice followed him, diminishing across the wide reaches of the outer Temple courtyard, dwindling to nothing like ripples on the beach of the island that was the Temple, a tribute from one of His holiest and humblest adorers to the ineffable Presence that dwelt within those walls.

'The rule is to be interpreted leniently,' Samuel was saying. 'He who writes two letters does not desecrate the Sabbath if he does so in forgetfulness or inadvertently, nor if he does so in sand or in the dust of the road or with fruit-juice or with anything that does not make a permanent mark. In all such cases he is free of either extirpation or scourging, but is liable only to bring a sin-offering in accordance with the Law.'

56

CHAPTER 8

The shoemaker's head was bent, his small beaky nose pointed intently at a piece of cloth which he was pounding on a wooden block. Samuel barely looked up as Nicodemus entered, but returned his greeting. 'I am afraid I talked too much,' he said.

He seized another piece of dark-blue material, some cast-off rag, tore it into a rectangle and folded it many times over until it formed a multiple strip. He placed it flat on the block, on the ground in front of his low stool, and hammered at it with a metal weight. 'The customer is off tomorrow early,' said Samuel, 'and I promised it for today.'

'I thought you were only a cobbler,' said Nicodemus. 'Whatever is this?'

Samuel laughed delightedly, his dark eyes gleaming, leaned forward and tapped Nicodemus on the foot.

He does not mean it is a shoe, thought Nicodemus. This is only his way of saying you must go further. 'It is not a shoe,' said Nicodemus, 'but what is it?'

'What goes further than a shoe?' asked Samuel, and then, to help his stupid friend, he added: 'if you are going to the Temple.'

Sandals, not shoes, in the Temple.

Samuel explained. A customer, a tourist from Parthia, had brought his old pair, but it was past mending, so he wanted it copied. Samuel showed Nicodemus the hammered strips of cloth: edgewise they were iron-hard. He placed a bundle of them together, flat to flat, hammered them once more until they became solid, and trimmed the ends to shape with a knife. He took a thin iron spike, glowing, from the fire, and bored two holes right through them. He fitted several sections together: the sole, he said, and you pass these leather thongs right through

them, bring them over the top and add a cross-piece for streng-
thening. A new pair of sandals, and extremely cheap.

'What are you going to charge?' asked Nicodemus. Samuel
told him, and he was shocked. 'You have a family to support,
Samuel, you cannot sell things at what they cost. You should
charge as much as people will pay you. Samuel, this can make
you rich.'

Nicodemus had seen the possibilities. Leather-soled sandals
were not only expensive, for the ordinary person, but if hard
they were dangerous and if soft they were uncomfortable on the
steep and stony roads of the city. The cloth-soled sandal would
be cheaper and far better, the ideal footwear also on the polished
flagstones of the Temple.

'Make me a pair for myself,' said Nicodemus, 'to start with.
I will pay you one-half the price of leather sandals.'

'I will make them,' said Samuel, 'but the price is one-quarter.'

'One-half.'

'One-quarter. Nothing else would be right.'

Nicodemus knew it was no use arguing. Samuel always won,
when once he had made up his mind. The only chance was to
catch him before he had time to consider, before he could
categorise the problem into the framework of the lawful and
not-lawful, immutable basis for the yet more fixed division between the right and wrong. Even when Samuel had got to this
conclusion, you still did not know exactly where you were, for
he thought in terms of others' rights but his own duties, and
would never do a thing, however lawful, if it took something
away from somebody else. Nicodemus had only managed by
great guile to get him out of his old living quarters in the poor
part of the city, but Samuel had obstinately refused to move his
shop. They rely on me, down here in Siloam, he kept saying: the
rich up there where you live can pay good prices, but these will
go barefoot if they can't find someone to do it for very little,
like me.

So Nicodemus changed the subject. 'Dear friend, you were so

distressed the other morning, you must be glad to hear that the woman has escaped.'

Samuel already knew. He threw down his tools and raised his eyes and his hands in a gesture of mixed delight and anger, relief and indignation. 'If it was God's will that she should escape the lawful penalty, then I am glad,' he said, unable to stop himself smiling. 'But,' he added, furiously scowling, 'accursed are her people!'

The woman's family, he said, lived down here, in Siloam. One of Samuel's customers lived next door and had heard them talking. Then he told Samuel, knowing he was a judge.

'They decided, the husband's family, to *sell* her to the *Romans*.' Samuel spoke the two words as if each would despatch the erring clan to everlasting tribulation.

'Impossible!' said Nicodemus. 'It is forbidden.'

'It is forbidden,' said Samuel grimly, 'but they did it.'

Nicodemus was appalled and disgusted. 'She must be redeemed at once. I will do it myself,' he said, 'there is only one dealer who could have taken her, and I will go to him now and buy her back.' Rising, he asked himself: But what happens after? Who will look after the wretched creature? But that was only the second step: the first was imperative, redeem a daughter of Israel from bondage.

'They shall die for it!' said Samuel, choking.

He seized a section of sole and drove the red-hot spike right through it.

They were guilty, Samuel did not need to remind his fellow-judge Nicodemus, of the gravest and most unforgivable offence against the Almighty. They had not only broken His Law but shamed Him in the eyes of the Gentiles. Samuel spoke the words like a curse: '*They have profaned the Name.*'

*

The sun was not yet setting, but the low tower of the High Priest's dwelling cast a long shadow down the slope, across the reddened umber roofs and the tawny walls of the houses, towards the valley and the viaduct which spanned it, and the visitors pouring out of the main Temple gate beyond.

Nicodemus was enjoying himself thoroughly, exercised, sweated, boiled, cooled, scraped, refreshed. With a large beaker of wine in front of him, undiluted and unscented and unspiced, he sat while the shadows absorbed his own house in the distance and then the walls of the Temple. He felt not exactly at peace but uplifted, en-shelled to some degree against the surprises of that day.

'You keep yourself in good form,' he said to Annas. 'You skip like a boy in the gymnasium.'

'Well, I can still keep up with the younger ones,' said Annas complacently, 'such as you.'

It had made a lot of difference, Annas said, the new water-supply. A proper swimming-bath in the cold room. Also, running water in the privies. Annas had tapped the new aqueduct to the Temple, Pilate's ingenious contrivance for humiliating the Jews. Nicodemus could not see how Annas did it: the aqueduct ran well below the house.

'It only needs some labour,' said Annas. 'Only a fifty-foot lift.'

Only some labour, thought Nicodemus, how many slaves with buckets of water, to fill a swimming-bath and flush the High Priest's privies, up a fifty-foot lift? Even though Nicodemus had the money, he could not bring himself to do it, yet neither could he bring himself to disapprove of those who did.

Nicodemus was in no hurry to pass on the news he had come with. First they talked of the glassworks at Sidon, and his forthcoming trip. Calculations however must wait till tomorrow: after the age of forty the eyes could not manage figures by lamplight.

At last, reluctantly leaving the safe neutral ground of business, Nicodemus spoke of the woman. All day he had been making enquiries, and now he was certain. She was in the hands of the Romans.

Annas showed more interest than Nicodemus had expected.

'How was that? Did she run away and ask them for protection?'

'Not exactly. The family sold her.'

Annas chuckled. 'Brilliant! A most ingenious method of disposal. It would have been appalling to have her on their hands.'

'But it is unlawful!' said Nicodemus, shocked.

'Of course! But they can always pretend they did not know it. Nine-tenths of our people don't know the Law anyway,' said Annas, with mixed contempt and indulgence.

'They take care not to learn it,' said Nicodemus, 'so that they can break it.'

However, he said, it would not help the family in this case, for Samuel was already after their blood.

Annas foresaw trouble. If Samuel got a bone he would never let go of it, and trouble meant publicity, something always bad.

The first thing, in any case, was to get her back from the Romans. 'How can we?' said Nicodemus. 'She is up there in the Palace. Bought by a woman, the dealer said.'

'There in the Palace,' might mean anywhere in several acres, hundreds of rooms, a score of courtyards, three gigantic towers and dozens of smaller ones, but Annas pinpointed her at once.

'The Tribune Festus is not married. The woman who took the girl away must be the freedwoman called Paula. She is much older than Festus. Have you any idea whether the girl is good-looking?'

'The dealer said she looked too sad to be pretty.'

'That sounds hopeful,' said Annas, musing. 'She will not always be sad.'

'I do not see what her looks have to do with her bondage. The Law does not say that only ill-favoured women have to be redeemed.'

Annas was pacing slowly, his face radiant, serenely over-riding the incomprehension of his friend. 'If only it could be true!' he muttered. 'If the Lord had magnified his handmaiden, to be the salvation of his people Israel!'

No, salvation was too much to expect, the Romans were all-powerful, but at least it could be a lot of use. Annas had already tried it with Pilate, and failed, for Pilate's wife was too vigilant: the next best thing to Pilate however was the Tribune Festus.

Annas stopped pacing and stood in front of his friend. He took a great decision, sadly for it was costly. '*You* are the man. You are the one to do it. See Festus. Also, if possible, the girl. You must postpone your trip to Sidon.' He stopped, admiring his own public spirit, wistful at the receding prospect of making a fortune out of window-glass, beautiful and transparent.

'What!' exclaimed Nicodemus. 'You want me to *enter the Palace*!'

'I know, dear friend, but it is for Israel. The uncleanness lasts only till the evening.'

Nicodemus was ashamed to find that what mattered was what other people would be thinking. In Alexandria it had been different, more civilised, more tolerant, but Jerusalem ... ! The Rabbi Nakdemon consorts with the Romans, they would be saying, Samuel and his other colleagues on the Council. Worse, there was his son Gorion.

'If I do,' he asked, 'what is it that you want me to find out?'

'What chance there is—or, better still, do your best to arrange it—to plant this woman where she will be most useful.'

Nicodemus was wilfully stupid. He did not wish to understand.

Annas continued, explaining as if for an idiot. 'Where *any* girl would be most useful. Straight into Festus' bed.'

'Do you not think she might detect a certain inconsistency? After all, for *that* she was condemned to death.'

'That was the Law,' said Annas, 'but this is important for Israel. Let her know, if you can, that her sin will be forgiven her. The High Priest says so, you can tell her that.'

'If I could even see her, which is not likely,' said Nicodemus, 'I could not possibly say that.'

'No, no, of course not!' said Annas. 'But you have experience. Everything hypothetical. Extreme sorrow at her captivity, but she shares the lot of many illustrious daughters of Israel in the past. Then console her: if the worst should unfortunately happen, there are compensations. Tell her—by the way, what is her name?'

'It is Esther.'

Annas was delighted. 'It is a sign. Lead round to the story of the other Esther, she must know it already.'

'The other Esther *married* King Xerxes.'

'Only because she was the concubine who pleased him best.' Annas was impatient with this quibbling. 'Anyway, she saved her whole people from slaughter.'

'Any other edifying stories about daughters of Israel?'

'I think just stick to Esther. Keep off Judith. We do not want any misunderstanding, striking off the head of our modern Holofernes, or anything like that.'

*

Samuel was delighted to hear of Nicodemus' errand, even though a Rabbi would have to set foot within Gentile walls: the angels would weep at this, but less than they would rejoice at the redemption of a daughter of Israel from bondage, even one so recently condemned to death by Samuel himself.

'God bless you, dear friend,' he said to Nicodemus, 'and bring her back safely.' Samuel was much affected at the thought. The lost one would be restored to her own people. Also, although she was no use as a witness, being only a woman, her return would make things much hotter for her family, whom Samuel intended to destroy.

As Nicodemus was leaving, Samuel pulled him back and pressed some coins into his hand. 'It is not much,' he said, 'but if ready cash is needed, use it.'

It was the day's takings, and tomorrow Samuel would go hungry. To refuse it was out of the question, and Nicodemus almost wept.

CHAPTER 9

'I am sure you are right, Paula,' said Festus, 'and they do not keep a pig in there. But if there is a misunderstanding it is their own fault entirely, for keeping people out.'

After the débâcle over the 'idolatrous' legionary standards, Festus had suggested and Pilate had commissioned a study of the Jewish superstition, but work on this, for lack of reliable material, had hardly yet begun. Paula, unfortunately, was less help than might have been expected. Her forbears in the Iturean country on the borders of Galilee and Lebanon had indeed bowed to the sword of the Maccabees and Jehovah, but her people always reverted at the first opportunity to their ancestral worship, one or another of the numerous Phoenician Baals who, in addition to being more homely than Jehovah, were easily convertible into one or another of the Greek and Roman pantheon, whereas the Jewish god was notoriously intractable and useless for international purposes, not being convertible at any rate of exchange into any other deity at all.

But what was the god of the Jewish superstition? No one exactly knew. Strabo had published something, but how far could you rely on the judgment of a scholar who also asserted that the surface of the Dead Sea was hilly? Strabo had spoken well of the priest Moses, who attacked his fellow-Egyptians for depicting God as an image. Later, however, according to Strabo, the Israelites started going downhill and became very superstitious.

The Jews did not keep an image in their temple, that was certain, but they might be worshipping, secretly, something else. Not that a reasonable man would regard this as likely, but their behaviour was suspicious. If anything at all inhabited the shrine of their temple, it was certainly mobile, probably small, and possibly living, for it had got away or been hidden by the custodians before Pompey could see it, when he forced his way inside. Then, before that, the Jews had been bitterly offended when that Greek fool Antiochus had sacrificed pigs on their altar. Putting all this together with the fact that the Jews held pig-flesh forbidden, it was easy to understand, said Festus, why so many people concluded that the holy place of the Hebrews housed a pig.

But, said Festus to Paula, we lack evidence. What we need is exact observation, personal if possible, but otherwise a reliable second-hand account from a witness. Failing that, the unbiased views of a member of the community are a lot more useful than the speculations of people like ourselves.

Paula knew that her role was that of a chopping-block in this kind of discussion. The Jewish girl, she reminded Festus, had not yet gone to Caesarea. The delay disturbed Festus, and he asked the reason.

'She is much too gloomy. She hasn't got over the shock. She walks and speaks and hears but she does not show feelings. She does not run or smile or weep.'

'She must realise it's her duty to be cheerful, or else she won't be fit to give away.'

'Since she's here, would you like to ask her questions?'

'Is she reliable, impartial, do you think?'

'No woman is impartial, in your sense, but she is truthful. She will tell you anything you ask her, because she does not care.'

*

The sun would soon be up now, behind the Mount of Olives, full in Festus' face, and he turned his chair to avoid it. Paula remained standing in a corner, while the Greek secretary seated himself at a table and unfolded his tablets of wax. 'This is long enough for pen and ink,' said Festus, and the secretary prepared it. 'Write,' said Festus, 'Subject: the Jewish superstition.

Information given by a female slave of Jewish origin named—what was her name, Paula?'

'It is Esther,' Paula said. Festus had asked her to stay while he dictated. She had interpreted, last night.

'Named Esther. The informant recited what appeared to be lessons taught to Jewish children and learned by heart, the truth of which she admitted she had no means of verifying.' He broke off. 'Is that right, Paula?'

'Yes, though she did not use those words.'

'The informant stated that the god of the Jews spoke to the leader of their people, Moses, on a mountain which according to her description lies in a south-easterly direction from Alexandria, forbidding the Jews to worship any other god except himself. However, since this appears to have been at a time prior to the foundation of the city of Rome, the informant was unable to state positively that the gods of the Romans were not included. Furthermore, she said, the god of the Jews had forbidden the making of images, of either himself or any other god, and threatened to punish the children of anyone who did so.'

Festus broke off, and added: 'Note, contrast inferior statement by Strabo.' To Paula, pleased with himself he said: 'A pity Strabo is dead. I'd like to tell him.'

He continued to dictate. 'Furthermore the Jewish god stated on the same occasion that he had personally created not only the earth but the sun and the moon and the stars, and that because he had completed this not inconsiderable labour in the space of six days and then rested for one day, everyone else should follow his example and observe each seventh day as a day of rest.'

He waited for the shorthand to catch up, and continued. 'Informant further stated that the Jewish god had forbidden a number of actions which need not be itemised in detail since they are reprobated by almost every tribe and people.'

'Including adultery,' said Paula. 'She was not likely to forget that.'

Festus continued: 'When questioned about the forms in

66

which the Jewish god showed himself, she said that she had never been told anything about that, except that he lived at one time in a sort of small portable temple as an exceedingly bright light totally concealed in an impenetrable cloud. She was unable to give any explanation of how this could be observed. Is that right, Paula?'

'What she said was: "I do not know". It seemed a sensible remark.'

'It comes to the same thing,' said Festus. He continued dictating. 'When asked whether the god lived at present in the Jewish temple she answered that he was generally supposed to do so, but she then recited an address reputedly made by a Jewish king to his god after the building of an earlier temple. The language of this seems sufficiently extraordinary to be recorded, since in some ways it resembles though it does not come up to the best thought of the philosophers. Reportedly, the Jewish king Solomon said: *Can you, O God, really dwell upon the earth? If the heavens and the heavens that are above the heavens cannot contain you, how much less this house which I have built for you here!* She appeared to be unaware,' Festus continued, dictating, 'that this cast doubt upon the validity of much else that she had been saying. Is that right, Paula?'

'She said, these things are beyond understanding. It seemed a sensible remark.'

'Not to a philosopher, Paula. But we must hurry.' Festus continued: 'Finally, she was asked, since nobody could give any reliable information on the subject, how she personally would picture the god. She replied that she hoped he would look like the kind gentleman who saved her from being executed. Is that right, Paula? It shows that the poor girl really has no ideas in her head.'

'It is what she said,' replied Paula. 'But it seemed to me a sensible remark.'

*

Festus had been enveloped in his toga, too impatient to allow of faultless draping by the slave. One of the advantages of life in the provinces, except on rare occasions, was escape from the tyranny of this unspeakable garment, huge and hot white woollen blanket, imposing gravity on the wearer who, if he moved without dignity and attention, could easily fall on his face.

This was one of those rare occasions, a first encounter, in an official residence, with a native dignitary. Festus was not sure of the reason for the visit. In any other province it would have been simple: prominent members of the native community called as a matter of course to pay their respects. In Jerusalem however things were different. The Jews would appear when summoned or—as far more often—when they had some impossible petition to present, but they would stand in the courtyard to finish their business and then they would go.

Nicodemus had remained standing, waiting for the Tribune Festus to appear. The reception hall was one of Herod's more showy constructions, two storeys high to the painted ceiling, and as long as one courtyard was wide. Nicodemus remembered it from his last visit, twenty-four years ago, before he left for Alexandria and before the Romans swallowed up Judaea. The marble pillars seemed to him no less marvellous, more so indeed, for now he realised what had gone into them, each one was different, twenty-four quarries laid under toll by the old Herod, in every quarter of the Roman world from the Atlantic to the Euphrates, greens and olives, browns and purples and, flanking the spot where Herod himself had held court—throne recessed into an alcove for protection against the treachery which he dreaded—two pillars of Verona marble, yellow-gold.

Festus seated himself between the golden pillars, at an angle. He and Nicodemus half-faced each other, on chairs which Nicodemus also remembered and now recognised, citrus wood brought from the Atlas mountains, carved and inlaid with ivory in Alexandria. A Syrian interpreter stood behind them, but Festus dismissed him as soon as Nicodemus began to speak.

This was the first surprise. Festus found himself talking not

68

as he had feared to a Jewish fanatic but to an Alexandrian gentleman, as cultured as a Greek, more urbane than a Roman, albeit in fancy dress. The ankle-length gown and barely shorter overcoat, and the rolled headdress, were less suited to the Palace than the Temple: Festus observed them from his window in the tower every day. The gold borders of the white coat however were something different, perhaps some badge of office. Festus decided to ask.

Nicodemus, misunderstanding, began to explain the fringes and the tassels, mementoes of the commandments ever to be worn according to the Law. Commandments, and the law, thought Festus, interesting, especially after what the girl was saying last night, but at this stage of our acquaintance I had better not press things: this is an honoured visitor and not a slave 'And the golden borders?' he asked.

They signified, Nicodemus said, a certain standing in matters of the Law. He himself bore the title of Rab, or Rabbi. 'A Master who teaches, that is all. As a matter of fact, I do not do much teaching.'

A teacher who does not spend time teaching, but is well qualified: Festus wondered whether, and how soon, he would dare to start working this rich mine. The gods, if they existed, had heard his prayer, if he had made one. Sitting in front of Festus was the informant of his dreams. For the time being, however, he must be cautious.

Nicodemus, he learned, during his years in Alexandria had not only prospered. He had gone on with his Law studies, and taken up with the philosophers as well. A man of two careers, therefore, just like Festus, or what Festus had been proposing for himself: Festus the natural philosopher, writer, historian, as well as Festus the Senator and Proconsul.

Learning that Nicodemus had made his money in papyrus, Festus summoned a secretary and showed Nicodemus a piece. The small sheet, little wider than the palm of a hand, showed smears and marks of ink lodged in crevices. This was serious: the material was costly unless it could be sponged and used two or three times over, and Festus' consumption was enormous.

Nicodemus fingered it doubtfully. 'How do you get it?' he asked.

'It comes in my monthly book-parcel from Rome. The bookseller calls it "Augusta".' The highest grade there was.

'You are being cheated,' said Nicodemus. 'This is "Hieratica".' Two grades worse. He asked what Festus paid, and the answer shocked him. 'I can arrange for you to get the best quality direct from the Lower Nile factory at wholesale prices, plus the cost of packing and transport. It would cost you something like three-quarters of what you are now paying for a third-rate product.'

Festus admired the sense of it. His visitor had deliberately, and wisely, passed over the perfect opening for a bribe. The faintest hint of a special favour, failure to mention a price, or the mention of only a low one, would have put them both in a difficult position. Nicodemus had done him a good turn, but nothing out of the ordinary, and nothing which could not in due course be repaid with equal straightforwardness and lack of meaning.

The opportunity was not long in coming. Nicodemus was perfectly direct and open.

'I have a question to ask, if you will allow me. It is about a woman of our race who has come into Your Excellency's household. This is a case where the laws of the Romans and the Law of our people differ. Where they conflict, the law of the Romans is stronger, for Rome is the master in Judaea.'

This was a good line for Nicodemus to take, Festus decided, not one which would be usual among the natives.

Nicodemus continued: 'Nevertheless, where the laws of the Romans and the Law of the Jews conflict, the Romans may sometimes decide to give way, in their wisdom. The woman Esther has been bought, quite lawfully, for Your Excellency's household. But it was unlawful for her to be sold by a Hebrew. Our Law obliges us to seek her redemption. Whatever the price paid for her, we would match it, or we would supply in her stead a foreign worker of equal value.'

Festus considered. The secret was out much sooner than he had expected, before the girl had been got away to Caesarea. The Jews being what they were, trouble could be expected if he refused to release her, while if he let her go the Jews would (or *should*, for they were not notoriously grateful people) place it to the Roman credit. However, Festus would lose a useful source of local information, as well as a valuable presentation piece for Pilate.

Festus said to Nicodemus: 'Will you excuse me while I consult other members of my household?'

*

Nicodemus, left alone in the vast reception hall, shuffled his feet on the piece of matting: it shifted, and disclosed tiling. He looked and saw the god Bacchus, rolling and rioting with the other little-clad revellers over the mosaic floor.

Herod, King of the Jews, Jew not by race but by adoption, arch-breaker of the Law of the Jews and arch-builder of the Jewish Temple, had admitted effigies of the heathen gods inside his own palace, and the Romans had covered up an image which, if installed by Pilate, would have led to a revolt. Simultaneous opposites, reflected Nicodemus, is that our Jewish people? What am I doing at this moment except two things which contradict each other? Or, rather, I do not know which of them I am aiming at, I am still only preparing the way for both of them. I have not—yet—been disloyal to either Samuel or Annas.

Nicodemus had left Festus the option, and he hoped that in the end the decision would be that of Festus, and he could report to either Samuel or Annas that nothing could be done. What the decision would be he had no means of guessing. This young man is deeper than most of them, thought Nicodemus, and probably honest: a bribe would be most injudicious. Annas was right, and he is worth cultivating, though not for Annas' reasons. If his curiosity about our customs and things in general is more than a show, it is good and to our advantage. It may be sincere, though he does not have the look of a scholar, more like the marble busts of all those Roman patricians, including his own Porcian clan: grave and severe—at least when they think someone is looking—close-lipped, fixed gaze, nose straight and uplifted, regulation crop of short hair, they do not laugh at themselves any more than we do, though at least they can mock each other as we do not.

*

Festus returned. 'Before we go further,' he said, 'I think you had better see her. This lady will escort you, and bring you back.'

CHAPTER 10

There was only one chair in the small room, and she stood with her back to the window, bowed slightly, mould of the marble figure beyond her, out in the courtyard, the princess mourning but tearless.

Moments of time past and time present ran together for Nicodemus into one act of being, an incandescence. They were all there at once: what he had witnessed, the procession in the Temple and the figure who arrested it; what he knew of and could picture, the semi-circle of judges who had condemned her, the devil's brood of her family which had trapped and deceived her, delivered her for death, and sold her; and the stoning which had happened only in desire or in imagination but which had acted not the less powerfully on events for that. All this and the present moment were together, and Nicodemus bowed and groaned for the victim, innocent in all but a trivial sense.

He rose and said to her, softly and tenderly as if it had

been his own daughter: 'You have nothing to be afraid of, my child.'

The effect of this was extraordinary. Nicodemus found himself holding with one arm a wildly sobbing creature who clung to him for support. He patted her gently, hoping she would stop soon and that no-one would see them. She was only a child, really, fourteen years old and not fully grown, but in the eyes of the Law she was a woman, of an age to have been twice married and to bear a sentence of death.

'I am sorry,' she said at last, backing away and sniffing less miserably. 'It was what the other one said to me. Nobody else has been kind.'

'What other, my child?' he asked.

'The other man when they were taking me away in the Temple. The one who made them leave me alone. I do not know his name.'

'His name was Jesus,' said Nicodemus. 'He seems a very kind man. Have they not been good to you here?'

'Oh, they are not cruel, and the lady tries to help me, teaching me my work. I meant, none of our own people.' She began to sob once more, but less wildly.

She told him the story, bit by bit. It was only her word but obviously the truth was as Annas had suspected. The trial was as Samuel had told him, and the sale as reported to Samuel and verified by Nicodemus himself. She described what Nicodemus had seen but only half-heard in the Court of the Temple. The words of Jesus puzzled him so that he questioned her, hoping that they might turn out to be different, and easier to understand. *Let him that is without sin among you be the first to cast a stone.* Nicodemus put the thought at the back of his mind for the present: it seemed to hold the seed of something new and extraordinary, but what it was he could not see clearly, nor was he sure that it was good.

Esther told him also of the scene in the Palace on the night of her arrival, the goodness of Festus in saving her at the last moment, and his mercy towards the slave.

Till now, Esther had been for Nicodemus only an object of pity, something passive, a helpless creature subjected to suffering extraordinary and undeserved. Now he looked at her with respect and humility, also pride in a daughter of Israel. To hold the man off like that, what courage! And then to ask for mercy on his behalf!

But this was another complication to the problem. Things were bad enough when Nicodemus had only to balance between Samuel and Annas, but now there was a third party, Esther herself. Esther was not a mere object to be disposed of —the Romans permitting—as the Law or the interests of Israel, however interpreted, might demand. Esther was an individual and deserved to be regarded, and although Nicodemus at this point could not see the answer, he determined that she should.

The most delicate part of Nicodemus' mission had yet to be accomplished. Nicodemus said: 'In your work here, you see the lady Paula, who you say is good to you, but do you also see the Tribune Festus himself?'

'Oh yes, Sir,' said Esther, in a normal tone. 'He saw me once at the beginning, and then he sent for me last night.'

Nicodemus said sadly: 'Did he want you to do anything special for him? Anything but your ordinary work?'

'Yes,' said Esther, and left it at that.

'Were you not sorry?' asked Nicodemus, giving her every chance.

'Oh no, Sir, I was quite glad,' said Esther cheerfully.

Nicodemus felt weary, disappointed. Perhaps he had got things wrong about her, and his sympathy was out of place. At least, this was something that should please Annas. 'Is it likely to happen again, do you think?' he asked her.

'The lady Paula said he was pleased and might send for me again.'

'So the lady Paula knew all about it?'

'Oh yes, Sir, she was there.'

Nicodemus was shocked at Roman depravity. 'I am surprised at that.'

Esther seemed puzzled. 'She had to be there to interpret. Although,' she added proudly, 'I do know some Greek.'

'She must have been rather embarrassed,' said Nicodemus frostily. 'Found it difficult,' he added, in case the girl did not understand the word.

'Oh no, Sir, the words were quite easy. I was just telling him what the Scriptures said.'

'Bless you, my child,' cried Nicodemus, ashamed of himself and full of relief. 'So the Tribune Festus only wanted to know about our Scriptures! Were you told his reason for that?'

'The lady Paula said he wants to know more about our people.'

Nicodemus thought he had heard enough. There remained the moment of decision: assuming anyone could do it, what ought to be done with the girl?

He started again: 'I came to the Palace on a mission. It was unlawful for your family to sell you, but the Romans can keep you if they want. I do not know if they will do so.' He drew a handful of coins from a leather pouch attached to his girdle. 'It is the price to redeem a daughter of Israel from bondage. If the Romans would let you, do you wish to go free?'

She added the words which were already in his mind unspoken: 'To a husband who deceived and betrayed me, a family which swore false witness to send me to stoning.' Nicodemus added to this mentally: a people whose rulers have sentenced me to death.

'But,' she went on sadly, 'I wish only to do what is right.' She looked at him intently and Nicodemus for the first time took in her features, now that her expression had once more come to life: dark eyes much too large for a face which dwindled to such a small chin, and full red lips which were no longer childish, under the short fringe of black hair cut straight across the forehead, the serving-maid's style as drab as the serving-maid's dust-coloured working garment.

She put to him a question worse than any which he had been dreading. 'I will do what you say is right. What is it?'

What is right? Not in the abstract and not in the general, but what is the right course for one individual, here and now, in circumstances which are hideously tangled and which we do not know completely?

Not what is lawful or unlawful, for everything that she could do would be unlawful in some degree or else the cause of stumbling. In her way of life with the Romans she must break the Law continually, eating and drinking, work on the Sabbath. If she returned to her people, how long could she continue? The lawful sentence against her had not been cancelled. Her family, having tried twice to despatch her, would not fail a third time, but if they did, or if Samuel's retribution overtook them, what was left for a lone woman, penniless, discarded? Perhaps only life in the streets, something far worse than the single action for which she had been condemned unjustly.

With the Romans, also, she might perform service for Israel, even if not by the means that Annas intended. Who could say that Annas was wrong on one side of his calculation? Was the ritual uncleanness of a single individual, or perpetual breach of the food and sabbath laws, even the violation of the great commandments, to weigh heavier than services thereby rendered to God's whole people? The Israelite is not only an individual, but a part of Israel.

These were the sort of questions to which the Rabbi Nakdemon, like the Rabbi Samuel and perhaps even the Rabbi Jesus, was supposed to know the answer. Yet even the noble saying of Samuel the other day in the Temple was not much help: to do all the commandments of God for the love of God was all right —perhaps—for people like Samuel, but this girl must abandon some in order to do others. For her, the question was: which?

Nicodemus glimpsed at this point something full of terror. The Law was God's Law, eternal, existent before all things were created. Nothing could change it, nothing take away from it, only more could be discovered. Yet could there one day—and this was the terror—arise a situation in which the Law provided no answer? Not that the Law ceased to exist, but that it had no application?

Nicodemus refused to follow this further. The practical question remained: were there any commandments which a captive child of Israel must always, everywhere and at all costs follow, even at the cost of death?

Nicodemus said: 'My child, if you do not want to return to your people, remain with the Romans. Keep the Law where you can, but if you are forced to break it you may do so, only die rather than worship heathen idols.' No need to add that innocent life is not to be taken, but he hesitated over the third absolute prohibition, all sins of the flesh. Then she added it for him: 'The other man in the Temple told me I must be careful, and not let it happen again.'

CHAPTER 11

Samuel took it better than Nicodemus had expected, perhaps because he had had time to simmer, waiting till the cleansing from Gentile contact had made his friend safe to approach. It was not until the late afternoon of the following day that Samuel visited him, after closing the shop. Now, Samuel sat with Nicodemus in the small library opening inwards on one of the courtyards, big enough to have accommodated Samuel's whole house. Nicodemus had planted a bay tree in one corner, and also rosemary by the pool, raised from cuttings given him by Annas from Italian stock imported forty years ago by Herod. They gave great pleasure to Nicodemus, the rosemary and the bay: for the whole year they were green and pleasant, unlike the bed of Egyptian roses which at this season only, and sometimes again in the autumn, filled the courtyard with their scent.

Samuel sniffed, faintly disapproving, for roses meant dung,

and dung meant reptiles, and reptiles meant defilement, and although nothing had yet been decided against the keeping of gardens, there was already a distinct current of opinion among his more rigorous colleagues in favour of precautions of that sort.

'There was nothing for it,' said Nicodemus, speaking of Esther. Festus had listened, courteously, he said, and had even allowed him to see her, but in the end he had refused to release her: she was already promised to someone else, important, who would treat her well.

Samuel went straight to the point which Nicodemus had tried to pass over. 'Did she want to return?'

Nicodemus said not, and Samuel said slowly and sadly: 'It is not to be wondered at. I cannot find it in my heart to blame her. The shepherd rejoices more over the return of one lost sheep than over all the others which remain to him, but the lost sheep will not return if it has been driven out by the flock.'

Nicodemus said: 'They have behaved wickedly, in selling her, the family, but no doubt they will plead ignorance of the Law.'

'Ignorance!' exclaimed Samuel scornfully. 'Yes! No doubt they are common people, who do not trouble to learn the Law, so that they can more easily break it, but they knew enough of the Law to bring the woman for trial and to produce witnesses, all exactly in form according to the Law. No, they appealed to the Law and they shall be punished by the Law, full measure.'

'Then,' said Nicodemus, 'in this case where can you find the witnesses?'

Samuel said: 'They must be punished, and therefore we must find witnesses. There is the dealer, for a start.'

'He will not talk,' said Nicodemus.

'He must be persuaded,' said Samuel implacably. 'There are ways and means of bringing pressure. His record is not clear with the tax-collector, I am sure.'

'At least, you will do nothing to annoy the Romans. What they have done is lawful, and they will not give her back.'

'No,' said Samuel regretfully, 'this is no fault of the Romans.'

'Do you think that all our people will understand, that this is so?'

Samuel said, after a pause: 'I hope so, but I am afraid of the Zealots. In this sort of thing they are quite mad.'

'May God forbid!' said Nicodemus, thinking of crosses.

'May God forbid!' said Samuel, thinking of his son.

Samuel was proud of his son Simeon, who had gone up in the world, being apprenticed to a goldsmith, but he was uneasy in other ways. Simeon said little about his doings but much about his feelings, and it was common knowledge where such feelings led. Nicodemus had the same problem, with his son Gorion, and so did probably half the fathers in Israel, preferring, if the truth was what they feared, to remain ignorant till the last moment which, if it came, would be like the end of the world for them, waking one morning to hear their son was missing, another Zealot on another cross.

Samuel returned to the subject of Esther. 'Did you speak to her, about her duty and the commandments?'

'I reminded her of idols. There was no need for the second: she is no murderess. As for the third, she knew of it already.' Nicodemus glanced sideways at Samuel, wondering how he felt towards Jesus. 'The new Rabbi in the Temple had told her to be more careful, not to let it happen again.'

'Indeed,' said Samuel, 'I am very glad to hear it. I like the sound of that. It fits in better with other things he has been saying.'

'I can tell you exactly what happened,' said Nicodemus. 'I got it from the girl herself.'

Samuel turned in his chair and looked at Nicodemus intently. 'Tell me,' he said, and Nicodemus knew that every word he said and every intonation would be remembered: the mind that carried the whole of the Scriptures word by word and letter by letter would absorb at first hearing and for ever a new brief anecdote.

Samuel listened, and returned to the words of Jesus. *Let him that is without sin among you be the first to cast a stone.* 'The Clerk of the Court,' he said, 'did not hear clearly, or else, when he reported, he got mixed up.' In a different tone of voice, rather puzzled, humble, Samuel asked: 'What do you think Jesus meant by that?'

'One thing strikes you at once,' said Nicodemus. 'He was not being obstructive. He was not judging, he gave no opinion. He only invited other people to decide for themselves.'

'Or to judge themselves,' said Samuel quietly, sinking into thought.

'To pass judgment on themselves is one thing,' said Nicodemus, 'but to make their own judgment on a matter already judged by the Court is another. Which do you think he meant?'

'I do not know,' said Samuel, simply. Nicodemus had never seen him so perplexed. 'Some day I would like to ask him. But meantime one thing is clear. As you said, he was not obstructing. It was the execution-party which obstructed judgment. They had a sentence to carry out, and they failed to do so.'

'And since the witnesses and the family were in the party, they are guilty of obstructing the Law.'

'Exactly,' said Samuel. 'For that the family also are guilty. They shall be punished also for that.'

Nicodemus stored this up to tell Annas, who would be annoyed at the prospect of still more publicity but also mightily amused. The next thing, Annas would say, is for Samuel to get hold of Jesus as a witness, to testify against the execution party for its dereliction of the Law.

Nicodemus said: 'I am glad you think highly of Jesus. He seems to be well-spoken of.'

Samuel exploded, to the alarm of Nicodemus. 'Well-spoken of!' he cried shrilly, wagging his small beaked head. 'My friend, you do not know what you are saying.'

Nicodemus made calming gestures and noises, but Samuel continued unappeased. 'I have been listening to him in the Temple, teaching, and I have heard stories.' He drew breath and continued, calmer, on a lower note. 'Hillel was just too old, you did not know him, but I am one of the last of his disciples. There were others after him but I still look to him as my Master.' It was an understatement. Samuel and Gamaliel were the great heirs of the greatest Master of Israel, and both of them had all his sayings by heart.

'You are setting a high standard,' said Nicodemus, trying to placate his friend. 'To judge the new Rabbi by Hillel's standard, is that fair?'

Samuel looked at Nicodemus in surprise. 'You should see and hear him yourself,' he said gently. 'A greater than Hillel is here.'

CHAPTER 12

A few drops of rain sizzled in the torches, flaring in the gusts which at this season, after the hot east winds had faded, generally announced the last storm of the year.

The smoky yellow flames borne aloft in iron cages showed up the unevenness of the roadway, by the shadows, and Nicodemus and his companion were obliged to watch their step. They had already passed the High Priest's palace, the only residence in that street of great houses where an occasional window opening outwards leaked faint light on to the street. Otherwise it was a dark canyon between blank-faced stone walls, wooden gates shut fast at every entrance, only a crack of light as they passed the shuttered window of each porter's lodge. It was not far from midnight, and Jerusalem was asleep, even in that grand quarter where lamps were not a luxury. Life would begin again long before daybreak, and the hours of darkness were for sleep.

Not much could be done by lamp-light, except for reading, but even with several lamps burning it was not easy, and they made the room so hot. Only a dedicated scholar would attempt it: Nicodemus now seldom, Samuel sometimes, and also the person whom they had just left.

'Does your master often receive visitors after nightfall?' he asked his companion.

'Oh yes, Sir. He receives them at any time, either by day or night.'

'Does he get much sleep, in that case?'

'If there are no visitors, he reads a lot at night, or sometimes he just stays awake, thinking.'

Yes, a scholar of the stamp of Hillel, thought Nicodemus, only he is more fortunate, he does not have to work all day for a living, he seems to have friends who look after him, who will always offer him a bed. But that is as it should be: people of that sort should be looked after, should devote their whole time to the Law. How much better it would be for Samuel if he had money! Or could be persuaded to accept it! Nicodemus himself was lucky, though he did not devote all his time any longer to study of the Law: he knew he was not in the class of Samuel, or of Jesus, he was only a run-of-the-mill and middle-of-the-road Rabbi with no claim to distinction, one who would never be quoted after he was dead. He would be remembered, if at all, because of other people, because of words which men like Samuel had said to Nicodemus once. Or, perhaps, because of the words which he had heard that evening from the lips of Jesus. He himself did not matter: he was only the person to whom Jesus had spoken, a ruler of the Jews who came to Jesus by night.

His thoughts were interrupted by a stumble: the young man had slipped. Ah, leather soles! thought Nicodemus with satisfaction. He himself was delighted with Samuel's new style sandals: as he had expected, cloth-soles were far safer in these streets.

His companion seemed to have hurt himself, and was limping. Nicodemus kindly took his arm. He was much more free and easy with servants than some people: Annas would have strongly disapproved. Kindness but not familiarity was a good practice: taking the arm erred on the side of familiarity but the man was limping, it was dark, and there was no-one to see. Also, he seemed to be someone whom his master trusted, for he had been allowed to stay in the room.

'How long has your master had you?' asked Nicodemus, by way of tiding over any embarrassment which the young man might feel at accepting this kind of help.

'I have been with him for only a few months.'

'Indeed! You must be a good worker. What is your special work?'

'I was brought up in fishing.'

Nicodemus was puzzled. 'That is something unusual,' he said.

'Oh no, Sir, not where we come from.'

'From Galilee, is that? Yes, I know there are many fishermen, but . . .' Nicodemus did not finish the sentence. To keep a slave especially for fishing? There was something queer about that. He changed the subject. 'You are a son of Israel,' he said, making a flat statement: you never knew with these Galileans but the Rabbi Jesus could be trusted to make sure. 'Do you know that your master ranks as a teacher of Israel?'

'Oh yes, Sir!' cried the young man, once more losing his balance.

'You must watch your step,' said Nicodemus, 'the stones are slippery here.'

The other continued: 'They say there has never been anyone like him in the lakeside cities, not even Capernaum.'

'From what I have heard, that seems quite likely. Not even Capernaum.'

'Yes,' said the other, happily. He seemed a volatile young man. 'And what an honour for our family!'

'So you are related!' Nicodemus concealed his huge blunder.

'Yes. The mother of Jesus is my mother's sister.'

'And your name? I did not hear it.'

'My name is John.'

'Did you understand what your master was saying?' asked Nicodemus. The young man's intelligence was probably limited, and his education more so, but the family connection might help.

'Not much,' said John without hesitation, and added disconcertingly: 'Did you?'

'There is a great background to what he was saying,' said Nicodemus, who did not want to start a course on Scripture, suitable for an advanced class in the Temple, at midnight in the middle of the street.

'I would like to know more about it, but how can I?' asked John.

Nicodemus recognised the authentic cry of the student, fisherman or not, and the authentic teacher in him responded. 'How old are you, lad?'

'Eighteen years old this summer.'

'And how much have you learned of the Law?'

'Why, nearly all of it,' said John proudly. 'Until I was fourteen I stayed at school.'

Nicodemus reflected: And I, from the age of six I was stuffed with the Law like an ox, and at the age of fifteen I began my studies in earnest, and I continued my studies while I was working, and went on with them when I came back to Jerusalem at the age of thirty-four, and they now call me Rabbi, but still I do not know it 'nearly all'.

Nicodemus said gently, for he was beginning to like the young man: 'Anyone who wants to learn will always find a way, and people to help him, if he wants it hard enough.'

They had come to the entrance. One of Nicodemus' torchbearers had already hammered and the porter inside was drawing the bolts.

Nicodemus began to speak: 'It was good of the Rabbi Jesus to send you with me,' and then he stopped. For the second time in a few days he experienced time running together: Rabbi Jesus speaking the unfathomable words in the Temple, Rabbi Jesus tonight in the lamp-lit roof-room hard by the city wall, between the Palace and the house of Annas, the gusts of wind blowing up suddenly, rattling the shutters and ceasing before starting up again from somewhere else, the young man sitting motionless in the corner, missing no word of the wind and the spirit but not understanding, the present moment poised on Nicodemus' own threshold but also this time a sense of something future, not to be grasped or apprehended except that the decision to be taken in this moment would be most tremendous for both of them, both Nicodemus and the almost unknown young man who was on the point of parting.

John turned, ready to leave, and again stumbled. Nicodemus said: 'You have hurt yourself, you are limping.'

'It is nothing, Sir,' said John. 'If you are kind enough to send one of your torch-bearers with me I can manage.'

To let him go, or not. That was the decision.

Nicodemus withdrew the foot which he had already placed within his own threshold, and took John's arm again. He said: 'Your leg will become worse if you do not rest it. You must stay here for the night.'

*

There was little ceremony at the mid-morning meal, and they would only sit and not recline at table, but Nicodemus was nervous. For himself it did not matter, or not very much, if the young man did not know how to behave. It was son Gorion who would be upset: Gorion was well-mannered enough not to make a scene of it, but he would soon withdraw politely, pleading indisposition, and since Gorion observed punctiliously the fourth of the Commandments it would be almost impossible to have the matter out. To honour his father meant not to argue with him, only to let him see that you knew he was wrong. Life in the household would become more difficult, relations worse between the learned but much too tolerant father and the twenty-year-old son whom Nicodemus knew to be strict and suspected of Zealot leanings. Marriage with Samuel's daughter, Nicodemus hoped, would soften him, but meanwhile he spent too much time in the company of Samuel's fanatic son.

John however passed the test to which, unconsciously, he was being subjected: hands held with fingers pointing upwards without even looking to see what the servant was doing, then reversed so that the second waters ran down from the wrist, and —a special mark, this one—the third pouring with the fingers again upraised. Over the blessings he did not hesitate or stumble, they were automatic, and this was what mattered even to Gorion, not whether the precise number of benedictions reflected the rule of the great Doctor Hillel rather than Shammai.

Gorion contented himself with listening, uninterested for the most part in tales of Galilee or those misguided enough to live there, exposed to Gentile infection, far from the pure citadel of Judaea. Nicodemus looking at his son, grave and narrow-minded, blamed himself. The boy would have been altogether different if he had stayed longer in Alexandria, instead of being uprooted at the critical age of twelve from that broad and fertile nursery-garden of Jewry in the Dispersion, and transplanted to the harsh earth of Jerusalem, deep root-run perhaps among rocks and a clean soil but a thin one. Three years with Philo in Alexandria, and Gorion would have been a different person, wiser and more broadminded, knowing the world outside, not less conscious of the incomparable, heaven-towering splendour of Jewry but, because more conscious of the world in which Jewry must struggle for existence, better equipped for the battle by which Jewry continued to survive.

Gorion might have been more like this boy, even, thought Nicodemus, glancing at John: he would have been much better educated and not so innocent, obviously, but perhaps as open, as generous, as willing to learn. What a contrast! and not only of looks: the severe, reserved and inward-turning expression of Gorion, the hard mouth and black beard already strongly grown, and John, reactive, outward-looking, eager, the features still unmoulded, candid or even childlike, the fair-coloured beard still only a down. Would to God, thought Nicodemus suddenly, that this one was my son!

Gorion showed interest at one point only, when John was telling his father about another preacher, the one near the

Jordan, who went about saying that the Kingdom of Heaven was at hand and therefore Israel ought to prepare itself and repent. Gorion said: 'And did this man say anything about *how* the Gentiles are going to be driven out of our kingdom?' Nicodemus interrupted: 'The man sounds perfectly orthodox, my son, only he has put it the other way round. If all Israel cleanses itself from all sin, *then* the Kingdom of Heaven can be expected.'

Gorion was scornful, though outwardly deferential. 'In the world as it is . . .' (What do you know about it? Nicodemus wondered) '. . . surely that is the same thing as saying that the Kingdom of God will *never* be established, and the Gentiles will *never* be driven out, and Israel will *never* be ruled by its own king in its own land.'

They had forgotten John, but now Gorion addressed him: 'What did your teacher, the Rabbi Jesus, say about that?'

John hesitated. 'He too speaks of the Kingdom of Heaven and says it is coming.'

'Nothing more precise?' asked Gorion. 'A teacher with such a reputation must have said more than that.'

'Sometimes,' said John, 'he says the Kingdom is already here.'

Nicodemus again interrupted, to avoid a clash. 'A literary exaggeration,' he said, 'a device to focus the attention of the listener on something which, if not actually present, may be just round the corner. Or, if it is not just round the corner, men ought to act as if it were.'

Gorion lowered his eyes, as if to conceal his contempt for this evasion. 'Your master,' he said to John, 'is by all accounts a man of great understanding.' He implied, perhaps, that his own father was not. 'If he counts on the coming of the Kingdom he must have good reasons. Does he expect a national uprising against the Romans? Would he support it?' An extraordinary thought occurred to him. 'Or would he start it?'

John looked at him, astonished. These were depths which he

did not know existed. Could that be the explanation? John said, simply: 'I do not know.'

For Gorion the matter was ended. A simpleton had been speaking of an unknown quantity who might or might not turn out to be useful, in some minor role. 'If you will permit me, father,' he said to Nicodemus, 'I will go to the Temple. Gamaliel is speaking, and I am going with Samuel's Simeon, and with Saul.' He took his leave gravely, politely.

*

John approved of the bay and rosemary courtyard, with the roses and the pool. The sun struck towards them through the columns, for Nicodemus had so designed it, the library and the portico outside it facing to the south. Street noises came very muffled, over an intermediate courtyard this side of the boundary wall. Voices were barely audible, but the hooves of donkeys could be heard.

'The Rabbi Jesus,' said John, luxuriously stretching, 'is sorry for rich men, but it must be nice to be rich.'

'But the Rabbi Jesus accepts things from rich men.'

'Oh yes, but if someone offers you a good thing it is silly to refuse.'

'Not always, surely,' said Nicodemus. Something was missing in that.

'Only refuse for a good reason.'

That was it, thought Nicodemus, the wisdom of the Rabbis put in homely language. A man on the Day of Judgment will have to account for every good thing which he might have enjoyed and did not.

'Another saying of Jesus?'

No, John had thought of it himself.

Not bad, for a simple fellow with no learning, but John surprised him again. Sometimes, John said, the reason why you do a thing matters more than the thing itself.

But do not tell that to the Rabbis! Not unless you are one of them yourself and can hedge it all around with qualifications. The Doctors might think you were subversive. The Law does not care about your reasons. It is your duty to obey the Law.

Later, perhaps, it would be kind to drop a word of warning in the ear of the Rabbi Jesus. John, for himself, was too insignificant to matter, but what he said might be held against his master. Better for Jesus to stop his followers talking. Let Jesus speak for himself.

John's attention, like a child's, wandered. He looked around the walls. Hundreds of cylindrical leather containers stood upright on rows of wooden shelves. The caps of some of the containers were off, and the ends of the wooden rollers were showing, and the edges of the papyrus rolls.

John moved around the shelves examining the lists of contents, a few of them Aramaic, which he read easily, many Hebrew and some Latin which he could not decipher, and the rest Greek. 'I can talk Greek,' said John, 'but I cannot read it easily. You have many books by Greeks.'

They were not all written by Greeks, said Nicodemus, but it was the common language. His friend Philo, for instance, was a Hebrew, but because he was also a philosopher he wrote in Greek.

'And can you understand all that he writes, this man Philo?' John asked innocently.

'No-one can ever be sure that he understands a great teacher properly,' said Nicodemus, amused. 'Why, your master himself was not so easy last night.'

'No,' cried John, 'and you said there was a lot behind it. Can you tell me what you mean by that?'

'The Rabbi Jesus is a Master of Israel,' said Nicodemus, 'and I do not think that I or anyone else could explain him, only sometimes I see where he gets his thought. I asked him, last night, to make sure about one thing, and although he did not give me the answer I expected I know that I am right. Can you remember what I said?'

Nicodemus was testing John for his memory-training. Without a memory, a student was like a leaking pot. John repeated it exactly: 'How can a man be born when he is old? Can he enter a second time into his mother's womb and be born?'

It was word-perfect. Nicodemus said: 'The answer was obvious, only Jesus did not give it. An ordinary Rabbi would have answered: No, but just as a Gentile convert becomes as a new-born child when he is received into the house of Israel, so the son of Israel will be as a new-born child in the Kingdom of God.'

John did not question this piece of information: he absorbed it and, like a child, proceeded to the next. 'You asked also about the wind,' he said.

'Which is both the wind of the air and the wind of the spirit. Yes, he paid me a great compliment there,' said Nicodemus, with satisfaction. 'His answer—what was it, do you remember?' John again repeated the words exactly: 'Are you a teacher of Israel and yet you do not understand this?'

'Quite right. He meant that anyone with my training in the Scriptures was bound to know the answer, and so he went on to something else.'

'And what did he mean,' asked John, 'by being born of the spirit?'

What indeed? thought Nicodemus. Perhaps I know something, but perhaps not much more of what matters than this eighteen-year-old lad. Of one thing he was certain: he had been right when he greeted Jesus: 'We know you are a teacher come from God.' It was on impulse that he had said it, but it was the good impulse at work in him and not the evil impulse, he was sure. But why had he said it? Not for the reason which he had given immediately afterwards, justifying this extraordinary breach, at the first moment of the first meeting, of any well-mannered reserve. He had said that no-one could do the signs which Jesus did unless God was with him, but this was patently untrue, at least on the lips of a man of education. The signs done by Jesus were indeed remarkable, but so were the feats of various other people who, quite certainly, did not have God with them: sorcerers or magicians, familiar with the name of JEHOVAH only as a wonder-working spell.

Nicodemus' mind was absent, and inhabited again the lamp-lit upper room. Two or three lamps only, and those flickering, perhaps that was partly why he could not then make out, or now remember, the features, save for the beard and the long curling sidelocks proper to any conservative Rabbi, and dark eyes in a face which was also dark and probably lean. Semi-darkness, Nicodemus had often noticed, blurred features but heightened expression, and his recollection of Jesus, sitting at arm's length with not even a table between them, was not of appearance but of pure expression: expression of whatever might be within him, with no limits, present to excess. What he knows, he knows more surely, and unless we know as he knows, we do not know at all. When he suffers, it is with a suffering which would extinguish us. When he loves, you are surrounded. When he speaks, there is no answer: either you turn away altogether, or you accept him as he is.

Impression, guesswork only, maybe, but Samuel had spoken truly. Jesus was someone greater even than Hillel.

None of this, however, was much help in his problem, how to answer John. What did Jesus mean, by being born of the spirit?

'Sit down, lad,' said Nicodemus, and began teaching. He spoke of the pouring out of the spirit in the last days, and of the sprinkling of water and the gift of the spirit, and the cleansing of the spirit: he spoke of Isaiah and Joel and Ezekiel, and the books of Ecclesiastes and Jubilees.

'After all that, my son,' he said finally, 'I have not told you your master's meaning, only that what he said is full of meaning and deeply rooted in the heart of Israel.'

'Jesus must know almost as much as you do,' said John. 'He only finished his Law studies last year and we were expecting him to settle down and get married, but instead there is this.'

'I am sure that Jesus knows a lot more than I do,' said Nicodemus.

'Oh no, Sir,' said John politely. 'He hasn't read books in Greek.'

'The things that matter are not all written in Greek.'

'If Jesus speaks like this,' said John, 'it is all right for another Rabbi, but what about ordinary people?'

'Last night he was speaking to another Rabbi, but he often speaks to ordinary people.'

'I think I would understand better what he says to ordinary people if I could understand what he says to another Rabbi.'

Nicodemus pondered this extraordinary remark: surely humble and not conceited, but was it true or false, profound or shallow? He answered: 'Come and see me whenever you are in Jerusalem and your master can spare you. Tell me of the doings of the Rabbi Jesus and his teachings, and I will tell you how it looks to another Rabbi. But I can only offer you learning. Understanding is something else.'

CHAPTER 13

Annas, as Nicodemus had expected, savoured it enormously. 'The Doctors can make this last for years,' he said. 'Friend Samuel is now after the blood of the family for failing to carry out the Court order and execute her. He is also after them for having sold her to the Romans, contrary to the Law. Can they be prosecuted under *both* the charges? And if only one of them, under which?'

'The answer seems to me quite simple,' said Nicodemus.

'No doubt,' said Annas. 'But it can be argued, and if it can it will. If the woman is dead in the eyes of the Law, can anyone be punished for selling her thereafter? You see how it could go.'

Annas was pleased however at one thing, and surprised at Nicodemus' political sense. Nicodemus had not told Samuel the truth about the Sanhedrin's blunder. Samuel, said Annas, was too honest. If he knew there had been a miscarriage of justice he would have the whole matter reopened. It would not help the woman, and only discredit the Court with the Romans.

Annas said: 'The worst thing we have to fear now is some mad action by the Zealots, if the Tribune Festus keeps our modern Esther. What did you find out in the Palace?'

It seemed to Nicodemus too casual a way of referring to his dangerous mission, his self-sacrificing dash into the stronghold of the Romans, which it was unnecessary for him to admit that he had enjoyed. This insufficient consideration of his feelings consoled him for the measure of concealment which Nicodemus now realised he must exercise towards his friend. Already he had been less than wholly frank with Samuel, and now it was the turn of Annas.

'The Tribune Festus told me that he must keep her. He had promised her to someone important who would treat her well.'

Annas was pleased. 'That sounds like Pilate, but I'm sure it isn't. Confidentially, we have already tried to plant someone in his household, but Pilate's wife got rid of her at once. No, the important person is quite obviously Festus himself. What else did you discover?'

At this point, thought Nicodemus, the region of half-truths begins. 'It was rather a delicate subject,' he said, 'and one could not expect more than a hint.'

'A hint of the right sort can be as good as a direct statement, and sometimes even better. I can see you succeeded, perhaps better than you think.'

'Well, first of all,' said Nicodemus, 'I was lucky enough to be able to see the woman, and see her by herself.'

'Alone!' exclaimed Annas, admiring the finesse of it. 'That must have needed some arranging. Congratulations, my friend!'

'It was not really difficult,' said Nicodemus modestly. 'Anyway, we had a long private talk. I discovered that she is happy to stay there, and she seems to like Festus himself.'

Annas was delighted. 'What else emerged?'

'Nothing that I myself would regard as in the least conclusive.'

'Perhaps someone else could judge. What was it?'

'She said that Festus had sent for her, only the previous night.'

'Anything else?'

'She said she had enjoyed it.'

'Well, what else do you want?' asked Annas, barely able to conceal his impatience at such caution. 'A blow-by-blow account of what went on in bed?'

'Also, she gathered from the woman Paula that Festus was pleased and would probably send for her again.'

'And yet you say it is not conclusive! Why, you have had a total triumph, my friend!'

'No, no,' said Nicodemus modestly. 'I had nothing to do with it.'

'Never mind. At least you have ascertained the facts. This is extremely valuable.' Annas appeared to be already calculating how best to exploit this new asset.

'No,' Nicodemus persisted, 'you really should not jump to conclusions. The evidence is *not* complete.'

'What other conclusion could there possibly be?' asked Annas. 'You could not exactly ask her point-blank what happened.'

'As a matter of fact,' said Nicodemus candidly, 'she told me.'

'The hussy!' exclaimed Annas. 'Disgraceful! What was it?'

'She said he asked her about our Scriptures.'

Annas roared with laughter, so that Nicodemus rose and shut out the princely twilight view of the stone-walled city. What things happen in upper rooms! he reflected. The other night Jesus, only a hundred paces from where we are sitting: the soft voices, the lamps, and the wind of the air and the spirit; and now the High Priest of Israel, so delighted with an imagined act of adultery that he could be heard out there in the street.

'Magnificent!' Annas bellowed. 'That girl has wit and character. I should like to meet her. What a wonderful invention! The Roman master sending at night for a slave-girl, to discuss the Hebrew Scriptures!'

The laughter continued, while Nicodemus waited. At last Annas said, controlling himself, 'The suspense was dreadful. You have a talent, you told the story beautifully, my friend.'

Annas said: 'That leaves only one thing, Jesus. Did you see him, as I asked?'

'I went by night, as you suggested. It was an interesting talk.' Better to dole out the truth in small doses to Annas. Otherwise Annas would convict him of lack of judgment, and Nicodemus would be discredited himself.

'And what did you think? Is he worth grooming, for a seat in the Sanhedrin?'

'He makes a favourable impression. Samuel, as well as Gamaliel, holds him in great respect. He is no ordinary person.'

'It does no harm to be a little out of the ordinary,' said Annas, 'provided it is not extreme.'

'Of course he is rather young,' said Nicodemus, 'thirty-two or thirty-three.'

'Several years under age, but that will change,' said Annas encouragingly. 'Anything else?'

'Also he is not married.'

'That is something worse. The Sanhedrin cannot be expected to make an exception. He ought to look for a wife immediately, if he wants to sit on the Court.'

'He only finished his Law studies recently, so that explains why he is late.'

Annas was relieved. 'Any signs of his taking interest in women?'

'Oh yes, he takes a lot.'

'Good!' said Annas. 'He sounds quite promising, is that your own impression?'

'Oh yes, distinctly. But there is one point to watch. He is not what you would call safe and predictable. Not a comfortable sort of man to have about the house.'

'Well, if that is a point to watch, let us watch it,' said Annas good-humouredly. 'Just keep in touch with him, and let me know, my friend.'

Part II

AUTUMN, AD 28

CHAPTER 14

The tide of spectators flowed less and less strongly at this time of day, in the evening, as the week of the Feast wore on. On the first night movement was difficult in even the outer Court, and the first Court inside the Temple proper was a solid jam, but in mid-week there was no need to arrive hours ahead of time to make sure of admission. The excitement of the great harvest festival was waning, the children of Israel were getting tired of camping in booths on the roofs or outside the walls in the olive-groves and vineyards, and the dwellers in Jerusalem were beginning to wonder how soon their relatives from the country would go home.

There was no longer such a press to see the spectacle, and there was now much less to see: the torch-bearing dancers and the singers had been for the first day only, and there was not much now at night except the illuminations, the kindling of the fourfold four-branched lampstands, pillar-high in the inner courtyard, out of sight of where Nicodemus was sitting, beyond the brazen gates.

Nicodemus watched the trickle of fathers and children, few in numbers for another special reason, for this was the eve of the Sabbath and barely an hour to sunset. Samuel was already gathering himself to depart, from his seat away to the left down the long colonnade of the Court. It was only at festivals that he would be here at this time in the evening, an hour which he could most profitably have spent in his shoemaker's shop at this season of pilgrim custom, but which he insisted on spending in the Temple, making himself available not only to his nucleus of students but to any visitor, whether seriously enquiring or only curious.

Nicodemus himself would not have been there but for a message, brought only just now by John. There had been no time to question, for John was hurrying: Jesus had sent him on ahead. They waited now for the next thing to happen, and Nicodemus asked him the reason, but John could not explain. They had stopped at a house on the Bethany road, about two miles away, belonging to friends of one of the Rabbi's followers, Simon, not Simon Peter but the Simon who had been a Zealot. There they had seen a young man Simeon, the son of Rabbi Samuel, and this had thrown the Rabbi Jesus into great distress. 'He was not discourteous, I hope, to Rabbi Jesus?' asked Nicodemus. 'Oh no, Sir,' said John, 'but he said he had no message for his father, only one which he had sent already, that he was ailing and would stay with friends till after the Sabbath.'

'If that is all, it does not sound very alarming,' said Nicodemus.

'Rabbi Jesus,' said John, 'generally knows when people are speaking the truth.'

There would be more chance to ask John later. It was five or six months since Nicodemus had seen him, and exaggerated rumours had reached Jerusalem all through summer. Now Jesus was here, and according to John he had no plans to leave at once. Nicodemus hoped to borrow John from his master, whom for reasons at present unknown he was about to see himself.

They entered the Court from the opposite direction, coming as if from the Mount of Olives, through the eastern gate, and they walked quickly down the colonnade to where Nicodemus and John were standing. John moved to meet them. 'Rabbi Jesus,' he said to Nicodemus, 'thanks you for coming. He has something to say to Rabbi Samuel, and it is not yet too late.'

Nicodemus admired the delicacy of it, the tact. The subject so tremendous, but so outrageous a request. Put directly to

Samuel it could throw him into shame or embarrassment, but by using an intermediary Jesus was helping Samuel—to agree without shame at the injury to his principles, or to refuse without embarrassment at administering a rebuff.

*

Nicodemus caught Samuel just as he was moving: his students had already gone, and he was alone among the pillars, his long white coat reddened by a shaft of the setting sun. Samuel looked tired with the extra period of teaching. He needed the Sabbath's repose.

'Rabbi Jesus told me something which you should know immediately. It concerns your son.'

Samuel did not ask the obvious question: why does Jesus not tell me himself? The indirect form of approach to a much senior Rabbi might be a token of respect.

Nicodemus continued. 'He saw Simeon less than an hour ago, in the house of a Zealot friend.'

'I know,' said Samuel. 'I do not like his company, but he sent a message. He is unwell and will stay there till after the Sabbath '

'The Rabbi Jesus thinks it is more serious.'

'Is Jesus a doctor as well?'

'Yes. Some of the tales are true. He said: The powers that I have are from the Holy One, blessed be He.'

'All good powers are from the Holy One,' said Samuel. 'Blessed be He. Has he then the powers of healing?'

'Those around him assure me it is true.'

'But Simeon is not sick. He is only not strong enough to come home this evening. Tomorrow is the Sabbath, and it is more than a Sabbath day's journey.'

'Rabbi Jesus considers that this is not an ordinary sickness. It is a sickness of the mind.'

'Is there anything to show it?'

'It shows in his appearance. He looked like a woman: he had shaved off his beard.'

'Simeon must have had a reason. Can Jesus see into the mind?'

'It seems so. The Holy One, blessed be He, has given him power to cast out evil spirits.'

'Evil spirits!' cried Samuel. He turned his back towards the spot where Jesus was waiting among his group of followers some fifty paces distant, lest Jesus should see the indignation in his features and feel hurt. 'Does he suggest that my Simeon is possessed of an evil spirit?'

'I understand your feelings,' said Nicodemus, with sympathy. 'I told him that this only happens to members of the lower classes. But he did not agree.'

'And what does he think is the nature of this "evil spirit"?' asked Samuel, with irony in his voice.

'It is one that leads the victim to do mischief to others.'

Samuel was silent, unconvinced but not wholly disbelieving. Whatever came from Jesus was worthy of respect.

'If this is true, the boy must be brought home immediately after the Sabbath, and I will consult the Rabbi Jesus about a cure. But until then, nothing is possible.'

'Rabbi Jesus considers that something should be done immediately.'

'How can it? Sabbath begins in half an hour.'

'Jesus believes that he can cure Simeon, but you must be present.'

'It is beyond a Sabbath day's journey!' exclaimed Samuel. 'And to effect a cure!'

Then the implication of this came home to him. 'So Jesus must hold that this sickness is mortal! But that is not so. Simeon may be unwell, but even if he is held by an evil spirit, there is no danger to his life.'

'What you say is reasonable,' said Nicodemus, 'and with my mind I believe it, but a man with the powers of Jesus knows more than I do, and if he says something without giving a reason he may all the same be right.'

'I am deeply grateful for his kindness,' said Samuel. 'He is a merciful man, and on the day after the Sabbath I will go with him gladly, and if he is kind enough to do so he may try to heal my son. But tomorrow I cannot do it. Tomorrow is the Sabbath, and Simeon's illness does not endanger his life.'

＊

Nicodemus returned to Samuel with a message. 'He begs you to think once more, for the sake of your son. Life and death are in the hand of the Holy One, blessed be He, and what man can know that this sickness will not kill, or that it will not kill to-morrow?'

'He says "for the sake of my son",' said Samuel, 'and I would give all I have for him, but I cannot transgress the Law, God's commandment. I will seek out the Rabbi Jesus and go with him to my son on the day after the Sabbath.'

Nicodemus said, 'Jesus said: *The day after the Sabbath may be too late.*'

Samuel bowed his head and turned away. 'We are all in the hands of the Almighty. But thank Jesus for me, all the same, most humbly.'

＊

Nicodemus took his leave, having delivered Samuel's last message. The features of Jesus, by day, were no more to be held in memory than by the dim lamp-light of the upper room. When, Nicodemus wondered, shall I really see him? See him as he *is*.

An intense flash of light blinded him for a moment, and he was startled until he saw where it came from, just behind the head of Jesus, the setting sun reflected in the flat polished face of a brazen gong, swinging in the breeze.

As his eyes cleared, he caught on the face of Jesus, gazing after the retreating Samuel, another of those densely pure expressions: interior suffering and intense compassion, deeper surely than anything called for by Samuel himself.

Also, he caught a whisper: 'If only he knew, *but he cannot.*' Jesus was talking to himself.

CHAPTER 15

There was a commotion but Festus took no notice. The talc windows of his chair gave light enough to read, but shut out views of anything outside. The bearers slowed, and Festus was joggled, but he remained the captive of the masterpiece in his hand. Apenninus, forty years a beekeeper, had committed his observations to writing, before his untimely death, and they formed uncommonly good light reading for a journey as well as excellent raw material for Festus' own book.

Bees are the most marvellous of all insects, and alone appear to have been created in the image of man. They have their own code of morals, form themselves into political communities and hold councils, at which they swear loyalty to their king.

The obedience which his subjects manifest towards their king is surprising. He issues his orders continually through bodyguards and lictors, and idleness or disobedience is invariably punished with death. Without a king the swarm cannot exist, and yet if more than one king is found in their community they instantly put all but one to death.

Exact observation, that is the thing, thought Festus. Deduction was all very well but often led to unreliable results. So did analogy, though analogy was very tempting: substitute 'Jews' for 'bees' in this passage and it gave you food for thought. Bees they were, of a sort, it was true, producing honey, though they were not the tame sort with which Apenninus had got so well acquainted, more like the wild and ferocious African variety with which he had been experimenting just before his death.

But did the Jews have a king? Certainly not Caesar, whatever they might for reasons of tact pretend. Was he perhaps the secret inhabitant of their Temple? That would explain a good deal of the mystery with which they surrounded him, a wise precaution against inquisitive Romans.

The procession had halted, and there were voices. It was no longer possible to read. Festus thrust the roll back in the side-pocket of the sedan-chair and opened the window. They were still only half-way from the Palace to the Fortress, on the roundabout route outside the walls. Golgotha was behind and to the right of them, and they were just entering the garden-suburb north of the city wall. Six out of the eight mounted men of his escort were still facing forward, towards a growing and unfriendly native crowd. The other two secured the rear, and in the middle, a few yards away from his chair, a dozen foot-soldiers were holding a struggling figure clad in a black woman's dress.

'There has been an attempt on your life, Sir,' said the one in command of the escort.

'Are you certain?' asked Festus. 'I noticed nothing myself.'

The officer, a junior centurion, was pleased with himself and unwilling to surrender his success. Three others, he said, had got away after making a distraction. This one, the prisoner, was to do the work.

'But a *woman!*' exclaimed Festus.

'A man in woman's clothes.'

Festus was extremely reluctant to be the object of an attempt at assassination, because he knew what must follow, and it never did any good to political relations.

The centurion, seeing Festus still doubtful, showed him the short curved dagger: both edges razor-sharp. It was the weapon of the dagger-men among the Zealots, a lightning kill and the instrument hidden once more in an instant under the patriot's robes.

'Let me see the prisoner,' said Festus. They brought him forward, exhausted now and bruised. 'He had shaved himself,' said the centurion, 'so as to wear these clothes.'

'Do you admit it?' Festus asked the prisoner. 'I do,' the prisoner said.

There was no escape. 'The usual. Tomorrow,' said Festus. For this he had not only Pilate's authority but his orders. He closed the window. Then he opened it again. 'Omit the usual preliminaries.' For such mercy he had no authority, but there was no point in torture: no Zealot ever spoke, except to give false information.

Festus closed the window again and took out his book.

Bees also excel all other insects in the valour with which they will repel an intruder, plunging their sting into him even though knowing that this must result in their own death.

*

Samuel returned slowly to life again, from the grave which had held him for a week, crouched on his bed in the corner. Visitors came and sometimes he saw them: they spoke and sometimes he heard. Life was there, but his mind was absent, conversing with Simeon in his childhood, and recalling the sorrows of Job.

Nicodemus came each day to sit with him, but only on the first day did Samuel speak, when Nicodemus told him of the favour he had begged of Festus: the merciful despatch of Simeon after only one day of suffering, and the return of the body. Samuel had muttered, like Job: 'Let the day perish wherein I was born,' and Nicodemus, lest he vex or tempt his old friend like the vain counsellors of Job, had hastily departed and taken on himself the burial of Simeon and the support of the family while Samuel was not earning. Also, conspiring with Samuel's wife, he had 'repaired' Samuel's rather primitive dwelling, making improvements which Samuel could never afford.

Now, on the seventh day, which was the second day after a Sabbath, Samuel roused himself and refused the food which was brought to him, for this was one of his two weekly days of fasting. Then Nicodemus knew that Samuel was himself again, and they were able to speak.

Samuel had other visitors also, and told Nicodemus of one of them, so that Nicodemus knew it was now safe to mention Simeon. 'Jesus came to see me,' said Samuel, 'and at first I did not know what to say to him.'

'What could you say?' asked Nicodemus. 'What should I say if one day it is Gorion?'

'It came to me suddenly,' said Samuel, and fell into an abstraction, muttering as if to himself: 'Though he slay me, yet will I trust in him,' and 'Shall we receive good at the hand of God and shall we not also receive evil? Blessed be God for ever and ever.' Nicodemus regarded these admirable sayings as a form of self-administered stupefying drug, to dull the pain. Samuel continued, aloud: 'I said to him: If I had gone with you to Bethany, on the Sabbath, my son would not have died. Yet, if I had gone, I would have transgressed the Law by intention, and it makes no difference that *the truth was hidden from my eyes.*'

Samuel continued: 'I said: I obeyed the Law as I saw it, not knowing what it would cost, but if I had another son to lose, and did it knowing, I could do nothing else.'

'And what was the answer of Jesus?'

Samuel said severely: 'There could be no answer. There is none.' Then he added, his face softening with a gentle radiance: 'But he is a man of tender feeling. Jesus wept.'

CHAPTER 16

Festus knew that the upper classes of the subject nations could generally be counted on to collaborate against violent subversion. All the same, there was a risk. Luckily he had been getting on well with Nicodemus, and he had a reasonable pretext to invite him to the Palace. The supplies of papyrus direct from Alexandria had been arriving, and he was delighted, but his bank required more details on how and where to pay.

Since their first meeting, in the formal robes which both of them detested, they had reverted to their normal dress, which was the same for both of them, save for the narrow purple stripe of the equestrian order on Festus' white tunic. They met this time in Festus' private office, high up in the highest tower which like the great lighthouse at Alexandria rose in stepped stages, diminishing near the top. Nicodemus remarked on the resemblance, and Festus thought to please him by praising Alexandria, a greater city in some ways even than Rome.

Alexandria, said Nicodemus, was not only a place for enjoying oneself and making money. It was the meeting-place of Jew and Gentile. There, if anywhere, the wisdom of the Greeks and the thought of Israel might one day mingle. In Jerusalem the wise men of the Jews spoke only to Hebrews, but in Egypt his friend Philo expounded the Hebrew religion, like a philosopher, for all the world, in Greek. Festus, immediately on the track of a new source of information, demanded the name of Philo's publisher. It was exactly what he needed, for the work commissioned by Pilate, the Jewish superstition described in Greek.

Nicodemus, smiling, said that he would write for copies himself, it would be quicker. 'This time,' he said, 'you must allow me. Accept it as a gift.'

Festus accepted instantly. This was no bribe but an offer of friendship.

It was a good omen. He proceeded to the point. Recent events, he explained, had revealed a situation which might be as distasteful to the Jewish rulers as to the Romans. Terrorism and subversion was a threat to everyone interested in stability and peaceful government, Jews as well as Romans. Nicodemus agreed: he could have written Festus' speech for him, but he knew that Festus had to make it. Festus was every ruler, Babylonian or Persian, Macedonian or Seleucid, Ptolemaic or Roman, speaking to every native chieftain. Festus continued:

'After the recent deplorable incident'—he gestured out of the window at Golgotha—'the accomplices escaped but were later reported in a house near Bethany, a well-known resort of Zealots. None of the inmates are of consequence, but there was a report of a visit to the same establishment by a person of some importance, less than two days before the incident occurred.'

'Do you know the name of this person?'

'He is a Galilean, who has been making quite a stir in his own country. His name is Jesus.'

'I know him.'

'I thought you might,' said Festus, more comfortably, 'and that is why I ventured to ask your opinion. If you think it is in the interests of your own people to tell me, I should be very glad to hear it. But if you do not, I shall perfectly understand.'

'I can tell you at once,' said Nicodemus without hesitation. 'I am certain that Jesus has nothing to do with this movement.'

'One of his followers is a known member.'

'Or used to be,' said Nicodemus. 'Yes. I am certain. Jesus is a great Doctor of our Law, gifted with extraordinary powers of healing. Nothing more than that.'

Festus persisted: according to reports from all over Galilee people thought Jesus was something different, not only a Zealot but a Zealot leader. The common people, said Nicodemus scornfully, will believe any silly rumour.

Jesus, if he was a Zealot, was clearly not going to be given away by Nicodemus. Festus turned to the other side of the matter, the interests of science. Did Nicodemus know anyone who had actually witnessed a cure by Jesus? With his own eyes, that is, not just what someone else said, or what they thought might have happened. Nicodemus said yes, a young cousin of Jesus.

Festus summoned a secretary, for note-taking.

'Where would you like to start?' asked Nicodemus. 'What disease interests you most?'

'I am particularly interested in diseases of the mind,' said Festus. 'Possession by evil spirits.'

'Any aspect of it in particular?'

'The medical technique.'

'Jesus' method was the same in each instance,' said Nicodemus. 'He said to the demon "Get out of him".'

'And the demon did?'

'It did.'

'The doctor spoke only to the demon and not to the patient?'

'Yes.'

'No laying on of hands? No fumes and no anointing? No incantation?'

'Not a touch. Not a thing. Not a word.'

'That sounds remarkably elegant,' said Festus. 'A most advanced technique. The only other really authentic cases which I know of involved a lot more effort. At Ephesus, for instance, they shut the patient up and smoke him in some horrible vapour, and utter secret spells over him—they seem to mean something to the devil, but they would sound like gibberish to you and me.'

'It is certainly simpler than anything to which we are accustomed,' said Nicodemus. 'Cases of course are rare, so perhaps it is unsafe to generalise, but the exorcist usually wears a seal enclosing the root of a plant which King Solomon had discovered to be useful for the purpose, and he holds this to the nose of the sufferer and draws out the demon through the nostrils, meanwhile reciting incantations which Solomon also had composed.'

'How long would it take, that process?' asked Festus.

'I have never actually witnessed it, but I suppose about an hour.'

'At Ephesus the standard time is sunrise to sunset. The priests base their charges on that, but they make a reduction for the easier cases. What is Jesus' fee?'

'Not a penny.'

'From one point of view, I suppose, that is reasonable, since apparently it takes no time at all. But a Greek doctor would certainly ask something. He sounds unusual, your Jesus.'

'He is.'

Festus was dictating, and broke off. 'It would be helpful to have a little more detail. How did the fact of possession manifest itself?'

'In one case, in Capernaum, the man was just unbalanced, and took no notice of what anyone said. Another man, in Gadara, refused to wear clothes or to live among other people, and nothing was strong enough to hold him. A boy in Magdala was given to foaming at the mouth, and when he was in a fit he did not know what he was doing.'

'Interesting, that last one,' said Festus. 'It sounds like epilepsy. But there are other cures for that.' He addressed his secretary. 'Bring in Aristotle.'

Festus explained to Nicodemus. 'He is my doctor, an excellent Greek. Actually he is from Galatia, and I inherited him from my great-uncle, but you know how it is, no-one counts as a real doctor unless he calls himself Greek.'

Aristotle entered, a grizzled Gaul with blue eyes and the remains of reddish hair-colour. By his clothes he was a freedman, so it must have been Festus who set him free. At first glance he was a man of education: possibly also a eunuch, to judge by a certain soft fatness.

Festus said to Aristotle: 'We were discussing cures for epilepsy. What would you normally recommend?'

Aristotle told them. Festus got him to repeat it for the secretary, and handed the formula to Nicodemus.

'Jesus has helped us, indirectly, in our researches,' said Festus, 'and I would like to do something for him in return. If you see him, perhaps he would be interested. He has his own methods, obviously, which sound economical and efficacious, but in case of failure he might like to fall back on this.'

Nicodemus read: In milder cases, pound three berries of hyssop in squill vinegar and take for sixteen days consecutively. If this does not succeed, take powdered betony and bruised leaves of cinquefoil, infuse in wine with an ounce of Attic honey and take for thirty days.

Nicodemus said: 'I expect that Jesus will prefer his own methods, but he will be grateful for your thought.'

Festus said that Aristotle should stay and listen: he was always anxious to learn. Last year he had been sent to Samaria for a course with another great physician. But Simon Magus had been disappointing, and charged a high fee for simply letting students watch. Yet he had a tremendous reputation, and ranked as a son of one of the gods.

'Simon Magus is a Samaritan,' said Nicodemus with distaste. 'He cannot be one of the sons of God.'

Festus noticed the change of wording: the sons of God, to a Jew, must mean something, but not the son of a god. 'These things,' he said, 'work differently with the Romans. My "deified" great-great-uncle used to say that where gods can become men, men can become gods.' Festus paused on the word 'deified' and smiled slightly, and Nicodemus catching the point smiled back. Festus' forbears had had the foresight to marry into the Julian house, but Festus had mentioned Augustus Caesar not in order to glorify his own connections but to bring that kind of deity down to earth.

Festus decided that it would spoil things to carry this further, to mention that he himself was the son of a god, descended on his father's side from Zeus and through his great-grandmother from no less a person than Aphrodite. The family board had said so, and who should doubt it?—hung up in the hall of their Roman house until removed by his grandfather, a modest man who never boasted.

'According to our view of things,' said Nicodemus, broad-mindedly admitting for the sake of the Gentile that this was not the only possible view, 'all sons of Israel can become sons of God. Although,' he added wryly, 'it sometimes does not seem likely that many will do so.'

'Not even Jesus?'

Nicodemus conceded that the Rabbi Jesus would almost certainly qualify as a son of God.

Hopefully, Aristotle asked whether Jesus accepted disciples. What chance of going on a course?

There were no medical men among his followers, said Nicodemus, and he did not know if Jesus' method could be copied. Paradoxically, the more complicated a procedure, the easier it was to imitate. The difficulty with Jesus was that everything seemed so simple.

'Sometimes,' said Nicodemus, 'he does not even see the patient.'

'Then he sends some charm, or amulet, or remedy?'

'Not in the cases I know of. One of them you could check. It was one of your own people, seconded to Herod's guard in Capernaum. The patient was a young servant belonging to the centurion.'

'A good master, then,' said Festus approvingly. 'Naturally he could not afford to keep his own doctor, so he went out to look for one. What was the disease?'

'It was a very high fever, the sort which in those parts is generally fatal. By our reckoning it was on the fifth day of the second month after the month of Passover. The time of the cure was exactly one hour after mid-day.'

'How did they know the time so exactly?'

'The circumstances were curious, and there was a double check. The officer had gone to find Jesus at quite some distance. The boy was cured while they were still together. Jesus did not go to the house.'

'Aristotle,' said Festus reflectively, 'have you ever heard a thing like that? This is a cure at a distance.'

'Nothing that I would call authentic,' said the doctor. 'It is said to have been not unknown in antiquity, among the gods, but there are few details.'

'Just so,' said Festus. 'A notable achievement.' He said to Nicodemus: 'I shall do as you suggest, and make enquiries. If this is substantiated, it should be recorded. Now, what did Jesus say?'

'He said it was on account of the officer's faith that his wish would be granted.'

'His faith?' said Festus, puzzled. 'His faith, in what?'

'My informant could not tell me. If we knew, we still wouldn't know how Jesus did it. But I agree it is important. Faith, in what?'

CHAPTER 17

Samuel came to terms with life again. Nothing can break him now, thought Nicodemus, since this has left him unbroken. Would I have survived like that, he wondered? Not only the death of your only son, but knowing that in a way you were the cause of it. But Samuel, like Job before him, did not curse God and die. Had God spoken to him, as to Job, out of the whirlwind?

Best of all, Samuel's admiration of Jesus was undiminished. They had found themselves on opposite sides in an argument where each was equally right from his own standpoint. Nicodemus, hearing his friend admit it, wondered if the insidious Greek spirit, life-robbing or life-renewing according to the point of view, had filtered even into Samuel too. Samuel would have rejected the charge with horror, but Nicodemus had a nose trained in Alexandria for these things. The Law, God-given, was eternal and never to be cancelled, but what if the Law should lead to precisely opposite conclusions for different persons? In what sense can both be right?

Nicodemus was careful not to disturb his friend with such speculations, but nourished him rather in his re-found confidence and devotion.

Samuel, because of his prostration, had left off teaching for a while and returned to it only slowly. This had left more elbow-room for his colleagues, for the Rabbis by a delicate convention avoided overlapping, and adjusted their timetables with deference to the elders among them, of whom Samuel was the chief.

Jesus, separated from Samuel's pitch among the pillars only by that of Nicodemus, was one of the beneficiaries of Samuel's absence, and Samuel spoke to Nicodemus of his teachings.

'I have no patience,' said Samuel, 'with people who go round saying that Jesus does not respect the Law.'

They were sitting in Nicodemus' bay and rosemary courtyard, towards evening, for Samuel was still taking things easy and stopped work early: he was now on his way back home after his afternoon visit to the baths. The air was cool with the freshness of the first days after the first rains of autumn. Cloud-shadows moved but did not linger. This was the true beginning of the year, thought Nicodemus. Harvest is over, and the heats of summer are past, and soon there will be the sowing of the grain. The cold and the wet will come, and they are needed, but that is only an interruption: when the earth seems dead, growth has already started and next year's buds are swelling.

'Who says that,' asked Nicodemus, 'about Jesus and the Law? Not the common people, I am certain.'

'I am sorry to say that it is some of our own people,' said Samuel.

'Surely not Pharisees!' exclaimed Nicodemus. 'Jesus is one himself.'

'They call themselves Pharisees, but they are a disgrace to us,' said Samuel severely. 'We have many goats among our sheep.' His face brightened with glee, unregenerate, thought Nicodemus, delighted. 'They don't like the things he has been saying about them, that's the truth of it,' said Samuel. 'Why, he has a sharp tongue, that one,' he said admiringly. 'Some of the things he has said of them are almost as strong as my own.' He chuckled. ' "Whited sepulchres!" Splendid! I wish I had thought of it myself.'

'So you think they are getting their own back, by accusing him over the Law?'

'I'm afraid so,' said Samuel. 'It is ridiculous. A man of that quality! Why, his very life is the Law.'

And he, like you, dear friend, thought Nicodemus, is the sort of person who makes the Law—no, not *makes*, for it is God who made it, but uncovers and expounds it.

Samuel continued: 'They only have to listen when he is speaking. Do you know who said this? "It is easier for heaven and earth to pass away than for one letter of the Law to perish"?'

'It could have been Hillel or Shammai,' said Nicodemus. He added, smiling: 'Or Samuel. But, so far as I know, it was not.'

'It was Jesus,' said Samuel. 'And have you heard what he says about ourselves, the Rabbis, the Doctors of the Law? Pay attention, he says, to what they tell you, for they sit in the seat of Moses.'

'An honourable position,' said Nicodemus wryly, 'but it doesn't fit all of us. I know quite well that I am too small for the seat of Moses. I can't live up to it. I do not set a good example.'

'If you feel that way, how much more I do!' exclaimed Samuel. 'But that too is what Jesus says. God help people if they only copy our example. We try not to copy it ourselves.'

Samuel continued. 'Come with me tomorrow and listen. We will sit in your place and appear to be talking, otherwise he will stop to make way for me and my classes.'

*

The crowd was much greater than Nicodemus had expected, eighty or a hundred deep in a semi-circle all round, bulging out of the colonnade into the open space of the courtyard, reaching sideways almost as far as where Nicodemus and Samuel sat. They were all standing, in order to get as close as possible to the speaker who, because they were standing, himself stood instead of sitting on the stone Master's bench. To hold back the crowd, some of the Rabbi's followers were standing in front of him. Nicodemus recognised some he had spoken to briefly, and of course there was John.

Someone near the front was asking questions, and Nicodemus pointed him out to Samuel. 'I will get Gorion to speak to that young man,' said Nicodemus. 'He may listen to him. He is always misbehaving.' 'Oh, let him alone,' said Samuel tolerantly. 'Saul is a great persecutor of his elders, but he is a student of Gamaliel's, and he may develop. I think I managed to put him in his place some time ago, and we can rely on Jesus to look after himself.'

All the same, Nicodemus was shocked at Saul's tactics. He was trying on Jesus exactly what he had tried on Samuel. If there was any difference in the answers he would quote one Rabbi against the other.

'Rabbi, we know the heaviest of the heavy commandments . . .' Before he could continue, Jesus said: 'So let us hear it from your lips.' Saul recited it, as before, correctly, and continued: 'But is there a second?'

Jesus wasted no time. 'Have you not heard it spoken by a great Master of Israel, in this very place?'

A well-informed person, thought Nicodemus, though these things get reported very widely.

Saul remained silent, and Jesus continued: 'So what is it, my son?' Saul looked resentful but came out with it dully. 'Rabbi Samuel taught us: "And the second commandment is: Thou shalt love thy neighbour as thyself".'

'This do,' said Jesus softly, 'and thou shalt live.'

Saul pulled himself together for another attack. 'Rabbi, is there a third of the great commandments?' Samuel was smiling, pleased a little with the tribute to himself but much more at the skill of the Rabbi Jesus. Nicodemus felt almost sorry for Saul, exposing himself. No doubt the reply by Jesus would be as devastating as Samuel's though for wisdom and beauty Nicodemus did not see how it could come up to Samuel's standard.

Jesus said: 'I will tell you which is the third commandment if you will tell me which is the greater, the first or the second.'

Saul did not need to consider. At once he replied: 'The first, of course. Thou shalt love the Lord thy God.'

'No,' said Jesus. 'If a man love not his brother, whom he hath seen, how can he love God, whom he hath not seen?'

There was a silence. Saul bowed his head. This door was shut.

Jesus waited. Instead of the usual buzz growing stronger there was still silence growing deeper, as the crowd stopped fidgeting and shuffling its feet. Then Jesus spoke: 'On these two commandments hang all the Law and the Prophets.'

Samuel turned to Nicodemus. 'You remember what I told you?' he said, delightedly. 'He is greater even than Hillel.'

Saul was uncrushable. 'Rabbi, who is my neighbour?' Not quite the question which he had put to Samuel, six months earlier, but it had the same intent. Jesus said:

'A man was going down from Jerusalem to Jericho, and he fell among robbers, who stripped and beat him, and departed, leaving him half dead. Now by chance a priest was going down that road, and when he saw him he passed by on the other side. So likewise a Levite, when he came to the place and saw him, passed by on the other side. But a Samaritan, as he journeyed, came to where he was, and when he saw him he had compassion, and went to him and bound up his wounds, pouring on oil and wine; then he set him on his own beast and brought him to an inn, and took care of him. And the next day he took out two denarii and gave them to the innkeeper, saying: Take care of him, and whatever more you spend, I will repay you when I come back.'

Jesus paused. There was no sound. He continued:

'Which of these three, do you think, proved neighbour to the man who fell among the robbers?'

Saul said, for he could say nothing else: 'The one who showed mercy on him.'

Jesus said: 'Go and do likewise.'

There was again silence, complete, broken at last by astonished whispers: 'What, a *Samaritan*?'

Nicodemus whispered to Samuel: 'Saul could not bring himself to mention the word "Samaritan". The story stuck in his throat. He has far to go, that young man.'

Some distance for himself also, he reflected: until the very end, he had thought that Jesus was missing the point of the question.

The young man, however, had not yet surrendered. He was the most persistent objector whom Nicodemus had ever seen.

'The priest and the Levite,' he said to Jesus, but also addressing the crowd, 'did well if they thought the man was dead, for the Law forbids them to incur defilement. In the eyes of the Law, the Samaritans are sinners. In the Kingdom of Heaven, who shall first enter? He who kept God's Law all his life and avoided defilement, as he thought, by a dead body, or he who sinned continually against the Law but this once did an act of mercy?'

Jesus answered, almost exactly as Samuel had done to a similar question. 'The ways of our Father in Heaven are more merciful than man's ways,' but then Jesus began to diverge from Samuel. 'To what is the matter like?' he continued.

'It is like to a man who had two sons, and the younger of them said to his father, "Father, give me the share of property that falls to me." And he divided his living between them. Not many days later, the younger son gathered all he had and took his journey into a far country, and there he squandered his property in loose living. And when he had spent everything, a great famine arose in that country, and he began to be in want. So he went and joined himself to one of the citizens of that country, who sent him into his fields to feed swine.'

There was a murmur at the mention of the unclean animal. Jesus continued:

'And he would gladly have fed on the pods that the swine ate, and no-one gave him anything. But when he came to himself he said, "How many of my father's hired servants have bread enough and to spare, but I perish here with hunger! I will arise and go to my father and I will say to him, 'Father, I have sinned against heaven and before you; I am no longer worthy to be called your son; treat me as one of your hired servants'." And he arose and came to his father. But while he was yet at a distance, his father saw him and had compassion, and ran and embraced him and kissed him. And the son said to him, "Father, I have sinned against heaven and before you; I am no longer worthy to be called your son." But the father said to his servants, "Bring quickly the best robe, and put it on him; and put a ring on his hand, and shoes on his feet; and bring the fatted calf and kill it, and let us eat and make merry; for this my son was dead, and is alive again; he was lost, and is found." And they began to make merry.'

Jesus paused. Saul, with ineffable boldness, asked: 'Rabbi, the son did well to return, but what of the son who did better and remained with his father?'

Jesus continued:

'The elder son was in the field, and as he came and drew near to the house, he heard music and dancing. And he called one of the servants and asked what this meant. And he said to him, "Your brother has come, and your father has killed the fatted calf, because he has received him safe and sound." But he was angry and refused to go in. His father came out and entreated him, but he answered his father, "These many years I have served you, and I never disobeyed your command; yet you never gave me a kid, that I might make merry with my friends. But when this son of yours came, who has devoured your living with harlots, you killed for him the fatted calf!" And the father said to him, "Son, you are always with me, and all that is mine is yours. It was fitting to make merry and be glad, for this your brother was dead, and is alive; he was lost, and is found".'

This time, even Saul was silent.

'Make way for the Rabbi, please,' cried one of the disciples. 'The Rabbi has to go now. The Rabbi will attend the evening sacrifice.'

Long after the crowd had dispersed Samuel sat there with Nicodemus, marvelling. 'My own story,' he said, 'the King and his wastrel son. But how much more beautiful, how much deeper he has made it!'

There were tears in his eyes. 'The Holy Spirit has not spoken since the last of the Prophets,' said Samuel. 'Israel has been too sinful. Israel is too sinful still, and I cannot bring myself to believe that the Holy Spirit is again speaking. But if I could believe it of any man, I would believe it of Jesus.'

Nicodemus said soberly, as the implication of this tremendous statement struck him: 'You mean, you could almost believe that Jesus is a Prophet?'

'Yes,' said Samuel, 'I could, *almost*. But he is still young and he will go on teaching. There will be time to judge.'

'Myself,' said Nicodemus boldly, 'if he were a Prophet, I would not hesitate to place him above Malachi or Haggai, or even Zephaniah.'

'If he were indeed a Prophet,' said Samuel gravely, 'I would place him even higher. Greater than Habakkuk, perhaps even level with Amos or Micah.'

CHAPTER 18

Israel had been lucky, and Annas knew it. Pilate had left early for Caesarea, so that Festus was in charge. Festus had more sense than Pilate, and after the attack there had been no reprisals. All the same, Annas was worried. Next time might be worse.

'They are mad, these people,' he said to Nicodemus, in his palace. 'The Zealots will cut the throat of Israel in the name of religion. One would think they had never heard of Esther, in whose honour they get drunk once a year.'

They might even try to kill the modern Esther. Nicodemus consoled him: she had, he heard, already gone down to Pilate. Annas was not consoled: 'I know Pilate's wife better than you do, or Festus. The girl will soon be back.' And back, he comforted himself by supposing, in Tribune Festus' bed. This arrangement, so favourable to Israel, was one which the daggermen must not be allowed to disturb.

Nicodemus asked how he could stop them. By reason, in the first place, Annas said. Messages to various people in the movement, explaining what was what.

'Only in one thing you might help me,' said Annas. 'The only quarter where I have no connections myself.'

'What is that?'

'Could you speak to the Rabbi Jesus?'

Nicodemus laughed. 'You cannot be serious. Jesus a Zealot leader! And you were thinking of him as a candidate for a seat on the Sanhedrin!'

'And still am,' said Annas equably. 'But you yourself said that there were things to watch. You know that he visited the house from which the attack on Festus was mounted, less than two days before the attempt?'

Nicodemus explained, patiently. Things were the other way round.

'I hope you are right,' said Annas, 'but I have to assume you are not.'

Nicodemus was amused. 'Very well, if I do speak to Jesus, what am I to say? There is no point in putting it indirectly. He will know exactly what you mean. You, the High Priest of Israel, request the Rabbi Jesus not to arrange the assassination of a girl whose life he saved not long ago, because this same girl, by committing with the Romans the sin for which she was condemned to death by the Supreme Court of our people, may be performing an act of service to Israel.'

Annas said: 'You are unfair to me, my friend. Jesus is not mad, like most of the Zealots, and he would not give orders in this matter, only have influence. Also, the assassination of Pilate or Festus is more to be feared than that of Esther.'

'With that amendment, would your argument commend itself to the Rabbi Jesus?'

'If he is the sort of person I am looking for,' said Annas, '—and I have had very high hopes of him—it would.'

'I see that you and I have different opinions about the Rabbi Jesus,' said Nicodemus. 'In your position it might be hard for you to meet him, but I have been seeing quite a lot of one of his followers and I think he trusts me. If you want to know more about Jesus, that is the way to do things, and this man will talk more freely if he thinks you are only a friend of mine, visiting my house.'

*

John was disturbed for only a moment to find a stranger in Nicodemus' library. He took him on trust as a child takes a friend of its parents. A year ago, thought Nicodemus, he would never have dreamed of having such a grand acquaintance, but now he takes me and my house very much for granted, not appropriating us for his own purpose but treating me as another father and my house as another home. 'This,' he said to John, 'is a friend of mine on the Council. He is also an admirer of the Rabbi Jesus, though he has not met him yet.'

John took in the visitor without curiosity: evidently another of the same sort as his host, much smoother and more elegant than anything to which he was accustomed, even in the circles where Jesus now sometimes moved.

John addressed Annas directly. 'Are you too a Rabbi, Sir?' he said.

Annas laughed: 'No, lad, I am not clever enough for that. If you want to ask questions you must ask Rabbi Nakdemon.'

'Or Rabbi Jesus,' Nicodemus said.

'Rabbi Jesus, I hear, is most learned,' said Annas keenly. 'I have heard stories of his teaching of the Law.'

'Oh yes, Sir,' said John happily, 'and he does not teach only the Law.'

'Indeed! What else then?' asked Annas. 'I do not believe the stories which some people tell of him, that he is sometimes disrespectful of the Law.'

'Oh no, Sir,' cried John, 'he is most particular.'

'Then how do these stories arise? For instance, people say, his followers do not wash before they eat.'

'That is a lie, Sir,' said John warmly. 'Nearly all of us are very careful. There are just one or two who know no better. The Rabbi is always telling them, but sometimes they forget.'

'But,' said Annas, 'these stories go further. They say that the Rabbi actually defends them when people point it out.'

John smiled broadly. 'No, Sir,' he said. 'He does not defend them, ever, but he crushes the other side flat. I wish you could see it,' he added, familiarly, as if to an equal, forgetting the quality of the man to whom he spoke, admittedly not up to being a Rabbi but still one of the Sanhedrin members, an elder perhaps.

'Can you give us an example?' asked Annas.

'Why, yes!' said John. 'Once it was in Capernaum, after a Sabbath morning meal to which we were all invited. Our host said nothing, he was too polite to hurt anyone's feelings, but when we were walking home another guest caught up with us and got talking to the Rabbi, and after telling him how much he had admired his sermon in the synagogue that morning he said he was puzzled how one or two of us could slip up on an easy little thing like the pouring of water when an hour or two earlier they had been listening to the Rabbi speaking so beautifully about the Law.'

'And how did the Rabbi Jesus answer?'

'He didn't say a word in their favour,' said John. 'He was very polite. He said he was sorry that anyone's feelings should be hurt, especially when it was someone who he could see cared so much about the Law. "I do that!" said the fellow, pleased with himself. "Yes," said the Rabbi, "every bit of it! Even the newer parts that Moses never heard of, like this washing of hands before we eat. It isn't as if Moses had said anything *against* it either." "No," said the fellow, "there can't be any excuse." "Of course, if he had," said the Rabbi, "it would have been different, just as you say. I'm glad you agree with that." The man wasn't going to say anything, but the Rabbi made him, and he had to say Yes. "Well," the Rabbi said, "we agree on that, so let's see if we agree on something else." Then he told him of a story he had heard in Jerusalem at Passover, about some man who had a sick father, no longer earning. "The commandment of Moses says what, about parents?" asked the Rabbi. "The son should help the father," said the other. "No exceptions, then?" said the Rabbi. "Only not," said the fellow, "if he has already promised his money to the Temple." "Who said so?" asked the Rabbi. "Was it Moses?" "No, there wasn't a Temple in those days. The Rabbis told us, just like anything else." "Only a few years ago," said the Rabbi, "and it goes against Moses. So how can it be the Law?" "But it *is* the Law," said the man, "everyone says so." "Indeed!" said the Rabbi, "but you said just now that a rule of Moses is stronger than a rule of the Rabbis." Now the man was trying to get away, because he didn't like what was happening to him, but we were standing all around. "How is *your* father?" asked the Rabbi, very kindly. "Not very well," he said. "I'm sorry to hear that," said the Rabbi, "I'd be glad to look in if I'm passing." "Oh no, I couldn't trouble you," the fellow said. "No trouble at all," said the Rabbi, "I like helping." "I'll see he's all right!" cried the fellow, quite sudden. "Good!" said the Rabbi, "then I really am delighted, because now everything's all right." Well, by that time we all knew, and the fellow knew we knew, that he was the man in the story, and that he had been meaning to let his old father rot. "As for the other thing you mentioned," said the Rabbi . . . "Oh, it really doesn't matter!" said the other. "Oh but it does," said the Rabbi, "because it is the Law." "Oh never mind, I just mentioned it in case you hadn't noticed." "Thank you," said the Rabbi, "as a matter of fact I had." "I'm sorry I have to be going," said the man. "Go in peace, then," said the Rabbi, "and my blessings to your father, and my blessings on yourself".'

Annas listened with delight. 'That was magnificent. Exactly what ought to be said.'

'Then you are not a Pharisee, Sir?' asked John, puzzled. 'They are the ones who keep on about the Law.'

'No, I am not a Pharisee, young man,' said Annas, 'but I am just as careful as they are about the Law. Only, I reckon, just like your Rabbi Jesus, that the Law is the Law handed down by Moses, and although a lot of what the Rabbis say is good and useful it is not really the Law. I agree exactly with Jesus.'

Nicodemus looked uneasy. 'There are different opinions,' he said.

Annas laughed, and said to John: 'The Rabbi Nakdemon is right. The Pharisees do have different opinions, and they hold them very strongly. They are dangerous people, young man, to anyone like your master. Warn him to take care.'

John was out of his depth. 'I will explain afterwards,' said Nicodemus. 'My friend is right, and Rabbi Jesus should take care.'

'Well, finish your story,' said Annas. 'What happened in the end?'

John said: 'We heard, it was true, the man changed his mind and started helping his father. It was the same man, of course.'

'Your Rabbi seems to have good sources of information. And his followers, who did not wash their hands?'

'What he said to the other man was nothing to what he said to them later. They told me afterwards, they wished they were dead.'

'Anything else?' asked Nicodemus, 'anything Jesus said?'

'He said one thing that none of us could understand properly. He said: *Blessed is the man who knows what he is doing, but if he does it in ignorance he is cursed and a transgressor of the Law.*'

'What do you make of that, my friend?' Annas asked Nicodemus. John watched the two intellects at work, far above his head. 'Is it not something rather profound?' Annas said.

Nicodemus was disturbed. Philo had said something not unlike it: things contrary to duty in themselves may be done in the spirit of duty. But Philo was already much too liberal for the taste of his colleagues. And even Philo would never nibble at the Law. Indeed, he had said you must not do it: however much you know and love the inner meanings, you must not neglect the Law's commandments, and most particularly not the Sabbath.

'What Jesus could mean is this,' Nicodemus said to Annas. 'If you break the Law simply because you have not bothered to learn it, or you are careless enough to forget, then you are guilty. But if you neglect a command of the Law only in order to obey something more important . . .'—But what *is* more important? he wondered—'. . . then you are free.'

'Not only free and innocent, but praiseworthy,' said Annas gravely. 'It is fine teaching.'

'It is fine teaching,' said Nicodemus, 'but it is dangerous.' Nothing like this had yet come to the ears of Samuel: what would happen when it did? Perhaps Samuel would accept it if the commands were positive precepts and not prohibitions, and in twenty years' time the Doctors would sanction a new particle of the Law: The washing of hands is suspended by this, that and the other. But if the commands were prohibitions . . . ? 'Thou shalt do no manner of work on the Sabbath . . .' Only the most dreadful necessity suspended the Sabbath law: danger to life, for instance, or the continual service of the Temple, or the Mosaic precept of circumcision on the eighth day after birth. The Masters of Israel, but only collectively and over long periods, had sanctioned exceptions such as these, and no new Rabbi could go around adding to them, just—it seemed—as he pleased.

Nicodemus said slowly: 'If Jesus applies that to the Sabbath, my friends will be uneasy indeed.'

Part III

WINTER, AD28/29

CHAPTER 19

'Sit down, Centurion,' said Festus, 'and warm yourself.' The man was frozen, and he edged the stool closer to the charcoal glow. Midwinter in Jerusalem could be chilly, and snow could lie as it had lain now for a day or two on the Mount of Olives, making the limestone masses of the Temple in the foreground look dirty, but this was no worse than much of Syria and better by far than the highlands behind Tarsus or Smyrna.

Age perhaps was something, for this was obviously another of the long-service veterans, probably nearing the end of his term, hoping to settle comfortably in some town-colony, among a thousand others like him, lording it among the natives, a person of greater consequence the further he stayed from Rome. Festus had seen many of them in Syria. They had gone half-native themselves, and they mostly had a bit of native in them to begin with, Roman father, local wife.

Festus was right: the Centurion's home-town was Tarsus, his father a tradesman there, and he had signed on again after twenty years of service, with lighter duties. He had served in Antioch, Beirut and Damascus, and for the last fifteen years he had been stationed in Galilee, in Tiberias and lately Capernaum.

That would account for it, then, the blue feet of the Centurion. The Upper Jordan Valley was not as hot as Jericho but it was mild and glorious in winter, a small paradise compared with the highlands of Judaea.

'Not accustomed to this sort of winter, then,' said Festus. 'How do you like the change?'

It was an unfair question, put by a commanding officer, but

Festus did not see himself as a soldier, and this was not a military occasion. He had sent for the man as he sent for every officer newly posted to the Jerusalem garrison, to size him up as a source of information. This time it seemed that he had been lucky. The man might know something about that curious incident of which Nicodemus had told him, and which Festus intended to check.

'Jerusalem is very different from Capernaum, Sir,' said the Centurion valiantly, warming his chilblained toes. 'I shall get used to it here.'

'And your family?' asked Festus.

'Had to leave them behind in Capernaum, Sir. No married quarters in Jerusalem yet.'

'Will they be all right there?' asked Festus.

'Oh yes, Sir, we have plenty of friends. Even the natives are good to us, though of course they will never visit.'

'You got on well with the natives, then?' asked Festus astonished. How absurd it would be to ask that question here: the garrison shut up in its mighty fortress next to the Temple, all contact best avoided with a brooding and fanatic population, his own relationship with Nicodemus a rare exception and a happy chance. That is what we lack, thought Festus, high-grade information of almost any sort. It is no use relying on our third-rate lower-class informers who are probably in the pay of the other side as well.

'Oh yes,' said the Centurion, smiling at recollections of a happier time. 'I always said, be friends with them and they'll be friends with us.'

'And how does Jerusalem compare?'

'I've only been here a week, Sir, but I wouldn't try it. They strike me as hard and bitter, and they hate us.'

'If we can't talk to them here, how can we find out what they are thinking?'

'Ask in Galilee.' The Centurion explained. Half the people in Galilee spent half their time in Jerusalem anyhow, at some religious feast or other, and they talked when they got back.

And what about the Zealots? They were the ones who mattered. Galilee, said the Centurion, was the place to find out about the Zealots. They felt safe there, and made it their headquarters. No regular Roman troops were stationed there, only a handful of Romans like himself seconded to serve with Herod's local forces.

'You seem to know a lot about it,' said Festus. 'You must have picked up a lot during the last fifteen years down there. How did you report it?'

'Direct to Caesarea, once a month, until the change of Governor.'

'And since Pilate's arrival?'

'They seemed to lose interest. Told me to look in at the office if I happened to be on leave there, once or twice a year.'

Pilate can't know about that, thought Festus, it must be one of the jackals in his office, bone-idle or can't be bothered, or else in the pay of the Jews. But if in the pay of the Jews, then the Centurion is in danger, and especially in Jerusalem, for they will know what he has been reporting. They will have his life.

Festus saw what should happen. He said to the Centurion: 'Your posting here was not promotion. Am I right in thinking you would rather go back? Never mind about saying what a privilege it is to serve under me. Think, if you like, that you could be serving me in Capernaum.'

'Since you put it that way, Sir,' said the Centurion frankly, 'I would rather go back.'

'I do not know who arranged your posting,' said Festus, 'but I will speak to the Governor. If His Excellency agrees to reverse it, you will return to Capernaum, nominally seconded to Herod Antipas, but your real work will be to follow public opinion and keep track of nationalist movements. You will report on them not to Caesarea but direct to me.'

As the grateful Centurion was leaving, Festus remembered something he had forgotten, and called him back.

'Is there more than one Centurion in your neighbourhood?'

'I am the only one.'

'Was it your boy who was cured of a fever, by a man called Jesus?'

'It was.'

'What made you try him?'

'I had tried several others, but they could do nothing, and he had a good local reputation, so I thought I would ask.'

'Did he see the patient?'

'Oh no, Sir, it would have been no use asking, the Jews won't go into our houses.'

'So he cured the boy from a distance?'

'He did.'

'Did that not strike you as remarkable?'

'I hadn't heard of it done very often, but no, it didn't strike me at the time because of all the other things he had been doing.'

'Which were just as unusual?'

'So it seems.'

'Some time you must tell me more about them,' said Festus, 'but now only one more question. Did the doctor say anything about why he would try to help you?'

'He said it was because I believed.'

'Believed what?'

The Centurion was puzzled. 'I can't remember.'

'Perhaps he meant you believed he would do it?'

'Yes, I expect that was it,' said the Centurion. 'Yes, it sounds quite likely. I'm sure that was what he meant. I knew at once when I saw him, he wasn't a quack or a twister.'

'Would you go to him again?'

'Oh yes. If I was in the same trouble I wouldn't waste time trying any other doctor. I would go straight to him again.'

*

Festus descended. Even with the brazier burning and the shutters fastened, it was too cold up in the Tower.

He sat in a cubicle designed by the old Herod as winter quarters, facing across a courtyard due south, and the low

129

winter sun ducked into it, under the eaves of the colonnade outside. An octagonal bronze charcoal-burner, lion-footed, provided heat that was actual, and the forge of Vulcan in a fresco, heat of another kind.

During the winter Festus kept here a handstock of his library, containers ranged in wooden racks along one wall. Lamps burned all day on the tall bronze lampstands, by the table and in the corners, for there was not always sun.

Festus wrapped his cloak more closely round him, and robbed the other armchair of its cushions, to pad his own more warmly. Then he sent someone to find Paula: he had a question to ask.

She sat on the upright chair, across the table, no lines on her face and few shadows, in the glow evenly reflected round the walls of the chamber from a single shaft of sun. Festus forgot for a moment his question.

'You are beautiful, Domina,' he said.

At the word 'Domina' she started. 'I wish I were,' she said, smiling with a rueful pleasure, 'but it cannot be, and one day you must get married.'

She would not be the Domina of a future Senator and Pro-consul: her age opposed and her station forbade it, but all her life now she would remember, he had once addressed her as his 'Lady', truly though only in jest.

Festus told her the curious story of the Centurion and the healer. 'He said something odd to the Centurion. Do you know if he said anything on the same lines to Esther, something about "having faith"?'

'The simplest thing,' said Paula, 'would be to ask her.'

'How can we, when she is with Pilate?'

Paula said: 'She is back.'

Festus was astonished. 'But did they not like her?'

'Pilate liked her, too much.'

'What do you mean?' asked Festus.

'I will bring her in. You will see.'

*

'Is this the girl?' asked Festus, doubtful. 'Yes, I see.'

Wonderful what a few things will do for a woman, Festus thought. Instead of the slave cut, the hair done up quite simply with a single tier; instead of the straight-sided coarse grey garment, a properly tucked and folded white robe; a single silver ornament in the belt-buckle; and around the eyes the faintest shading of kohl.

'You did this?' he asked, admiring Paula.

Paula had. Festus continued. 'Yes, I can understand why Pilate's wife took against her. Perhaps a little—shall we say—outstanding for the part?'

But this created a problem. Esther, re-installed in the Palace, might cause trouble with the Jews. On the other hand, and rather more certain, she could be useful, at a low level, over native affairs.

'On the whole,' said Festus, 'I can't say I'm sorry that our plan miscarried, Paula. How about you?'

Paula looked at the child, standing just inside the door, unmoving except for the too-large black eyes restlessly following the exchange of speech. Festus thought, for the second time, Paula is pleased, and this is a daughter.

'No,' Paula said, after a long pause, for the question was not an easy one. 'I am not sorry she is back.'

'But what are we to do with her?' asked Festus. 'Could you make use of her yourself?'

Paula said they must talk in Latin: Esther's Greek had improved quite wonderfully. 'My needs are very simple. Not full-time, for sure. An hour or two in the morning, and then the afternoon at the baths.'

'Not enough to keep her busy.'

'I am not very busy myself.'

A brilliant notion came to Festus. 'Would you like to get out of the Palace more, Paula?' He explained his idea. Paula could go about in the streets accompanied by Esther. Both of them spoke the language, and both of them would be veiled. 'And,' said Festus, 'you may pick up useful bits of information, over-hearing the natives talk.'

Women of the better class did not go about in the streets, so they must dress like poor women coming in from the country, and the carriage must drop them at a safe distance outside the city. All the same, said Paula, speaking in Latin, there is danger, in spite of the veils. If Esther were recognised, some madman might kill her. 'If she is worried,' said Festus, 'promise her something. Some kind of reward.'

'We need not promise anything,' said Paula, 'only look after her, make sure she is not treated like any female slave. Remember the first night we had her!'

'I shall never forget it,' said Festus. 'It was a bad night's work, it cost me a very good bearer. But at least make sure of one thing, take away her knife.'

'She carries it always,' said Paula. 'She will guard it with her life.'

CHAPTER 20

In front of him Festus saw a happy man, the Centurion re-
planted in his warm and comfortable lakeside hot-house before
his roots could shrivel in the harsh cold soil of the Jerusalem
highlands. In that blessed country the early grain harvest was
already gathered almost before the almond had finished flower-
ing in Judaea. Already the days were hot enough to make uncomfortable the warm springs of Tabgha which, according to
valuable information imparted by the Centurion, were not only
cleansing but curative, specific for fevers and quinsy, rheumatics
and the shakes. Soon the cooling baths of Capernaum would
draw on the cold Jordan waters, snow-fed from Hermon, entering the Lake. In that blessed country Jew would speak to
Gentile, and the Jewish kinglet broadmindedly encouraged the
pleasures of civilisation.

Also, the mountains around the Lake were populous, green
and fertile, and networked with the feeders of the main Damascus
road. At any given time half the Galileans were working like
horses, and the other half—it seemed to the Centurion—
bustled about continually, telling each other the news.

This was the Centurion's second visit to Jerusalem since
midwinter. Festus asked for his report.

'Shall I start with Herod and his doings?'

'Not if it has to do with his women. I am sick of that.'

'In a way this has,' said the Centurion, disappointed, 'but
perhaps not in the way Your Excellency thinks.'

Festus smiled. 'What then?' he said.

'His wife has played a dirty trick on him. Got him to cut off somebody's head. He didn't want to do it, but she had made him promise.'

'Bloodthirsty bitch!' Festus muttered. A thought alarmed him. 'It was not your doctor man, I hope?'

'No, Sir,' said the Centurion, 'that was my own first thought. Only a rather crazy fellow who never cured anyone. It probably isn't much loss.'

'No trial, I suppose?' said Festus.

'No, it happened at a party. They sent and cut off his head.'

'A curious form of entertainment, even for a Herod,' said Festus.

'Herod was very sad. He said this man John was as good value as a troupe of performing monkeys.'

'Then what was the excuse?'

'The woman said he had spoken of her slightingly.'

'That was tactless of him. What did he say?'

'He said she was an incestuous whore.'

Festus smiled. 'For some of that family it would be a compliment. Was there any public demand for his death?'

'Oh no, on the contrary, this John was very popular. People agreed with what he said.'

'So Herod has executed a free man without trial, and without the voice of the people as his excuse. The act of a coward, or tyrant.'

'It is not the way we do things, Sir,' said the Centurion more tolerantly, 'but that is how these people behave.'

'It will be a black day if we ever imitate them,' said Festus. 'The right thing in such cases is to whip the man and let him go.' He recollected himself: it was hardly in place to talk high politics with a subordinate, however able, of such a junior rank.

'But this man, I suppose, was not one of the Zealots?' asked Festus. 'Anything new about them?'

'Too much,' said the officer. 'It doesn't add up as it should.'

'Rather too much than too little,' said Festus. 'Till now, we've had nothing at all.'

'Well, Sir, to start with the most serious, there are plans for some kind of rising, not this year but it seems like next year's Passover. About a year and a month from now.'

'In Galilee or in Judaea?'

'In Jerusalem itself. The usual thing, the bandits mixing with the pilgrims.'

'Anything else about tactics?'

'Nothing so far on that.'

'What about weapons?' asked Festus.

'They are not going to risk using the pilgrims' baggage. They are worried by the searches we have been carrying out. They are going to try something quite fresh, the wagons with offerings for the Temple.'

'We can easily look in those.'

'Begging your pardon, Sir, not unless you are going to find something. It will be sacrilege against their superstition, if you don't.'

'Then what use is the information if we cannot conduct a search?'

The Centurion explained: it was simple. There was a weakness in the plan. The offerings to the Temple were firstfruits, but even in the hot low-lying coastland around the Lake, Passover was too early for most of the firstfruits: barley would be ready and in some years even wheat, but not figs or grapes or pomegranates, let alone dates or olives. So, apart from grain, the wagons would be loaded with other kinds of offering, normally presented to the priests' households locally and not sent to Jerusalem at all, baskets of doves from the dove-valley above Magdala, jars of oil and of wine, and fleeces of sheep.

'This coming Passover,' said the Centurion, 'in a month, they are doing a trial run. They are loading half a dozen wagons with this stuff which is unusual, and if it does not make our checkpoints suspicious they will do the same next year, only with weapons hidden underneath. So, this year we need only watch them, and next year do the search.'

Festus admired the Centurion, and hardly less himself.

Between them, the Centurion by his efforts and Festus by giving him his head, they had hit upon something fairly serious. No revolt had any chance of succeeding, but far better to nip it in the bud. Festus asked the officer how he had got the information.

'A little from informants,' said the Centurion, 'but nearly all of it by a trick. Herod had given me a couple of bandits to look after. They are the source.'

'But how could you get it by torture?' asked Festus. 'These people never talk.'

'Oh no, Sir, torture is useless. I treated them very well. A nice room with beds and a window, and meals.'

'You left them together, then?' asked Festus. 'That would make it even harder. How did you get them to talk?'

'They didn't talk to us, Sir,' said the Centurion. 'We just waited. They got bored, and talked to each other, and they didn't know we could hear them.' He explained. Naturally, the prisoners tapped all the walls to make sure they were solid, but there was an old drainage channel under one corner, and a chink between the floor and the stone footing of the wall. The channel had been enlarged by the Centurion's interpreter, to make a listening-post. No other person was in the secret, and the interpreter was absolutely safe: he hated the bandits because they had slaughtered his family for helping the Romans.

'Most ingenious!' said Festus. 'I shall see that you are suitably recognised for this.'

The Centurion begged him to say nothing. People would talk. If the bandits got to hear about his special arrangements, any future prisoners would be on their guard.

'Very well,' said Festus. 'I will tell nobody, except the Governor himself.'

What else had the Centurion discovered? Were the names of the leaders known?

'Not yet,' said the Centurion. 'Maybe the prisoners do not know them, or they may have sworn never to speak them aloud. That is what we need most, the names of the leaders.'

He continued. 'That is what worries me. Absolute silence by some people, and others are shouting aloud.'

'Shouting the names of the leaders?'

'One of them, at least. You will not believe it. It is the doctor who helped me, Jesus.'

'It doesn't make sense,' said Festus, remembering Nicodemus. 'A man like that a bandit!'

'Just what I thought, Sir, but it is not quite as mad as you might think. I don't know how much you know about their superstitions, but the common people are always talking of some great leader who will come from nowhere and drive out the Romans. They call it establishing the kingdom of their god. It's mostly silly uneducated talk, but some of them take it quite seriously.'

'And they think it might be Jesus?'

'Yes. He's not a bandit, but he is a leader, and people run after him. I've seen them, not in the streets but across the Lake on the east shore, a few miles from Capernaum. Clambering up the hills after him, like a herd of goats.'

'What were they doing that for? Could it be training?'

'Not with women and children, Sir. I've no idea. And there are no villages. They wouldn't find anything to eat. It seems he did some cures up there, but why should he go half-way up a mountain to do it?'

'Medicinal springs, obviously,' said Festus. 'What happened after?'

'He gave them the slip during the night and got back to Capernaum somehow, but a lot of them followed him there. Then they started drifting away again. That made me suspicious. He might have told them to go away and not make things so obvious, or else the Romans would get Herod to shut him up as a trouble-maker.'

'Or,' said Festus, 'they might have decided that after all he was not their leader.'

'It could be,' the officer admitted, 'but it doesn't add up properly. He is the sort of man whom people do follow. No,

I fancy he is the one who did the telling. People wouldn't leave him, unless he wanted them to, for some reason of his own.'

'Now we are only guessing,' said Festus. 'You have done very well already, Centurion. Now go back and get some more facts.'

CHAPTER 21

It had been a bad winter for Nicodemus, for news had been scarce.

First there was son Gorion, disappearing for a week or two at a time. Gorion, in the intervals left by what he considered his religious duties, worked for a firm of grain-merchants, and his business could take him anywhere. Nicodemus was not surprised at his absences, only at his silences. Gorion, it seemed, had got over his distaste for Galilee, for he mostly travelled there, though not around the Lake where dealers were plentiful and the harvests were early. He was vague about his transactions and the people he had seen.

Nicodemus never forgot the words of Annas, but he shrank from the ultimate question, lest the answer should take away the last ground for hope. Gorion, he was all but certain, was involving himself with the Zealots, whom the Romans called bandits or terrorists and treated as such, and Nicodemus consoled himself by supposing that Gorion's role was unimportant and only on the fringe.

Then there was Jesus, also in Galilee. Annas and Samuel had both seemed ready to hail him as the hope of Israel, though for opposite reasons, but that was five or six months ago, and Jesus had not stood still. If the accounts going round in Jerusalem were to be trusted, Nicodemus was right to have misgivings. But reliable news was impossible to come by, and Nicodemus waited impatiently for the next visit of John. The winter rains were now finished, and Passover was approaching, and Jesus must be in Jerusalem soon.

*

John came when the first roses were opening in the sheltered courtyard. 'The Rabbi will be here tomorrow,' he said, 'and I have arranged his lodgings with Azzai and Mary.'

'I have kept a room ready for you,' said Nicodemus. 'I have been waiting. You must stay here tonight.'

Nicodemus was amused to see how easily John took to a new way of living, the world where you visit the baths without leaving the house, and served by more than one attendant. Afterwards they sat in the library, for the evenings were still too cool outside.

Nicodemus examined John closely. The difference was not only in the beard, now much more strongly grown. John had a restless look, inattentive as if exalted. Nicodemus did not like it. The more exalted the master, the more important that his followers should stay firmly on the ground. That Jesus was something exalted, Nicodemus by now had no doubt. Perhaps it was going too far to think of him as a prophet—the race of prophets had been extinct for several hundred years—but at the least he was a most remarkable person. People like that were entitled to a few aberrations, but the more aberrations they had the more they needed to be protected, from others who did not understand. That was why they needed good solid people around them, outstanding for common sense.

If John had fallen victim to illusions he would be useless, and Nicodemus must try to prick them gently. But first he let John talk.

He was appalled, to begin with. The credulity was greater even than he feared. Then he began to notice: John had a special technique. Which side is he on, the story-teller? Is it he who is credulous or you who are simple for thinking so? The misunderstanding, is it real, is it deliberate? Are the characters speaking the truth without knowing it—perhaps even their own

139

condemnation—thinking it is something else? Are you, the listener, yourself a character on the stage and in the story, without a speaking part?

Impossible to imagine that this was something conscious. The boy was far too young, open and artless, lacking in education too. Yet the talent was there, rich ore waiting for the hand to draw it out and refine it, something which seemed to Nicodemus very precious and rare. In all the Greeks, he had met nothing quite like it, yet it could take a Greek polish and sharpen at the edges.

Nicodemus arrived suddenly at a surprising conclusion: Jesus was not the only unusual one. This young cousin might not be in the class of Jesus, but he too had something extraordinary in him. Perhaps it ran in the mothers' family, they were sisters, John had said.

But if only he were my son! thought Nicodemus. What treasure, and what one could do!

'So,' said John sadly, 'it all came to nothing in the end, the movement. The Rabbi sent them away.'

'He could hardly do anything else,' said Nicodemus, 'if he didn't want to fall foul of the Romans. Herod would have treated him like the other John.'

'Perhaps then the Rabbi didn't really mean it,' said John, brightening, 'only that it was better to wait.'

'No,' said Nicodemus, 'my guess is that he meant something quite different, that he was not the man at all.'

'That is what he *said*,' said John, clinging to hope. 'He would not let them treat him as their king, but perhaps he meant that all the same he was.'

'Their *king*?' said Nicodemus. 'What did they mean by that?'

John lowered his voice reverentially, but not very much: he saw no great difficulty. 'The Messiah,' he said.

Nicodemus recoiled from the thought: he could not bring himself to speak the word. Unquestionably the great national leader, Messiah or whatever people chose to call him, would one day appear, and free his people from the yoke of the Gentiles, but it would be folly to expect any such thing to happen in one's own lifetime, it would produce a tremendous upheaval in one's way of life and upset all one's foreign connections, and nobody counted on it seriously as a practical possibility, except the ignorant common people.

'Tell me,' said Nicodemus, smiling, 'your master has cast out many evil spirits. Has he ever cured a man of claiming to be the Messiah?'

'No,' said John, 'but he has cured several of calling *him* that.'

'The Rabbi Jesus is too great a teacher,' said Nicodemus, 'to want to be thought of like that.'

'Oh, do you think so, Sir?' asked John, disappointed. 'We sometimes hoped. We hoped that it might be he who would redeem Israel.'

'Someone has been getting at you, lad, with quotations,' said Nicodemus. ' "Redeem Israel *from all its sins*", is what the book says, not redeem it from the Roman tax-collector. Also the Psalmist is not speaking of a man but of God himself.' Nicodemus spoke severely: 'My son, there have been lunatics who called themselves "Messiah", and some of them the Romans laughed at and they were forgotten and others raised a few hundred or a few thousand armed men in rebellion and were crucified. My son, forget it: it is a title mis-used by foolish men.'

'But,' said John, 'the Rabbi once used it of himself.'

'When was that, and how?' cried Nicodemus, startled.

'He was talking with a woman, whom he had asked for some water. He went on talking when it was all over, as he usually does, and they got on to quite a different subject. The Rabbi said to her: *The hour is coming when neither on this mountain nor in Jerusalem will you worship the Father*. He said: *The hour is coming, and now is, when the true worshippers will worship the Father in spirit and truth, for such the Father seeks to worship him. God is spirit, and those who worship him must worship in spirit and truth*. Then the woman said: *I know that the Messiah is coming, and when he comes he will show us all things.* Then Jesus said: *I who speak to you am he.'*

Nicodemus listened, absorbed. 'One thing is certain. The man who spoke those words is not a man of war. Listen, my son,' he went on, carried away, 'the man who said that is a great teacher, one of the greatest ever in Israel. He is not a commander in battle, shedding the blood of the Gentiles. But where did this happen? I am puzzled. Where is the mountain?'

'The woman was a Samaritan, at Jacob's Well.'

Nicodemus was relieved. In one way at least the Samaritans were more sensible than the Jews: they thought of the 'Messiah' only as a teacher. John took little comfort from this. He said that he and his friends had been badly disappointed, when Jesus sent the crowds away and everyone else had left.

'What did Jesus say to you then?'

'He asked us if we too were going to leave him.'

'But you didn't.'

'No, Simon said it, not the one who had been a Zealot but Simon Peter. He said: "To whom shall we go? It is you who have the words of eternal life, and we have come to believe that you are God's Holy One".'

'Well said!' exclaimed Nicodemus. ' "God's Holy One" puts it very neatly. Yes, I do not at all disagree with that. Jesus is quite as great a man as Samson, even if not as Aaron. Your Simon evidently knows the Scriptures well.'

'Not really,' said John, 'but he has a knack of saying the right thing to the right person.'

*

'All the same,' said John later, before retiring, 'it was much more exciting, and everyone would be with him. Do you think there is really *no* chance of his being the great leader?'

CHAPTER 22

Nicodemus had worked hard on behalf of Samuel, and had won. The Cause of the Parthian Sandals had ended this morning, and he hurried down to the Lower City to tell Samuel in his shoemaker's shop. Now Samuel could go ahead with the orders, hundreds and hundreds of pairs, all suspended while the Sanhedrin deliberated over Samuel's conscience. Were the sandals lawful, or not?

Samuel himself had raised the question, to the annoyance of his friends. The new style of sandal was a goldmine, or could be if Samuel would only adjust his charges, but last year on the Day of Atonement Samuel had conceived an awful doubt. The mixture of flax and wool in one garment was forbidden, if woven or spun. Did the law apply also to rags when hammered together? Samuel, as the maker, could tell the difference between rags of linen and of wool, but not so the customer when all was hammered solid. If doubt could exist the rule was clear: take the side of strictness. Thus, while it was lawful for Samuel to manufacture and sell the sandals, the sandals might not be lawful for customers to purchase or wear.

Fortunately Samuel himself could be excluded from the discussion, on the ground of his interest, which would have led him to vote against himself. None the less, Nicodemus had had a struggle canvassing, and the majority had been small. It had taken almost six months to reach a decision, and only now had the Opinion of the Learned been issued, for the benefit of the petitioner Samuel, shoemaker and Doctor of the Law. The purchase and wearing of the sandals was lawful if the sandals were made and guaranteed by Samuel himself.

In other words, thought Nicodemus, they have granted Samuel a monopoly. But he still will not charge!

Samuel received the news gratefully, sitting in his one-and-a-half room shop by Siloam, but seemed less cheerful than Nicodemus had hoped. 'You could take another apprentice,' said Nicodemus. 'There is no end to the orders. You can be rich.'

Samuel smiled despondently. At least, Nicodemus thought, he has accepted the Opinion. When he was younger and even more scrupulous he might have refused to act on it, lest it should profit himself.

Samuel took out the strips of cloth from the corner where he had laid them several months ago, squatted on his low stool and began listlessly pounding them: listlessly he pounded his thumb.

It could not be Simeon's death which still engrossed him: Samuel had got over that. 'What is it, my friend?' asked Nicodemus gently. 'There is some trouble on your mind.'

'I cannot work,' said Samuel miserably. He got up and closed the door and window. They sat there in darkness, but for the light which filtered round the edges of the shutters. Would-be customers approached and retreated. The voices and footsteps were muffled outside.

'Have you not heard?' asked Samuel. 'Jesus has transgressed the Law. Not in ignorance, for he knows everything.'

'Impossible!' said Nicodemus, with more confidence than he felt. 'He is the greatest defender of the Law.'

'True, and yet he has transgressed the Law.'

'There must be some misunderstanding. Only his followers, perhaps.'

'No, he did it personally and he declared that he was doing it.' Samuel explained. Yesterday there had been another remarkable cure, but yesterday had been the Sabbath. Nicodemus reminded Samuel, as gently as he could: there had been another case, of a young man who was *not* cured on a Sabbath but whose sickness proved mortal the next day. 'No,' said Samuel without flinching, 'My son was sick unto death, though I did not know it, and Jesus would have been right to cure him, just as I was right to refuse.'

'Perhaps it is the same in this case.'

'No. Jesus admits it. The man was one of those poor creatures at Bethesda, nobody who is going to die ever goes there, nor anyone who is going to get well: they just lie around the pool and gossip, for years and years.'

'He might have died tomorrow. The day after the Sabbath might have been too late.'

'If only I could think so! But I cannot.' Samuel almost wept. 'Jesus said something dreadful: *Is it not lawful to do good on the Sabbath?*'

'He only asked a question,' said Nicodemus.

'But he answered it by his deed.'

Nicodemus saw that the clash which he had feared was drawing closer. Samuel's point was unanswerable, in his own terms. God had given six days for labour, and the rest on the seventh day was in honour of the Almighty, beside whom men and all their doings were of no account. To perform on the Sabbath an act of mercy which could equally well be done the next day was deliberate defiance of the Law given by the Almighty. It was to set the temporal relief of a minor human affliction above the infinite honour due to the eternal God.

If Samuel's story was true, and Nicodemus intended to check it, a considerable amount of thinking had to be done. Nicodemus did not think he was the man to do it, yet he saw none of his colleagues better placed than himself. You could not get away from the rock-bottom basis from which they must argue, all of them, even Nicodemus himself: the Law is God's Law, unchanging, eternal, and attack on the Law is attack on God himself.

You would have to get right away from Samuel and go to that old cynic Annas before you found anything else, and in moral questions Nicodemus did not much relish having Annas on his side.

'If the man is a Prophet,' he said, consoling Samuel, 'as both of us had hoped, he must have reasons which are not apparent. Let us wait and see.'

145

Samuel said: 'I will not join those who condemn him, on the strength of this alone. I hoped that it would be he who would bring Israel to repentance, and I will go on hoping till the end. But the Prophets condemned Law-breakers, and none of them condemned the Law.'

'He cannot condemn the Law if he is the Law's great champion.'

'There are things,' said Samuel, 'which I do not understand.' He sighed and rose, and changed his garment. 'I am going to the Temple,' he said. Outside, he refastened the door. Shoemaker Samuel was shutting up shop an hour early, a sign of the most extreme agitation of soul.

'Gamaliel may have ideas,' said Nicodemus, as they made their way upwards through the narrow crowded streets, the lively noisy smelly back-end of the city, poor one-storey habitations plastered over the steep hillside right up to the Temple. The man-made cliff of the outer Temple wall rose sheer above them, pale bastion reaching endlessly upward and to either side, blotting out the northern sky: it was a monument, Nicodemus reflected, without rival in Greece or Asia, Egypt or Rome, vaster even than the Pyramids of Egypt and like them indestructible, and like nothing else on earth the abode of the living God.

'Shall we be hearing next,' said Samuel sadly, bitterly jesting, as they entered the great tunnel mouth at the foot of the platform supporting the wall, 'that Rabbi Jesus is speaking against the Temple?'

They rose into the light in the midst of the great courtyard, the Sanctuary itself ahead, and very prominent on the curtain wall opposite the tunnel entrance, the warning carved in stone: no Gentile is to approach within this place, and whoever does so will be guilty of his own death.

Nicodemus left Samuel by the great basin of ablutions and made his way above ground to the main western gate, over the viaduct and towards the Upper City, and to Annas' house.

The streets and houses were an unrolling pattern, and the

people like cloud-eddies drifting by. Nicodemus knew where he was but his eyes were turned inward, examining scenes somewhere else. Jesus could not be wrong, but nor could Samuel. If there was an answer to this riddle it must lie in something else, not to be found in the framework of Rabbi Samuel or even of Rabbi Jesus himself. If the two were in dispute over the same matter, they could not both be right. Therefore, since neither could be wrong, they must be dealing with different questions, even though the questions looked the same.

*

Annas, as Nicodemus had expected, was amused and not affronted: he applauded Jesus' feat. 'It will help to cut your Pharisee friends down to size,' said Annas. 'Jesus is perfectly right. The Sabbath rest is the Lord's commandment, but all these details are not, they have only been worked out by the Doctors. They should not call it the Law.'

'But it *is* the Law,' said Nicodemus. 'Even Jesus has said so. The Doctors of the Law, he said, sit in the seat of Moses.'

'Did he say that they speak with the voice of Moses?' asked Annas.

'I do not know,' said Nicodemus, 'but my friends the Pharisees as you call them say so, and they speak for Israel in matters of religion, and you and your friends do not.'

'That is a different matter,' said Annas, 'one of politics. Speaking purely as a religious authority, if you will allow me'— both the men smiled—'I say that the Pharisees are talking nonsense, but as a politician I know that you are right. Samuel speaks with the voice of Israel, whether he is mistaken or not.'

Nicodemus said: 'Samuel has no doubt whatever that what he thinks is right.'

'They terrify me,' said Annas earnestly, 'Samuel and his friends just as much as the Zealots. They are utterly unshakeable. They know that they are right.'

'And therefore,' said Nicodemus, smiling, 'you have to

147

admit that they are only doing their duty. They do what they think is right.'

'No, no,' said Annas, much amused by the fancy. 'That is no way for a Jew to argue. You are no better than a Greek.' He continued: 'For the second time I say it, good luck to the Rabbi Jesus, but let him beware. If he falls foul of the Doctors I cannot save him.'

'Then you still want to save him,' said Nicodemus. 'To put fresh blood into the Sanhedrin? Or perhaps just to help your own party?'

Annas considered, frowning slightly. 'As you know,' he said, 'I am not often mistaken in my judgment of people, but I am not so sure about Jesus as I was. Yes, I do wish him well, and I hope he gets clear of his enemies, but there have been some disturbing reports.'

'Not just his views on the Law?'

'Oh no, this is something serious. You remember, I had suspicions before. A possible tie-up with the Zealots.'

Nicodemus examined his friend: could the High Priest, ruler of Israel for over twenty years, experienced politician, worldly-wise if nothing else, take this extraordinary story seriously? Apparently, Annas could.

'If you mean the crowds following him near Capernaum,' said Nicodemus, 'Jesus sent them away. I have it straight from one of his followers, the nice young man you met.'

'Exactly what he would do if he were implicated,' said Annas. 'The Romans are very suspicious of any assembly. And that is not the worst. I don't like all these references to the coming "Kingdom". Jesus is too intelligent to believe it, and he knows it must excite the crowd.'

'If I am the slightest judge of persons,' said Nicodemus, 'Jesus is not the man to preach a holy war.'

'Oh,' said Annas, 'but I think he is, and I admire him for it, but we simply have no chance.'

'*If* he is doing it,' said Nicodemus ironically.

'Yes, *if*,' said Annas. 'This is still only suspicion, and we need

148

more evidence. Perhaps you could talk to your friend Festus. The Romans will have their own means of information about subversive movements.'

Annas took Nicodemus' arm affectionately. 'It does not do to be starry-eyed about persons, in my position.'

'I hope I was not starry-eyed in my business,' said Nicodemus, laughing. 'The Alexandrian business-world was not a place for innocents.'

'No indeed, but this is politics,' said Annas. 'Much worse than business. You were only playing for a fortune. I am playing for lives.'

Part V

SUMMER, AD29

CHAPTER 23

'You have nothing like *that*, in Galilee,' said Festus with satisfaction, pushing over a basket. The Centurion examined the small golden fruit with interest, fragrant, flushed, furry, warm to the touch. 'No, Sir,' he said. 'Can they be eaten?' 'Eat one,' Festus said. He had become tired of hearing the praises of Capernaum ('Is there not a fishy smell there?' he had said once.) To believe the Centurion, Galilee was the garden of the Hesperides, rich in golden apples as well as more ordinary fruit. Festus had heard so much about Galilee that he was warming to Judaea, cold maybe in winter but peerless in summer, when the mist still hung in the lower branches of the olives at sunrise and the vines were drenched with dew. Let the Galileans keep their honey-pots and their fish-sauces, and they could keep their young Herod too.

'They are apricots, from Armenia,' said Festus. 'The old king Herod planted them, forty years ago. Stewed, the flesh is delicious. The stones, pounded and steeped in vinegar, are said to provide a lethal potion. Probably that is why Herod got them.'

'We have nothing like that in Galilee,' said the Centurion, obediently. 'But I am sure they would do even better there.'

'No doubt,' said Festus, beaten. 'Everything seems to do better there.' True also, he reflected, of the Centurion. In Jerusalem he would have been wasted. In Galilee he produced results.

'What have you found out this time?'

'The rebel plan, and the names of the leaders.'

Festus smiled, admiring the brevity of the report. 'You could expand that a little. How can you be so sure?'

'The same way as last time, listening, but a little extra touch. We had some more prisoners and I got one alone and said to him: Well, now you're finished, we know all about your Rabbi Jesus and what he is after, so why don't you save yourself a lot of trouble and help us, tell us about the rest. Then he looked at me, very frightened, pretending of course, and after a bit he broke down, still pretending, and said in that case it's no use and I'll tell you, just to save people's lives. Then he told me a lot of rubbish which we knew already about this doctor Jesus and his followers, and where they could be found.'

'Which you pretended to believe?'

'I wrote it down in front of him. Then I let him go back to his cell and the first thing he said to the man he shared with was what fools the Romans are, they have swallowed the story which we have been spreading. "Won't *our* Jesus be pleased!" the fellow said.'

'And you found out which Jesus?'

'Yes, Sir. Even if he'd stopped there we'd have had plenty to go on, we have lots of Jesus's on our list but most of them can be counted out one way or another. But he went on talking and soon we had the whole story. The man who matters is Jesus bar Abbas. Whereabouts at present unknown, but we have his description.'

'And this gang had been putting it about that Rabbi Jesus is really their leader?'

'They had.'

'It sounds grotesque,' said Festus.

'It does when you know it, but if we hadn't known it we might have believed what they said. After all, as I said to Your Excellency last time, the Rabbi Jesus *is* a leader, only not one of their particular sort.'

Festus said: 'If they have been putting this about in order to cover themselves, how do they know that Rabbi Jesus won't be arrested? As soon as he's in prison, he is no more use to them, except to throw us off our guard.'

'I reckon they know he won't do anything to bring it on himself,' said the Centurion. 'Until the bandits want it, he won't be arrested.'

'When will they want it?' asked Festus.

'They are cunning,' said the Centurion. 'This is their plan. Just before Passover next year they will attack the Jerusalem garrison. But their only hope is to catch our men in the open. Rabbi Jesus is the bait to draw us out of the Fortress. They know that he will be going up to Jerusalem a few days before Passover, like everyone else, and they reckon that he is quite likely to have a big demonstration anyhow but if he doesn't they will arrange it, and they reckon that what with this and the other rumours they will be spreading the Romans will be out in force and all eyes on the Rabbi Jesus.'

'A good plan!' said Festus, approving. 'These men are something more than bandits.'

Should they arrest him now, the other Jesus, bar Abbas? The Centurion thought so, as soon as they could catch him.

'On what charge?' asked Festus.

'Hold him without trial.'

'Some time he must be charged, and the only evidence we have is secret.'

'Sentence him without bringing the evidence, or else fake it,' said the Centurion.

'The Jews can behave like that, but not the Romans.' Festus reflected: he wished he could feel so sure of Pilate, who could bend the rules if he wished, and on occasion had done so, for his personal advantage. These doubts, however, were not to be shared with the Centurion.

Better leave him alone, Festus decided, to start his insurrection. The Romans would be waiting, and would catch the whole lot red-handed.

Better, too, for Jesus bar Abbas if he was killed in action, outright. Otherwise he would be crucified after days of torture, when it no longer mattered to the Romans whether he was crucified or not, for after the special squad had finished with him he would be no more use to anyone as a leader, and they might just as well hand him back to his own people.

CHAPTER 24

Festus was anxious about his visitor's health. The season of apricots was over, and there had been mulberries and figs, and now the first dates from the Jordan Valley had reached the Jerusalem markets. Paula, on one of her expeditions with Esther, had brought back a bunch, lest they be observed empty-handed leaving the market. They were long and, as dates go, tender, this particular sort, and Festus was distressed that Nicodemus would not touch them, nor the wine nor any other refreshment that was brought.

'My doctor will give you a prescription,' said Festus, Aristotle climbed the stairs. 'Abstinence,' he said, 'is the best cure for a temporary indisposition of the stomach.' Festus was displeased with the doctor, not showing off his best. 'No, no,' he said, 'let us have one of your special prescriptions. Spare no effort for our guest.'

But this 'indisposition' is not temporary, reflected Nicodemus, it is as permanent as anything can be. No Jew shall eat with a Gentile. It is the Law.

Aristotle designed a specific of juniper, crushed with honey, in wine. 'That sounds better,' said Festus approvingly. 'Is there nothing else you could add?'

'I could mix in some of the gold-leaf which I use for the Governor.'

'Excellent,' said Festus, 'do that. Nothing is too good for our guest.'

Aristotle descended. They were alone in the Tower. 'Aristotle

153

can cure you just as well as the doctor Jesus, of some things,' said Festus.

'They use different methods,' said Nicodemus. 'Aristotle is more traditional. But Jesus works very fast.' He repeated some of John's stories.

Festus asked: 'What, then, do your people think of Jesus?'

'He is a great healer, but that is not what matters. He is a teacher too. Some of us think he is one of the greatest teachers ever. He is in the line of our prophets, and he may even be one himself.'

Festus said: 'I do not know about your prophets. Are they like the augurs whom we have?'

Nicodemus did not wince: he was accustomed to this sort of misunderstanding. But to compare the Prophets of Israel, sons and servants of the Most High God and mouthpieces of His Holy Spirit, with Roman soothsayers and their sacred chickens . . . !

'Not precisely,' said Nicodemus. 'For one thing, their main task was not to foretell the future but to remedy the sins of the present.'

'It sounds like a dangerous occupation.' said Festus.

'It was, and sometimes it was fatal.'

'How many of them do you generally have functioning? We usually run a dozen or so at a time.'

'Our system is different,' said Nicodemus. 'Our prophets are fewer than your augurs. Including Moses and Elijah there were about a score of them, spread over a thousand years.'

'Before that,' said Festus, 'I suppose you were Egyptian. According to Strabo, your Moses was an Egyptian priest.'

What nonsense! said Nicodemus, and they spent a happy five minutes dissecting the reputation of the dead writer, polymath over an even wider field than Festus but insufficiently critical about his sources.

They came back to Jesus. If he was a prophet, said Festus, he must be something rare.

'Very. The first for hundreds of years.'

'Does that explain the crowds that follow him?'

The moment was approaching: Nicodemus had come for this. He said: 'It ought to, and in my opinion it does.'

Festus said: 'Then it sounds as if there are other opinions.'

'There is a lot of foolish talk. Ignorant people are spreading rumours. I know myself that they are nonsense. I wanted to make sure that the Romans think so too.'

'What are these rumours?'

'That Jesus is not only a preacher but a rebel, preparing our people for a revolt.' Nicodemus waited, but Festus said nothing, and he had to proceed. 'Unfortunately, there are some important people among us who actually believe this nonsense. I would like to go back and tell them that the Romans agree with me, they know this man is harmless.'

Festus again remained silent, thinking, and Nicodemus asked, his confidence shaken: 'Can I tell them, the Romans agree?'

'How important are these people you mention?' asked Festus.

'Very important indeed. They are in a position to destroy the Rabbi Jesus, if they suspect him of plotting. They are entirely on your side.'

A very small number, then, thought Festus, but important: it can only be the party of the High Priest. 'But you,' said Festus, musing, 'know that Jesus is innocent, and you wish to save him from these people you mention, so that he may continue with his teaching.'

'I do.'

Festus, to give himself time to think, rose and walked to the window: to the east the Temple and to the north Golgotha, mercifully vacant today. Jesus, he knew, was innocent, but it was perilous to say so, and impossible to reveal the secret of how the Romans knew. However, in the end things were bound to come all right for Jesus: there would be no need for further secrecy after next Passover, when the revolt was crushed, and in any case no serious harm could come to Jesus without the agreement of the Romans, who would never agree to condemn an innocent man.

Therefore, there was little that Festus dared to say to Nicodemus, but he would help him as much as he could.

Festus said: 'You can tell your friends that we have no particular ground for suspicion in the present, though of course we are always on the watch.'

*

'Did Festus tell you anything of his sources of information?' asked Annas. 'He evidently had some. That is the thing that counts.'

'No,' said Nicodemus.

Annas repeated the words softly: ' "We have no particular ground for suspicion in the present, though of course we are always on the watch." A good official answer, designed to give nothing away.'

Annas lifted his head suddenly and asked point-blank: 'If you were a Roman, my friend, and you were asked by one of a subject nation whether you suspected that someone else was plotting a revolt, and if in fact you had reason to suspect him, what would you say?'

'I do not know,' said Nicodemus. 'I cannot put myself in their position at all.'

'I can,' said Annas, 'because I am always doing it, and I am a ruler, of sorts, myself. I know exactly. I would not say: Yes, I do suspect him, because this might be reported and reach his ears, and he would be on his guard.'

'What would you say, then?'

'I would say: We have no particular ground to suspect him at the moment, but we are always on our guard.'

Nicodemus asked: 'If you were the Roman, and you knew the man was innocent, what would you reply?'

'I would say: No, we have no ground for suspicion. Why should I not? There would be no reason to dissemble.'

Nicodemus said: 'You make it sound plausible, but I know that you are wrong.'

'If you cannot upset my reasoning, why do you think I am wrong?'

'Jesus is, quite simply, not that kind of man.'

'We have to go on facts,' said Annas, 'and not on our guess at someone's nature, or on what we would like to believe. But what sort of man do you think he is, really?'

Nicodemus said: 'He is in the line of the Prophets.'

'You remember what happened to some of them, when they mixed in politics?'

'Oh yes, but surely you are not suggesting that—if Jesus were really a Prophet—'

'If Jesus were a Prophet and was about to ruin Israel with the Romans,' said Annas, without hesitation, 'the answer is, I would.'

Annas rose and went to the window: the Temple in the evening sunlight was lovely from his tower.

He yawned and stretched his arms: 'Oh, Jerusalem! We are a wonderful people. We are the only people who stone the Prophets, and the only people who produce Prophets to be stoned.'

Part VI

AUTUMN, AD29

CHAPTER 25

'No,' said Festus, 'I can reassure you. We know he is here, but we have no plans to arrest him. I discussed it with the Governor only yesterday.'

Months had passed, and Nicodemus knew by now that he could expect nothing better from the Romans, no general certificate of harmlessness for the Rabbi Jesus, but at least this was something. There was no threat to Jesus today.

It was towards evening, and half a mile away below them the lamps were already showing in the huge bulk of the Antonia Fortress, in Pilate's quarters overlooking the Temple, and the guards in the outer Temple courtyard could be seen going around with their torches, leaving points of light behind at every pillar.

Soon the great lamps would be lit, pillar-high in the first inner court of the Temple, not so much lamps as torches, enormous flaring wicks floating in gallons of oil.

On such a night as this, a year ago, in the midst of the same Feast of Tabernacles, Nicodemus remembered, he had been over there in the Temple, carrying to Samuel a message from Jesus about the sickness of Samuel's son. Nothing had happened then to cast a shadow between Jesus and Samuel, who then still looked to Jesus as Israel's rising star. Now the shadow had fallen and was growing, and there was Annas' absurd suspicion as well.

No more, for the moment, could be said about Jesus. Festus, when Nicodemus fell silent, turned to questions himself.

Gentiles, he knew, were forbidden on pain of death to enter the Temple, but could any Jew go anywhere inside?

Nicodemus was wary and answered briefly, for he saw where this might lead. Women in the first court only, men a few paces further, priests at the Altar, priests in the outer Holy Place daily, but the Holy of Holies, the inmost shrine, visited by the High Priest only, and on only one day of the year. 'For us, too,' said Nicodemus, 'death is the penalty of transgression. The place of the Holy One's Presence is holy and held in awe.'

'Your god,' said Festus, 'is evidently well-guarded, and no-one can approach him who is not a Jew. But is he in the same way limited? Does he address himself only to Jews?'

The question, Nicodemus knew, was neither irreverent nor superficial. Festus must share the views of any educated Roman about the so-called deities. The background to his thought was not the whoring, vengeful and jolly gang of Mount Olympus but the god of the Stoics, something not comparable, certainly, with the living God of the Hebrews, but a conception noble enough to commend itself to the philosophic mind.

Jehovah, when Nicodemus answered, must not be found wanting, by the side of the Stoic god.

'God by His nature,' said Nicodemus, 'is universal. Only, in what sense? Our wise men have not overlooked it. Have you read my friend Philo yet?'

Festus was ashamed not to have done so. 'Lend me your copies,' said Nicodemus, 'and I will mark some passages. Especially on the Word which is the mediator of God to all things and all men—not only to the Jews. And that God is the everlasting Fountain of life for all men—not only for the Jews. Also, that God is Light and seen by his own light only, by all men—not only by the Jews.'

'It sounds like the language of the philosophers,' said Festus.

'It is the language of a philosopher and of a great man of religion,' said Nicodemus.

'And have you many such?'

'No others who are both. We have our Doctors of the Law,

and one of them is an even greater man of religion than Philo, but he is not a philosopher. The Rabbi Jesus is not skilled in Greek.'

'A pity,' said Festus. 'Could he not learn?'

'Not unless we could persuade him to stop teaching for a period and to study, possibly abroad. It would be worth it, but there is no chance.'

'What a pity! He would have no difficulty in earning a living. If he took a Greek name he could build up a good practice as a physician anywhere, even in Rome. Also, it would keep him out of trouble here.'

'It would,' said Nicodemus, 'but trouble seems to be what he is looking for. I must tell you, that is why I came to see you. He is making more enemies than he need. Only the other day there was an incident. Some of my colleagues were extremely disturbed.'

'Another healing?'

'Yes, an eye-case. The trouble is, it was on our Sabbath.'

Festus said: 'It sounds like something that Paula heard this morning. Would you like to hear her account?'

Paula entered, accompanied by Esther: the two appeared to be inseparable. They greeted Nicodemus without embarrassment. For Paula there was no point of difficulty, and for Esther this was the man who had been kind.

It was the man's mother whom they had heard talking, said Paula, in the vegetable market outside the walls. 'She said God forgive her, she wished it had never happened, it made so much trouble for them all.'

'What was it?' asked Festus.

'It was her son. His eyes had always been bad, and the other day somebody cured them.'

'And how did he do that?'

'He made a paste out of some mud and some spittle.'

'*Fasting* spittle, I suppose,' said Festus. 'It is much more efficacious. In fact, the doctors say that for many purposes it is the only kind of spittle that will do.'

'I couldn't cross-examine her,' said Paula. 'We daren't push ourselves forward.'

'A pity!' muttered Festus. 'This may be important. I hope we can find out.' He went on: 'And what about the mud? Where exactly did this happen? Different ailments are best treated with different kinds of earth.'

'It was outside the bigger of the two underground entrances to the Temple courtyard, coming up from the lower city.'

'Ah! That pinpoints it exactly,' said Festus with satisfaction. 'We can send and take samples of that. And he applied this paste as a salve to the patient?'

'He did.'

'No spell or incantation?'

'No, nothing like that. He just told the man to go and wash in the Pool of Siloam.'

'And did that work?'

'Yes. When he came back, of course, people didn't believe it.'

'Why ever not?'

'Well,' said Paula, 'apparently it had been a severe case of blindness, much too serious, people thought, to yield to simple treatment like that.'

'How serious then?'

'The blindness was total.'

'Oh! Not just poor vision! And how long had he been like that?'

'The man was blind from birth.'

Festus was silent, and so was Nicodemus. Festus said: 'Your Rabbi has been excelling himself. Why, the next thing is we shall be hearing he has raised someone from the dead!' He smiled.

More seriously, he added: 'This makes it all the more important to find out whether the Rabbi had broken his fast that morning. Then we should have the prescription complete.' He thought for a moment. 'The only way to make sure is to ask him. But it will look better if we do not go empty-handed. Let us offer something in return.'

Aristotle was sent for. 'Tell me, doctor,' Festus said, 'what is the most serious sickness from which a human being can recover?'

The doctor did not hesitate. 'The madness of dogs,' he said, 'and that very seldom, and until recently never.'

'Have you ever treated a case?' asked Festus.

'Three times, but without success.'

'Then how can you say that cure is possible?'

'It is something very recent, Sir.'

'What is the prescription?'

'It is surprisingly simple, for such a malady. The root of the dog-rose is burnt and compounded with honey.'

'And it works?'

'Except in the month of the dog-star, Sirius. During that month canine madness is fatal to all.'

'You have not tried this remedy yourself, obviously. How do you know it works?'

'I read it in the last confidential bulletin of the medical faculty in the Pergamon Aesculapion. I am a subscriber.'

'But who discovered it?'

'It was not a discovery, but something really reliable, it was a revelation. The god vouchsafed it to one of his worshippers there, at night in the temple, in a dream.'

Festus was doubtful. 'Without proof of actual cure I would not like to recommend it to the doctor Jesus. We could only pass it on to him as a useful but not yet wholly proven prescription.'

Festus continued, to Nicodemus: 'Could you arrange for its transmission to the doctor Jesus, in return for the information which we need? You could say that in the book which I am compiling there will be a section on remedies for diseases, with full acknowledgment to the authors of all original prescriptions.'

Aristotle had gone, dusk had fallen, and suddenly across the city the sixteen great torch-lights flared up in the inner court of the Temple, casting the long shadow of the high-fronted Sanctuary right across the western slope of the city and the western city wall, across Golgotha and into the country beyond. As the evening chill fell, mists drifted low over the city, reflecting the light of the flames downward on to the houses, a faint and even dawning over the dusky town.

Nicodemus said to Paula: 'Was there anything else that Jesus said?'

'Nothing for certain,' Paula replied.

Esther said unexpectedly: 'The mother said she didn't believe it, because it was nonsense and nothing to do with the business, and her son couldn't see who it was speaking anyhow, so it may not have been the Rabbi, but whoever it was said quite distinctly: *I am the light of the world.*'

CHAPTER 26

The last day of the Feast of Tabernacles was over. Autumnal winds anticipated the Children of Israel in dismantling their tree-branch booths. The visitors from the country were dispersing, but not yet, it seemed, the Rabbi Jesus and his men. Nicodemus grew more and more worried. He had obtained no better assurance from Festus. Jesus was immune today but the Romans said nothing about tomorrow. Annas still clung to his absurd suspicions. Much more serious, and something that really hurt, the people whom Nicodemus most respected were split right down the middle, Gamaliel on one side and Samuel on the other, but Samuel was the stronger.

'Why does your master do it?' asked Nicodemus.

'He does not tell us,' said John, 'or if he does we do not understand.'

'All the same, remember what he says,' said Nicodemus. 'Later it may become clearer. But you are not the only people who do not understand. We see what he does, but we do not know why he does it.'

'He does good, mostly,' said John.

'But why on the Sabbath? Only the other day he did it again. The man had been blind all his life: why cure him on a Sabbath, what is wrong with waiting one more day?'

'I do not know,' said John, simply. 'The man himself did not object.'

'There is no doubt whatever,' said Nicodemus, 'that your master has broken the Law as we know it. Never mind the people who hate him because he knows they are evil: now there are others who are dangerous to him because they love him but they think he must be silenced because they love God more.'

Nicodemus continued, after a pause. 'These are the holy men of Israel,' he said hoarsely, 'they are sons of God if there are any such, Rabbi Samuel and some others like him. *They* are the ones who matter to your master. I love them all and I venerate them, no less than I honour your master. They cannot both be right, and yet they must be. What is the answer to this riddle? It is tearing me apart.'

Nicodemus was thinking aloud, not waiting for an answer, for who would expect one from this unlettered lad? John remained silent, and Nicodemus continued.

'It is not as if your master was saying that *he* and not the sages of Israel is the one to say what is the Law. That would be bad enough, but he goes much further. No, he praises the Law set out by the sages, and calls it the commandment of God, but he breaks that Law when he pleases. Nobody has ever spoken like that.'

'No,' said John proudly, 'that is what everyone is saying. Only this morning he drew away the crowd.'

'Where was that?' asked Nicodemus.

'In the outer Temple courtyard, where the procession comes up from the Pool of Siloam with water for the Altar, just before sunrise. It was not far from where the Rabbi teaches, and when people saw him they left the procession and went off to hear what he said. The priest was very annoyed, and he dropped the golden bowl with the water, and the music stopped, and they sent the police to move us all on, but they didn't, they simply stood there listening themselves.'

'And what happened about the procession?'

'The priest had to go back and fetch some more water, and when he got back he just went in at the gate without looking and they blew the trumpets as usual. Then when they started singing the Psalms of Praise inside the Temple, and we could hear it all in the court outside, the Rabbi made us all be silent, and towards the very end he made us join in where it says:

This is the gate of the Lord, and the righteous shall enter through it;

I thank thee, Lord, that thou hast answered me and hast become my salvation;

The stone that the builders rejected has become the head of the corner;

This is the Lord's doing, and it is marvellous in our eyes.

Then in a minute or two when it finished he sent them away.'

'What do you think he meant by that? The singing?' asked Nicodemus.

'None of us knew.'

'Was there anything else that you did not understand?'

'One thing he said when the priest dropped the bowl of water he was bringing to pour on the Altar. He said: *I am the fountain of living water, and if any man is thirsty, let him come to me and drink.* The same sort of thing as he said last year to the woman at Jacob's Well.'

'And none of you knew what he meant, and he did not explain it?'

'No, we just remembered. It must be just a manner of speaking, like that other thing he said to the blind man: *I am the light of the world.*'

'Anything else of the same sort?' asked Nicodemus.

'Last spring in Capernaum he was talking of bread to some people, the same ones who had had a meal with him in the mountains the day before.'

Nicodemus interrupted: 'I know the story. Jesus was the only person who knew there was enough food to go round.'

This was not exactly the story as Nicodemus had heard it, but he was afraid of hearing John repeat mere rumours, too close to sorcery for comfort although no wonder that ignorant people ran after Jesus if he was thought to behave like that.

John continued. 'The Rabbi said: *I am the bread of life and he who comes to me shall not hunger.* He said: *This is the bread which comes down from heaven, that a man may eat of it and not die. I am the living bread which came down from heaven: if any man eat of this bread he shall live for ever.*'

It reminded Nicodemus of something. He asked what time of year it was, how close to Passover? Then he rose, opened a small chest and reverently took out a roll. He opened it to the passage which must have been read in the synagogue on the preceding Sabbath. It told of the fruit of the Tree of Life in the Garden of Eden which, if a man eat, he shall live for ever.

'I promised you once,' said Nicodemus, smiling, 'that I would tell you how the teaching of Jesus looks to another Rabbi. But I think I need helping even more than you do, because it is just people like me and still more Samuel who are most likely to be misled. It looks as if the Rabbi Jesus was comparing himself to the Tree of Life. But it must be only a manner of speaking. The pity is, he can be misunderstood.'

'The Rabbi would never say he was anything he wasn't.'

'How else does he describe himself?' asked Nicodemus.

'That is another thing we don't understand properly. He always calls himself the "son of man". But so could anybody.'

Maybe, or maybe not, thought Nicodemus. And if not, what use to talk to this lad of the Book of Daniel, still less of Enoch? It would give him the wrong idea. Why does Jesus do it? Nicodemus wondered. It means nothing whatever to ordinary folk, and it only confuses people like Samuel and myself, who automatically run in our mind through the Scriptures, sorting the references and looking for the undertones—obviously he does not mean us to regard him as something better than an angel, but that bit about coming on the clouds of heaven is quite repulsive to an educated mind.

'It is rather a general description,' said Nicodemus aloud. 'At least, he never calls himself by that title you mentioned, the leader?' He could not bring himself to say 'Messiah'.

'Not personally,' said John, 'but a lot of other people are saying it.' John was hopeful. 'Right in the Temple they were arguing about his cures. Some people said he couldn't do better if he was the Messiah.'

'That has nothing whatever to do with it,' said Nicodemus sternly. 'Remember what I told you! Jesus is a great teacher and a great healer, but he is not a leader in war.'

'Could he not be both, Sir?' asked John, pleading. 'After all, he has never denied it, only told people not to go round saying so. And there are so many stories.'

'I know about the common people,' said Nicodemus, 'but they will believe anything. You, my son, are not one of them, and I cannot let you miss the truth. There are nothing but rumours behind this story.'

Surprisingly, John resisted. 'It can't be only rumours, Sir. There is one of us, Simon, not Peter but the one who was a Zealot. His friends are still mostly Zealots and he tells us: we must keep it all very quiet but he hears there is something big brewing, and our Rabbi will turn out to be a far more important person than we think.'

CHAPTER 27

The first heavy rains of winter had set in, not the light warm showers which herald the end of summer but driving, cold, unceasing, for days on end. A small fraction of the downpour found its way to the underground cisterns, and the remainder, becoming ever more brown and yellow, rushed down the streets, under and through the gates of the city, washing the rubbish dumps of Gehenna and filling the bed of the river Cedron, and away through the ravines of the Judaean wilderness to the Dead Sea.

In such weather Nicodemus got himself carried, in a chair. It was only a few hundred yards to the High Priest's palace but more than enough for a walker to get soaked. Even under the thick felt cover of his winter sedan-chair it was dripping, and he needed his own goat-hair travelling cloak.

On such days as this, ordinary men fastened all their shutters and huddled with lamps and braziers burning in the warmest room of the most sheltered courtyard. Annas however would not be dislodged from his upper chamber. He sat with his feet close to a bronze basin of glowing charcoal, listening with satisfaction to the rain outside, beneficial to his estates in the country, discouraging to brigands in their caves.

'When the rain stops,' said Annas, 'will you put in another trip to Sidon?' The glass-makers, good business-people, had been interested but they were still experimenting. Nicodemus, Annas said, should make them hurry, put on a trial run.

'I will start immediately the roads are dry,' said Nicodemus. He could afford to be away for the present. Jesus and his followers had left Jerusalem, and would not return for weeks.

'Splendid!' said Annas. 'Then you must hurry back and help me, over something else. We have to settle with the Rabbi Jesus, and it will not be easy.'

Nicodemus gave no sign of his feelings. It was a climactic moment in his life. At all costs, he thought, dissemble. Annas and I will be fighting on opposite sides, but I shall be stronger if he does not know it.

'You are a man of reason,' said Annas. 'You may not be altogether of my opinion, but you talk the same language as I do, and you can recognise facts. People like Samuel are utterly useless, in matters of common sense.'

'What are the facts which *you* recognise?' asked Nicodemus.

'Jesus is a first-rate teacher, and he talks a lot of sense. But all that goes for nothing. He is heading a revolt.'

'That is something simply impossible.'

'I too used to think so, but I cannot get over the facts. Reports have been coming in direct from the top Zealots, and all of them agree. Rabbi Jesus is the real head of the liberation movement—oh, these madmen!—and the true leader of the coming revolt.'

John's report of the absurd rumour spread by another disciple had prepared Nicodemus a little, but not for anything like this. He said: 'It still seems impossible. What does Jesus say himself?'

'What matters is that he does not deny it. You know people are always addressing him by this absurd title "Messiah".' Annas spat the word with distaste. 'Do you know of a single occasion on which he has denied it?'

Nicodemus was silent. Annas continued. 'No, he has not. He often tells people not to go about saying so, but that is an obvious precaution. Of course, he is much too intelligent to believe anything so foolish, but he knows that if the common people believe it they will follow him to the death.'

'Then what do you propose?' asked Nicodemus. 'Ask him to give it up? Assuming there is anything in it.'

169

'Things are gone too far,' said Annas, 'and in any case he could not do it. He is his own prisoner. He is far too exalted to listen to reason. His head is turned by now. I know that sort.'

'Then how can you stop him?'

Annas said, darkly: 'It is expedient that one man should die for the people.'

'What!' exclaimed Nicodemus. 'You would sacrifice an innocent man?'

'Innocent of what?' asked Annas. 'He has done nothing yet, but if we let him alone he will.' Annas continued, ever more gravely, 'You remember, I told you. Last time there was a big rising there were two thousand crucifixions. So long as I can stop it, there shall be no more.'

'You would arrest him?' Nicodemus was puzzled.

'That is the first precaution.'

'But how can you arrange it? Whenever he appears the crowds gather round him. There are many who would fight.'

Annas was more amused than impatient. 'We have experience in these matters. All we need is to know his movements, and when he is likely to be unguarded. It should not be difficult to find that out. Among so many followers there should be one man of sense, at least.'

'What do you mean by that?'

'Someone who has seen what the Romans do to crush a rising. Anyone who has seen a village sacked and men crucified for the sake of the Zealots. A man who would save his misguided master from bringing ruin on his people. An ordinary sensible Jew.'

Annas continued, 'With your connections among his followers, you could make enquiries. Just a brief note on the personal background of each.'

Nicodemus said nothing in answer, but had another question to ask. 'And if you could lay hands on the Rabbi Jesus, what then?'

'Ah! There we are really in difficulty,' Annas admitted, with a smile. 'If I were an absolute ruler, like the Romans, I know what I would do with him. I would ship him off quietly to some remote part of the Dispersion, with a comfortable pension, and licence to teach the Law. He would do great credit to our reputation for learning. Babylon would do.'

'Assuming that Rabbi Jesus would agree to go.'

'He could take his family with him,' said Annas. 'But that is only a dream. I cannot do it, because I have to take notice of other people. Your colleagues and mine, on the Sanhedrin.'

'A good many of them are in your pocket,' said Nicodemus.

'Yes, but what matters is the rest. Now that is where I rely on you, and you must help me,' said Annas. 'They are the sort of people that you but not I can talk to, Pharisees. Half of them are simply blind about Jesus. There is Gamaliel. There is Joseph of Arimathea.'

'They would ask you what accusation you are bringing,' said Nicodemus. 'What justifies you in silencing a man who, even if he is politically imprudent, speaks with the voice of an angel—perhaps even the Holy Spirit?'

'I think I know the answer,' said Annas. 'Jesus is not sound about the Law. That is probably the note to play on, and perhaps you could try it. A pity, because I think he is right.'

'Your enemies could accuse you of lacking sincerity.'

'I am sincere in myself,' said Annas, 'but this is not religion, it is politics.'

Annas resumed: 'There are so few people I can rely on. Some of my own agents have made things worse. Excess of zeal, I suppose, but they went beyond their instructions.'

'How was that?'

'They were told to ask him embarrassing questions in public, try to make him see the difficulty of his own position, provoke him into saying something unpopular or take the risk of backing down.'

'I should not care for the job of provoking Rabbi Jesus,' said Nicodemus, with a smile.

'I'm afraid that they were not up to it. They made fools of themselves. Then, they got angry and launched out into something ridiculous, quite without orders of course. They tried to make out he was guilty of blasphemy!'

Annas laughed scornfully. 'I had to get rid of the lot. I sent them on a journey with messages to someone or other, very far off.'

'A charge like that wouldn't sound very convincing,' said Nicodemus.

'A charge of blasphemy can sometimes be useful,' said Annas, 'whether true or not, but not in this instance, or at least not yet. It has only confused the issue. Jesus is not mad, and the people who matter to me at this moment know it. If I am any judge of people like Samuel, their trouble is not that Jesus is mad, or bad, but good.'

'I think you are right,' said Nicodemus.

'The charge would be one to bring only in the last resort, if ever,' said Annas. 'The idiots! "Making himself equal to God"!'

CHAPTER 28

Nicodemus found Samuel huddled in a corner, wrapped up against the cold. 'I looked in your shop and in the Temple,' he said anxiously. 'You are not ill, I hope, my friend?'

'Not of the body,' said Samuel grimly. His face was pinched, but not with the cold: it looked immensely shrivelled, like some forgotten pomegranate between the rolled white head-dress and the furry greying beard. Overmastered by sorrow, thought Nicodemus, but not as when he lost his son. This is something less sharp, though quite as grievous.

The room was small, four or five paces, and dark outside the radius of the lamp, for it was shuttered against the cold. 'Let me put this bowl where you are sitting,' said Nicodemus tenderly, 'water is dripping from the ceiling, on your head.' During Samuel's brief illness a year ago Nicodemus had started reroofing Samuel's house, but the tiling had not reached here before Samuel recovered, and there was only mud and wattle above their head. Other men, thought Nicodemus, would have moved their living quarters in such weather, to the driest part of the house, but not so Samuel, who used the only dry quarters for storage of his books.

Nicodemus tried warming his feet at the small charcoal burner, but decided they would suffer less acutely if tucked under him, protected by the hem of his cloak. Samuel appeared oblivious, his sandalled feet, unstockinged, resting on the damp stone floor.

Here, in the living, sleeping and eating quarters of one of the sages of Israel, in cold and damp and darkness, there were weighty matters to discuss.

'I cannot work. I cannot teach,' said Samuel.

'The rain will not last for ever,' Nicodemus said. 'You will feel better when it is dry.'

'I do not think so,' said Samuel.

'Also, it will be warmer.' Nicodemus tried again.

Samuel could not contradict him: the truth was evident. He remained silent: he was, it seemed, dis-witted, distraught.

'I am glad you have come,' he said at last to Nicodemus, 'and there is someone to whom I can talk.'

'What is it, dear friend?' asked Nicodemus gently. 'Is it some great affliction?'

'The Lord has afflicted his people Israel,' Samuel muttered. He spoke habitually in the language of the Scriptures without noticing, nor seeing, how this must strike the ordinary man.

Nicodemus said, in a matter-of-fact way: 'He is always doing it.'

Samuel said: 'I can understand—no, not understand but I can begin to see how it might be understood—that the Lord afflicts his people with afflictions, as he afflicted Job. But what should I say, my friend,' he continued, accusing Nicodemus as it were, 'if I had to stand up in the Temple and say why the Holy One, blessed be He, afflicts his people with good?'

'Whatever you said, they would listen,' Nicodemus said. 'But I would not care to be in your place.'

'And yet He has done it!' Samuel mumbled. He seemed in anguish of soul. 'He has sent a great light for Israel, and the light is leading Israel astray.'

'If you are speaking of the Rabbi Jesus, those things cannot both be true.'

Samuel said: 'I do not agree with those silly people who say that his works are of the devil only. No man who teaches as he does can be of the devil. His teaching, or much of it, is greater than Hillel's, as great as any Prophet's, that is certain.'

'Then how can he be leading Israel astray?'

'I do not know *how*,' said Samuel, 'but he is doing it. That also is absolutely sure.'

'For the sake of argument,' said Nicodemus, 'suppose that I do not agree with you. I am a student asking questions—though not the young man Saul! How can a man lead Israel astray if he speaks as a Prophet?'

'Though he speak with the tongue of angels,' said Samuel, 'if he speaks against the Law he is nothing. Jesus has spoken against the Law.'

'Against the Law, or against the Law as we declare it?'

'It is the same. It is the Law. The Law which he himself said shall never perish. The Law not given by any man, not even Moses, for even Moses only conveyed it.' Samuel was carried away, forgetting that his only audience was another Rabbi. 'The Law, which existed before time began, which can never be added to or altered, only revealed or discovered. The Law, attack on which is attack on God himself.'

Nicodemus said: 'Can you really say all that of Jesus? He breaks the Sabbath rule, certainly, but does it go further than that?'

'Yes, further, and all the way. By what he does, he claims the right to vary the Law as it pleases him, and vary it from day to day. So far, it is only the Sabbath, but there is no end when once you start. I tell you, friend,' said Samuel fiercely, 'this man could snatch Israel out of its whole framework, tear it away from the Law. The Law will still be there, for it is eternal, but the people of the Law will no longer be a people, they are nothing without the Law.'

Nicodemus did not reply, but remained thinking. Jesus did not defend Law-breakers: to that extent he was clear. But was he clear altogether? Those who attacked him he crushed by counter-attacking: what right have they to judge? Are their hands clean? Why do they think that they really know the Law? Questions like this were not debating points only but highly subversive, overturning not just one person but any practical system, for if judges and police must be spotless and infallible, offenders will generally go free. No, Nicodemus thought, on this I cannot argue with Samuel. Somewhere, I am sure, there is something that has escaped him, just as it still escapes me, only I know and he does not, something that makes all the difference must be there.

Nicodemus diverted the argument: 'Does it not depend on the sort of person Jesus is? He seems to me the very last person to want it, to tear Israel away from the Law.'

'But he is doing it, or will do it if he is left alone,' said Samuel. 'But yes, you are right, it does matter what sort of person he is, and he knows it.'

'How can you tell that?'

'He knows the vital question. By what authority does he do it, claim to vary the Law? He knows that even if he were Moses he could not. So he always evades the question, gets out of it by speaking of something else. If he answered the question at all he would be admitting that he has no power to do it.'

'You mean, if he said he was someone not greater than Moses?'

'Of course!' said Samuel, smiling for the first time that morning. 'There were some foolish people, sent I suppose by Annas, who tried to make him say he was something much greater than Moses! As if Jesus was mad!'

'In any case,' said Nicodemus, 'I suppose there is no hurry. There is a lot to be said for Gamaliel's principle: let him alone, for if he be of God you will not be able to overthrow him, and if he be not of God he will fail anyhow.'

'I would like to think so,' said Samuel, 'but the rot is spreading.'

'You do not mean these ridiculous rumours about Jesus and the Zealots?'

'I am not so sure about their being ridiculous,' said Samuel. 'Personally I do not think that Jesus is that sort of person, but Annas makes it his business to know about these things. Perhaps he has allowed foolish people to use him. But that is something different. What matters is the Law.'

'Then what do you think should be done?' asked Nicodemus. It hurt him to dissemble with Samuel: it had not done, with Annas.

Samuel relapsed, and the liveliness faded once more from his features. 'There is a saying,' Samuel said sadly: *'If your right eye causes you to sin, pluck it out, for it is better to enter the Kingdom of God with one eye than with two eyes to be cast into hellfire.'*

'We have many sayings to that effect,' said Nicodemus, 'but I do not recognise this one. Whose is it?'

'Rabbi Jesus,' said Samuel, 'is a light and the right eye of Israel, and he said it himself.'

Before Nicodemus left, Samuel said more brightly: 'One piece of news at least is good. The family who sold the woman into slavery are to be punished. The Court has agreed, at last.'

'What was the sentence? Not another execution without telling the Romans, I hope.'

'Oh no!' said Samuel, missing the point of irony. 'The Court was merciful. The whole family will be banished, after being scourged.'

'A heavy sentence enough. Was there no plea in mitigation?'

'A plea of ignorance, of course. They said they did not know what they were doing. They did not know it was against the Law.'

Nicodemus remembered that Samuel had never known of the greater transgression, the unspeakable iniquity of tricking the woman and bringing false evidence to put her to death. Samuel was speaking only of their sin in selling her into slavery. Perhaps they were really ignorant in that.

'A hard punishment, if it was only ignorance,' said Nicodemus.

'Ignorance,' said Samuel, 'is not enough excuse. If they had sinned deliberately it would have been death for them— Romans or no Romans!—and to that extent they have been spared. Their punishment is heavy, but no more than they deserve.'

CHAPTER 29

They stood there, facing the people, twenty-five paces away, across the rows of iron rings clamped in the marble pavement from which no amount of washing would remove the stains. The risen sun over the Mount of Olives was full in their faces. Behind them up the steps was the white and gold face of the Sanctuary, seeming heaven-high. To their right was the vast square block of the Altar, unhewn stones and solid, larger than many a house, and the smoke of the dawn sacrifice rose from the charred offerings on its surface, mercifully concealed from vision on the flat top far above.

The three of them looked over the back of the bullock at the people, packed across the end of the court and cramming in countless thousands the greater court beyond. One of them placed his hands on the head of the bullock and solemnly intoned:

Oh God, I have committed iniquity, transgressed and sinned before thee, I and my house. Oh God, forgive the iniquities and transgressions and sins which I have committed and transgressed and sinned before thee, I and my house, as it is written in the Law of thy servant Moses: *For on this day shall atonement be made for you to cleanse you; from all your sins shall ye be clean before the Lord.*

And the crowds shouted: Blessed be the name of the glory of His Kingdom for ever and ever.

Only, they were not really there.

Nicodemus knew it, because he himself could not possibly be there, and nor could Samuel, for neither was a priest. The third of them, Annas, could be, but he should not, for son-in-law Caiaphas was titular High Priest and acted publicly in this office. And in fact Nicodemus had witnessed Joseph Caiaphas doing it, on the real Day of Atonement, two or three months ago. For other reasons also this was clearly just a dream. Annas in the middle, Nicodemus on his right and Samuel on his left were always changing places, and Nicodemus knew all the time what the others were thinking. Annas he knew was bored with the whole proceedings, and also rather cross. The only thing that he really liked was dressing up in the morning, in that glorious golden dress, the gorgeous dark blue robe with tassels at the fringes like pomegranate flowers, blue and purple and scarlet, and bells of gold; the breastplate of precious stones set in the same Temple colours; the two-tiered linen turban, blue and white, lapped and crowned with gold, and the sacred Name inscribed on the gold frontlet. But even this he had now had to shed for the most solemn part of the day's ceremonies. The plain white linen robe which Annas was now wearing kept vanishing and reappearing, and for the split seconds of dream-thinking the blue and golden garments took its place. None of this, fortunately, seemed perceptible to the crowds.

Yes, Annas was cross, for although he held with the Day of Atonement, for Moses had ordained it, he did not hold with what the priests had made of it. 'I am so *tired*,' he kept saying to Nicodemus. 'Think of the indignity of it, they kept me awake all night, and that was after seven days' hard training and re-hearsals and separation from my wife, and they stopped me eating garlic lest it lead to lustful thoughts.' Yes, Annas had it in for the grim Temple officers who had marshalled him for this service. Annas would get his own back, and he did.

The bullock was now tied fast to the rings on the north of the Altar, and a priest had drawn up its head. Annas ran a finger along one side of the knife which was handed to him, and then handed it back. Incompetent fools, Nicodemus could hear him thinking, there is a rough place on the side of it which the animal may feel: do you want the High Priest's sacrifice to become carrion? They brought another knife, and another. Three times Annas sent it back, changing into and out of his blue and golden garments continually, with growing satisfaction. At last, he made the cut.

'See how dexterous they want you,' he said to Nicodemus. 'I can only begin the cut and then I must leave the knife in midstroke for someone else to finish, so that both hands are free for the bowl, to catch the blood. But I can do it, I am a better butcher than any of them. It is my profession, ruler as well as High Priest.'

Now they were quite suddenly standing near the people, and the two goats were at their side. Samuel was now High Priest, and he plunged his two hands into the wooden casket in front of them, groping for the two golden lots inside. One goat 'for Jehovah', to be slaughtered, and the other for the wilderness, to be sent away and perish there. But there was a disaster. The casket was empty. Samuel found nothing there. No goat to be sacrificed to Jehovah, and none to be sent away. The hourglass tells no time when it is empty, the sun-dial no time without sunshine, but now it was not the sun but Jehovah who had veiled his face.

This is all wrong, thought Nicodemus, we have done things out of order, the sacrifice of the bullock should have come after. It is our rightful punishment, the worst thing that could happen to anyone, not an angry answer but no answer at all. Samuel said: 'Oh Lord, do not leave thy people Israel desolate because they have done things in the wrong order. They did it unknowing. Restore to them the lots.'

179

Annas laughed. 'Try harder, Samuel.' This time, the lots were there, and Samuel raised his right hand to show the multitude. They bound a scarlet thread around the neck of the goat on the right of them, and scarlet wool around the other goat's horns.

Now Nicodemus himself was holding the censer, climbing the long ramp to the top of the Altar which it would be death in life for him to tread: he filled it with glowing wood from the heart of one of the fires there and descended, climbed the flight of steps to the Porch of the Sanctuary and, carrying the fire and a bowl of incense, passed inside. As in a dream, for it was a dream, he reminded himself, he passed leftward in the half-light between the small golden altar and the golden seven-branched lampstand, threaded his way through the double curtain at the far end of the high narrow chamber of the Holy Place and stood in the Holy of Holies, small, square, enormously lofty, bare walls, bare rock, and apart from the glow of his charcoal totally dark. One man, on one day of the year, could come here. It was death to anyone else. But, thought Nicodemus with a strange peacefulness, it is worth it. It is quiet inside.

He placed the censer on the rough bare rock in the middle and cast incense on the coals. The smoke rose and filled the room to the ceiling, at least Nicodemus supposed so, for you cannot see in the dark unless of course the smoke for some reason becomes luminous, as this appears to do. Does this usually happen? he wondered, Annas had never mentioned it, or any others who had been there, and he had better keep it quiet, or the people would know he had been there himself.

The clouds grew brighter and ever ascending. They rose through the roof and let in the sunshine, they dissolved the walls, and there was a vast space full of people, wider by far than the outer Court of the Temple, wider even than Jerusalem itself.

This is what comes of having things done by the wrong people, in the wrong order, Nicodemus thought, and retreated. As he expected, everything was normal outside.

Now it was the turn of the goat 'for Jehovah'. The animal

was dark and small. It did not seem to like what it knew was about to happen. Remains of the bullock still lay on the close-by tables. There was no removing the smell.

The goat was shackled and its head uplifted. Annas turned its face towards the people, but the face was that of a man, and the creature spoke.

'I am the lamb of God,' it said to Annas, 'and I take away the sins of the world.'

Annas was puzzled. 'Why do you think it says it is a lamb?' he asked Nicodemus, 'when it is really only a goat.'

Samuel was also in disagreement. 'It does not take away the sins of the world,' said Samuel. 'It is an offering for the iniquities, transgressions and sins of the people of Israel. The animal knows quite well. It only needed to listen to what the High Priest said.'

'Stop!' said Nicodemus to Annas, for the creature had the face of Rabbi Jesus.

But he was too late, and the blood was already flowing, running over the golden bowl and out of the ewers and buckets, and all the basins of the Temple, over the white stone paving around the Altar, down the steps into the next courtyard and through the Temple Gates into the outer Court, flowing and rising as it flowed, rising up the sides of the Altar and quenching the Burnt Offerings, submerging Nicodemus and Samuel and Annas and all the multitudes. 'I told you I was a good butcher,' said Annas merrily. 'No-one else in the world could shed such blood.'

Samuel said: 'Oh Lord, hold it not against thy people that blood has profaned thy holy city. They did not know the animal was made like that.'

At last the flood subsided. There were people but there was no city and no Temple. The land was clean and bare.

CHAPTER 30

Nicodemus did not know how much the dream had to do with it. Normally, dreams deserved great attention, being among the most reliable guides to human conduct. However, their interpretation required skill and experience, and a prudent man would take several opinions.

If only he could talk to his friend Philo, master of this subject too! Nicodemus, in his library, took down the great Treatises on Dreams, magisterial and scientific, but alas with an inadequate spread. Philo had concentrated too much on unusual situations. Jacob's dream at Bethel, with the ladder set between earth and heaven and angels going up and down, was certainly a dream of some interest, but ordinary people were not likely to find themselves in a similar position, waking up next morning to exclaim: Surely the Lord was in this place and I did not know it!

Philo was in Alexandria, and in Jerusalem no-one could be trusted. Rumour spread easily, and whatever else the dream might signify there was one thing which it clearly showed: Nicodemus and his friends were now opposed.

Nicodemus had now no doubt that he would oppose them, and soon he saw what to do. Annas, he knew, must be totally mistaken, and he had no compunction about fighting him, by Annas' own weapon, intrigue. The real problem was Samuel, for Samuel was a man of such exceeding goodness that it settled his whole course. He was a man, if there were any such in Israel, who rather than offend the Almighty would sooner pluck out his own eye. With such men there is no reasoning. Given the facts as they see them, they are quite immovably right. But even if the facts are not as they see them, then are they not still acting aright?

Nicodemus blamed his upbringing for these questions. Was he reasoning as a Hebrew or a Greek? If only Hebrew, he might think like Samuel and there would be no problem: he too would know he was right—that is, if he were as holy a man as Samuel, as humble a practitioner of the Law.

Samuel was right, at least, to act as he was acting, in defence as he believed of the Law, that is of God. But was it not right also for others to oppose him? No doubt it was, if Samuel did not know the facts. Without all the facts it was wrong to condemn anyone. There must be something still unknown. Impossible to acquit Jesus of gravest transgression, yet equally impossible to convict such a man, sage and teacher without equal since the Prophets, gifted with extraordinary powers.

What were the facts? Gamaliel's advice was the soundest. Let him alone and the results will show it, whether he be of men or of God. But if others were too impatient, there was another course of action, the proper process, the formal trial.

Nicodemus took his pen and listed them, the seventy-one members. The voting on the full Sanhedrin could be predicted fairly exactly if you knew the faction heads. His calculations were satisfactory, even better than he had hoped. Even if the evidence did not lead to acquittal, Jesus might still go free.

He embarked on an important round of visits.

Then, pleased with himself, he set off at once to see Annas: time was precious, for Jesus was once more in Jerusalem and things might happen. The great winter festival was only just over, the re-dedication of the Temple, and Jesus might remain for some days yet.

He found Annas unusually testy, unreceptive to counsels of any moderate course. 'That man,' he cried, 'is no politician. He seems to want to make enemies. Have you heard the latest?' Nicodemus had not, and Annas continued: 'He has practically attacked me myself. It is a perfectly legitimate income, and has been going on for years. Naturally the licence-fees for the money-changers and so on go up with the cost of living, and a surcharge is quite justified for the tourist high season at Passover.

But that was still confidential, some of the stallholders must have put him up to it, preaching in the Court of the Temple, against the so-called profiteering of persons in high office, unnamed.'

'Is this report reliable?'

'Oh yes, one of my people was listening behind a pillar, and he took it down.'

'No actual interference with business?'

'No. At least, not yet. But wait till the season starts. That man will stop at nothing. We shall have to do something soon.'

Nicodemus said: 'At least, he is not attacking the Romans.'

'No,' said Annas, 'but authority. Today me, tomorrow the Romans.'

'What do you propose? Arrest him, I know, but what then?'

'It depends on people like your friend Samuel. What does he think?'

There was no reason not to tell him, for Annas would soon find out. 'He considers that Rabbi Jesus is leading Israel astray, by speaking against the Law.'

'The false prophet accusation,' said Annas. 'That sounds perfectly satisfactory, a capital charge. But could we count on a conviction?'

'It would mean the full Sanhedrin meeting,' said Nicodemus. That was cardinal to his plan. The smaller panel of twenty-three might be packed by Annas. Nobody could tamper with the full body of seventy-one.

'I suppose so,' Annas said reluctantly. 'That is, for such a charge. Then let us go through the list and consider. Fifteen of them are mine, including Caiaphas. The other fifty-six are your kind of people, let us see who they would follow, Gamaliel or Samuel, Azzai, Joseph and the rest.'

'Or,' said Nicodemus, 'perhaps even me.'

'Yes, my friend,' said Annas, looking up with surprise at this showing of teeth. 'We must not forget you. But I count you on our side.'

Nicodemus said nothing. They counted. Nicodemus already

knew the result. Annas could not believe it, and counted a second time. 'There is some doubt,' said Annas. 'Apart from my people and Samuel's, there are these dozen whom we can count on with certainty.'

'I would not like them as allies,' said Nicodemus, 'speaking for myself. Those are the real time-servers, they hate Jesus just as they would hate anyone decent who sees through them, including Samuel or yourself.'

'Never mind,' said Annas, 'they are useful. It is people like that who make the world go round. If you know their price you can always buy them.'

'Their services will be free in this instance,' said Nicodemus. 'They hate Jesus. They will convict him on any charge.'

'But that still does not take us all the way,' said Annas. 'Gamaliel, Azzai and Joseph, how do you think they would vote?'

'On that charge,' said Nicodemus, 'Azzai would acquit him. Joseph would not convict, and nor would Gamaliel. I know. I have talked to them.'

'You mean that Joseph and Gamaliel would bring no verdict?'

'Gamaliel would abstain for certain. Joseph might possibly acquit.'

'Could we not detach some of their followers?'

'I have talked to their followers too,' said Nicodemus. He did not say what had passed between them: he did not wish to reveal his hand so soon, to let Annas see that his friend Nicodemus, on whom he counted, had been going round counselling abstention, supporting Gamaliel.

'And there is no chance?' asked Annas.

'At the best, from your point of view, they will be neutral.'

'Then the neutral bloc is enormous!' cried Annas. 'I have never known anything like it! There is no majority in sight!'

'No,' said Nicodemus evenly. 'You cannot convict Rabbi Jesus, on a turn-out like that.'

Annas was not beaten. 'Let us keep our eye on essentials. I do

185

not care so much about the Law. What matters is the Romans. We must stop the Zealot rising.'

Nicodemus said: 'I do not know how to stop the rising, but of one thing I am sure. The Rabbi Jesus has nothing to do with it.'

Annas said: 'The facts prove it. What evidence have you?'

'I know him, and you do not. He is not that kind of man.'

'Your feelings do you honour,' said Annas, not insincerely. 'I respect you for it. But I cannot set your feelings above the evidence, when two thousand crucifixions is the stake.'

'You are wrong,' said Nicodemus, earnestly but without bitterness, for his friend was sincere in his fashion. 'I know you are wrong, though I cannot prove it. It is not two thousand crucifixions which is at stake, but the good name of Israel. It is bad enough to sacrifice a Prophet, but much worse if you do it by mistake.'

'You are prophesying yourself, my friend,' said Annas. 'Perhaps it is not so serious as you think, and in fifty years' time it will all be forgotten. We are too close to these events.'

Annas continued: 'No, I see it quite clearly. It is our only course. Jesus must be arrested and handed over to the Romans. No need for a formal trial on our side, we can simply tell them that he is generally condemned by his own people and open to the Roman capital charge.'

Nicodemus said: 'The right course is a trial, full and open. The good name of Israel demands it, and demands there shall be nothing less. But the trial must be in our court and on our charges. There is serious matter for discussion, and it ought to be discussed. As for the Roman accusation, that he will lead a Zealot rising, there is nothing in it. Whatever your agents may tell you, it is false.'

They parted, still friends though having made no impression on each other. Nicodemus was well pleased. So long as he was there he could see to it: there was no majority, nor could Annas quietly hand Jesus over to the Romans pretending that his own people had washed their hands of him.

Now Nicodemus must explain to the Romans, make quite sure that they understood the whole question from the Jewish side. Whatever Annas might tell them, Jesus was not rejected by his own people, only by some of them, and many thought very highly of him indeed.

He sent his secretary to the Palace, to make an appointment. However, the answer was disappointing. Festus was ill.

CHAPTER 31

It was warm in the winter-room in the courtyard where Festus was convalescing, with the stove and his books, swaddled in his white toga used as a blanket wrapped anyhow, over innumerable tunics, thick woollen stockings and boots. The two women took off their cloaks.

'You will take a distemper,' said Festus, 'which Aristotle cannot cure. He will cure you of epilepsy or canine madness, except in the month of the dog-star, but not of a cold in the head.'

Festus was delighted with what they had brought him: a small glass phial of mud. 'It was Esther's idea,' said Paula. 'She worked it out so that no-one would notice. She just dropped something on the ground and then picked it up again, sticky all over with mud.'

Festus praised Esther, addressing her directly, a thing which he seldom did. When, Paula wondered, will he open his eyes and look? Festus, she knew, was sharp-sighted in many things that mattered, the mating-customs of elephants, the rhythm of volcanic eruptions, the leg-movements of centipedes: but he was extraordinarily unobservant in others, including one natural phenomenon which had been recognised immediately by Pilate, and also by Pilate's wife.

187

Sooner or later, Paula knew, it was bound to happen. The fifteen years' difference between her and Festus was nothing when he was eighteen or twenty, but ten years later there would be a generation's gap. Paula had faced it for the first time when Esther came back from Pilate and Festus had asked her if she was glad. Now she would not say anything different, for if it was not Esther it would be another, and Esther clung to her and she to the girl. Esther indeed was the problem, not Festus or Paula, for unless Festus renounced his ambitions Esther no more than Paula could become the 'Domina' whom Festus one day must have.

'Aristotle must take this mud and describe it,' said Festus. 'Then we shall almost have the blindness cure. There is only one thing missing, and Nicodemus was going to find out for us: was Jesus fasting when he made the spittle?'

'The lord Nicodemus tried to see you a week ago,' said Paula, 'but you were ill in bed.'

'I will send and let him know as soon as I am better,' said Festus. 'Not only because of the prescription, but I am feeling out of touch. You and Esther bring back useful gossip from the city, but you cannot tell me what their Senators are thinking, and Nicodemus does.'

Festus continued. 'Did you pick up anything new in the city?'

Paula said: 'Only another of these stories, about the Rabbi Jesus.'

'Another of these cures? I don't need all the details, if it is just a repeat.'

'It may be only a rumour,' said Paula, 'something that has got mixed up, a man who was really only sleeping.'

'What happened to this sleeping man?'

'He woke up again, when the Rabbi Jesus shouted at him.'

'That is not so strange.'

'Only some people said he was not sleeping, but dead.'

Festus said severely: 'This is the sort of thing that really ought to be properly established. Either the man was dead or he wasn't. It is quite wrong of people to go round spreading rumours, which are bound to be unsettling if untrue.'

Esther spoke, uninvited: 'Also, if they are not.'

Festus adjusted his thoughts: the girl had a mind of her own and was not disinclined to speak it. Should he put her in her place? He looked at Paula: she was smiling, as if saying, see what you have got!

'Ask her, Paula,' said Festus, 'if the man was not sleeping, what does she think happened?'

Esther did not wait for Paula to repeat the question. 'The Rabbi brought a man back from the dead.'

Festus said to Paula, in Latin, lest the girl should understand: 'Do you think she really believes that? It sounds to me quite mad.'

'These people are full of superstitions,' said Paula, 'but I do not think she is mad. In fact she thinks it is you who are simple, trying to work out the prescription for the cure of blindness. She has the idea that it isn't the mud that mattered, or even the spittle, what mattered was Jesus himself, and he could have done it with anything at hand.'

'She lacks education,' said Festus. 'She has no idea of science, or cause and effect.'

'She knows a good man when she sees one,' said Paula. 'That is more than some people can.'

This exchange was becoming unprofitable and Festus returned to Greek. 'Both of you think well of Jesus,' he said, 'as I do, but such a thing is extremely rare. In fact, all the cases I know of are considered doubtful. Among her own people, has such a thing ever happened before?'

'Oh yes, she told me,' said Paula. 'They had an augur once who used to do it. Elijah was his name.'

'This wise man of yours, Elijah,' said Festus, addressing Esther, 'is he one of those whom the Senator Nicodemus called a prophet?'

'He was the greatest,' said Esther. 'No-one else can be like him, and anyone who is like him will be Elijah come again.'

'How can that be?' asked Festus, kindly, not wishing to hurt the girl.

'The Prophet Elijah never died,' said Esther, 'but was taken up living into heaven. So there is nothing to stop him coming down to earth again.'

'And you think that Rabbi Jesus might be really the Prophet Elijah, because he has raised the dead?' Festus kept his voice neutral. After all, was this any worse than a lot of so-called educated people, Romans, who would never admit to believing it but would never stake their lives against its being true, the way those absurd Greek and Roman deities kept popping in and out of human bodies, or turning them into this, that or the other, whisking them here and there, all much less creditable and basically less credible than a plain straightforward raising from the dead? Would Festus himself stake his life against the girl's story? He looked at her long and closely. He would not.

'So he could be the Prophet Elijah?' he repeated gently. 'Does that mean that people will all the more run after him?'

Esther said: 'Yes, the men are saying that if he is not Elijah he must be the Messiah who will drive out the Romans.'

'Oh yes, I have heard of this Messiah,' said Festus, knowing for the best of reasons that Jesus was not. 'Who do you yourself think he is?'

Esther burst into tears. 'He is not any of them,' she said, sobbing. 'He is just himself, a special kind of person. All I know is that he was kind to me, and saved me from being dead.'

Paula said to Festus: 'That is not a bad reason. She is a woman. It is the men who talk this nonsense about a Messiah whom they imagine. It is the men who like playing at soldiers, so they think that nothing else counts. The women follow him because they think he is a special kind of person, just as Esther said.'

'You talk as if you know,' said Festus. 'Have you seen it? Have you been to his meetings yourself?'

Paula said: 'Yes. We have.'

CHAPTER 32

'Apart from the fact that it is a fraud,' said Annas, 'this can no longer be tolerated.'

'Your son-in-law is already going round saying so,' said Nicodemus.

'What exactly does he say?' asked Annas. Joseph Caiaphas, he feared, might have got his lesson wrong.

'Your own words,' said Nicodemus. 'It is expedient that one man should die for the nation.'

'Good!' said Annas, relieved. 'Exactly what I said. Entirely non-controversial.'

'Except for the man himself.'

'Even you will come to agree with me,' said Annas. 'The case is so crystal-clear. If we let him go on like this, all the people will follow him in the rising, and it will not seem just a local affair to the Romans but a nation-wide revolt, and they will destroy our people utterly.' Annas drew his friend to the window and pointed across the slopes of the city to the eye-filling mountain of masonry there. 'It is the greatest work of man in all the world,' said Annas, 'but the Romans would destroy that too. They would destroy our holy place as well as our nation. The life of one man is a small price for that.'

'Even the life of a Prophet?'

'Yes, even if he were a Prophet, and more than a Prophet,' said Annas. 'No matter what or who.'

'Some people,' said Nicodemus, 'are now calling him Elijah. He has done what Elijah did. Or Elisha under the mantle of Elijah.'

'It is as bad one way as the other,' said Annas. 'Even supposing it was true, that he had raised someone from the dead. But that is why I said just now that it was becoming fraudulent. Nobody rises from the dead.'

'According to your Sadducees,' said Nicodemus, 'but there are other opinions.'

Annas explained patiently. 'It is simple arithmetic. There would be nowhere for them to go, not even standing room in our country for all our people.'

'We are only talking of one person,' said Nicodemus, smiling. He disagreed with Annas on almost everything, and with Samuel on almost nothing, and he loved and honoured Samuel far more, but he much preferred talking to Annas. No point in explaining that a more sophisticated view of these things was possible. Better concentrate on the practical details. 'One person only, name Lazarus, place Bethany, time a week ago,' Nicodemus said.

'The principle is what matters,' said Annas. 'If one person can do it, so can everyone.'

'What can you do?' asked Nicodemus, smiling. 'To make sure that the Sadducees are not mistaken?'

'Now you are not being serious,' said Annas. 'This is very serious indeed. We shall have to lay him by the heels as soon as possible. He is hiding somewhere in the country, but he is bound to be here at Passover. Let us hope that nothing happens in the next three months.'

One thing will certainly happen, thought Nicodemus, and that is that the Romans will find out. As soon as I can see Festus they will know the whole story. Annas does not speak with the voice of our people. A fair trial by the Sanhedrin will show it. As long as I am here to see to it, Jesus will be safe.

*

Samuel was delighted, even though more alarmed than ever. Annas and his Sadducee party were thoroughly discomfited. Nothing could have shown up their ridiculous views more clearly, or supported better the teaching of Samuel and the rest. Samuel applauded the performance in principle, and if it had been any other time or performer he would have done so without reserve. Unfortunately it was the Rabbi Jesus who had

192

brought off this achievement, unparalleled since the time of Elijah, and the populace could easily be forgiven for imagining that he, like the Prophet Elijah, possessed supernatural powers. They would follow him all the more eagerly, in whatever direction he led, but the direction he was leading them in was the wrong one.

So, Samuel's alarm was greater than his pleasure. As Nicodemus had expected, nothing could make him change. His mind was already set and he moved forward with sublime certainty: the Law and therefore God required it, and nothing else mattered at all.

'We did not need it,' Samuel said to Nicodemus. 'Therefore, this action cannot be of God. We have Moses and the Prophets. If we do not follow them already we shall not do so, even if someone is raised from the dead.'

*

Son Gorion was absent: he almost always was, not saying where he was going or when he was coming back. Nicodemus was glad for the moment. It cleared the way for John, who, a less marked man than his master, moved freely to and fro. After only a few days of refuge in the country he had been sent back on some errand, and lodged naturally with his other patron here.

Nicodemus no longer trusted Gorion, where anything to do with Jesus was concerned. The Zealots, Gorion's attachment to whom he no longer doubted, seemed much less likely to do Jesus a mischief than either Annas or Samuel, but one could never be sure. Also, Gorion's politeness had failed to cover his contempt for the lot of them, useless, he implied, in any enterprise that counts. Lately, indeed, he seemed to have forgotten their very existence, so little did they figure in his scheme of things. This was not the least of the reasons for which Nicodemus disbelieved Annas. If Jesus were indeed the great hope of the Zealots, even their youngest member would not forget his name.

It was the evening of the day on which Nicodemus had seen

Samuel and Annas. He sat with John in the library, for it was cold, looking out on the bay tree and the rosemary, ever green and fragrant, encouragements much needed at the end of such a day.

'Tell me more stories,' said Nicodemus, to take his mind off the present. He listened with delight at the art of it, while the young man spoke. 'But you know that already,' John said, 'the story of the blind man here.' 'Never mind,' said Nicodemus, 'the way you tell it is different.' John continued:

'So for the second time they called the man who had been blind and said to him: Give God the praise; we know that this man is a sinner. He answered: Whether he is a sinner, I do not know; one thing I know, that though I was blind, now I see. They said to him: What did he do to you? How did he open your eyes? He answered: I have told you already and you would not listen; why do you want to hear it again; do you too want to become his disciples? And they reviled him, saying: You are his disciple, but we are disciples of Moses. We know that God has spoken to Moses, but as for this man, we do not know where he comes from. The man answered: Why, this is a marvel! You do not know where he comes from, and yet he opened my eyes. We know that God does not listen to sinners, but if anyone is a worshipper of God and does his will, God listens to him. Never since the world began has it been heard that anyone opened the eyes of a man born blind. If this man were not from God he could do nothing. They answered: You were born in utter sin, and would you teach us? And they cast him out.'

'Are you speaking, or is it the blind man?' asked Nicodemus.

'The blind man told me,' said John. 'Those were his words.'

John paused for a moment: had he been truthful? He added: 'More or less.'

More or less! thought Nicodemus. What worlds in that! Style and language make all the difference, not to the truth but to whether people notice. Put that story another way, and people will not even hear it: put it in John's way, and no-one will ever forget.

No, and it does not come from copying his master. No-one can copy like that. The young man has done something better: he is soaked in it.

Even when he does not understand . . . But how could he? he is not yet twenty, and at more than twice his age, with a hundred times his learning, can I say I understand? Things tumble out of him which he does not understand or question, picked up from his master as an infant learns from its parents, things which he will make much of, when he grows up. One day he will grow out of those other things, the childish fancies that make me want to shake him, and then we shall see.

'Your master,' said Nicodemus, 'has the gift of words above all others. He says things which you cannot forget, even if you do not know what he means when he says them. Think of some of the things you have told me, his sayings: *I am the light of the world.*'

'He is always talking of light,' said John. 'There was another thing. He said: *This is the judgment, that the light has come into the world, and men loved darkness rather than light, for everyone who does evil hates the light but he who does what is true comes to the light.*'

'I had not heard that,' said Nicodemus thoughtfully. 'He himself was the light, was he?'

'I suppose so,' said John.

Nicodemus fell into great agitation of mind. He rose, breathing heavily, and paced to and fro. 'So that men are not judged by anyone or anything, then,' said Nicodemus, 'but by themselves, by their own actions, whether they turn towards or away from the light.'

He continued, after much thought: 'My son, this is something new and vast beyond conception. Nothing like this has ever been heard in Israel. I am not sure that Israel can contain it. The Rabbi Jesus is as great as that.'

He broke off, stunned. But, to make sense, something is

necessary to complete it . . . but no, there is nothing that is possible . . .

He caught himself up, briskly: 'So, it is not so foolish after all, what some people are saying, that Rabbi Jesus is the Prophet Elijah.'

'I do not think he can be, Sir,' said John tentatively. 'We saw them together, once.'

'Another of your stories!' said Nicodemus, indulgently. 'Only, remember when you tell it to say it was only a dream.'

'It seemed quite real,' said John. 'Three of us saw it together.'

'It must have been all the same dream.'

'Well, it is true, we had been sleeping, but we all thought we had woken up.'

'What do you think you saw?'

'He was talking to Moses and Elijah.'

'*Moses* as well! For full measure! Are you sure that is who they were?'

'We only had the Rabbi's word to go on, when we told him, but he would not deceive us, I am sure.'

'The other two had the same dream exactly?'

'Simon anyhow, but we didn't have time to discuss it properly. There was a thunderstorm coming, and we had to get down off the mountain before we got wet.'

'What time of day was this, if you had been sleeping?'

'We left at daybreak.'

'So it was dark when all this happened. If it was real, *how could you see*?' Nicodemus thought this would deflate the imagination.

John answered: 'The Rabbi was bright all over.'

'Whatever do you mean by that?'

'Like Moses when he came down from the mountain, only much more so. None of us could look at him. His face was brighter than the sun.'

Nicodemus did not like this piece of imagination, even about something seen in a dream. John's words were perilously close to a description of the Shekhinah, the Radiance, the manifestation of the Presence of the living God.

'That shows it wasn't real,' said Nicodemus. 'But dreams are often important. It sounds like an important dream.' Worth submitting, he thought, together with his own, to his friend Philo.

'Perhaps you are right,' said John, 'and we dreamed it. But have you never dreamed a dream that was real?'

CHAPTER 33

It was again the Greek in him, Nicodemus supposed. The Rabbinical schools did not encourage it, fanatically suppressed it in fact, but once you had been exposed to it, the Greek way of thinking, there was nothing you could do about it. The thing was with you for life.

Nicodemus had remained in his library after his guest had gone to bed. It was now long after dark, and a servant had kindled the lamps. Nicodemus told him to move the tall bronze lampstands all together, and they stood in one corner, multiple flames merging into a single bright glow.

The pure Hebrew mind could not have done it, would have instantly shied away, at the least approach to mysteries so awful. Just as his friends here in Jerusalem shied off Philo, thought Nicodemus, when the processes of reason common to all men reached out towards the unreachable and unknowable living God of the Jews: just so, Samuel would be horrified at what I am now doing, setting up the most fantastic hypotheses, violating the holiest convictions, contemplating them purely as an intellectual exercise in order to knock them down. How quickly can we dispose of them by Socratic questions, in how many rounds?

It had begun with the extraordinary fancy that seized him, at something he heard from John: *This is the judgment, that the light has come into the world*, so Jesus had said. And men by their own deeds acted their own judgment: they turned either towards or away from the light. And Jesus—so John supposed, so let us go on that assumption—spoke of himself as that light. Now do a thing which only a Greek would dare, and go further, approaching the unapproachable in thought. If the judgment on men was to be of this fashion, and if the Rabbi Jesus was the light whose very being brought about judgment, then the light and Rabbi Jesus were something more than the Law. As a Jew, Nicodemus abhorred himself as a Greek for being able to contemplate it, even as the maddest of fantasies to be discarded at once. Grimly, ironically, he smiled at himself. Nothing is greater than the Law, unless it be God himself.

Annas had rightly called his own people idiots, trying to drive Jesus into such a trap. A greater than Moses, indeed! He would indeed have to be, and he would be, in this mad conception—not so mad that people could not conceive of it, for Annas' men had done so, but such that no-one could possibly retain it, unless he was mad.

Retain it, except in fantasy, to play with in the mind. God spoke, long ago, to Moses, and has spoken by His Holy Spirit to the Prophets, but never face to face. No man can see God and live. The brightness of His presence, the Shekhinah, had been a devouring light so intense that none could look on it, veiled in thick cloud on Mount Sinai or inside the Ark of the Temple. No living man could look at it, any more than the sun.

Absurd to entertain it for a moment, even in thought: the fantasy that the Unknowable and Unseeable, timeless Being, not to be contained in all the heavens and the heavens that are above the heavens, should permit his essence to appear on earth, at a single time and place, inhabiting not even the inmost cell of a shrine or the topmost peak of a mountain but the frame of an ordinary, walking, breathing, eating, talking man. Would it not be to place Himself on the level of the absurd Greek and Roman deities, demons or spirits or whatever they might be?

The thought might have theoretical attractions, from one

point of view: it made things hang together a lot better in what one had heard of his teaching, and various things that had been puzzling would naturally fall into place. But the same could be said of anything whose meaning was hidden, and it was unphilosophical to drag in the Explanation of All Things wherever there was anything to explain.

Mad to think of it, for anyone, and for a Hebrew doubly mad. Nicodemus laughed suddenly as he saw the horror, something far more abominable and far more certain than any Greek tragic fate. The fantasy, if it were more than fantasy, would lead to this: God thus appearing and thus speaking must be rejected by his own people, the people of his Covenant, the Jews.

Not by all of them, but by the best and holiest, even more than by the worst, and the more zealously they served Jehovah in heaven the more certainly they would reject him on earth. God had given them the Law and measured them by the way they observed it: then—in this fantasy—veiled and unrecognised he informs them that other things are sometimes more important and that a certain man, to all appearances mere human, is the one who can tell them all about it, is able to vary the Law. Samuel is bound to reject him, and Samuel would be right.

Is Samuel to be convicted of offence unspeakable because he is less versed in the thought of the Greeks than Nicodemus, less wise in affairs and less tolerant than Gamaliel, more learned in the Scriptures and more zealous a follower of the Law than the common people who run after Jesus though they do not understand what he says? Samuel is the tragedy, not Annas who is only an accident. The best and holiest of Israel, by following God's commandment, will cast out their God.

Nicodemus found himself becoming enmeshed with his fantasy. The creature of his imagination was becoming real, and he turned and fled, glancing with tortured fascination over his shoulder. If it caught him up, he would be mad.

It was past midnight and the lamps were flickering. One by one they began to go out. Words kept darting at him out of the darkness of the room and his memory. 'I am the light of the world.' Jesus had said it. 'God is Light, and not only Light but the Light of all lights. God is Light and seen by his own light alone.' Philo said that. 'The Lord is my light and my saviour,' David said that.

I am the Fountain of Life, God said to the Prophets. God is the everliving Fountain, said Philo. Whoever drinks of the water that I shall give him, said Jesus, will never thirst again, and the water that I shall give him will become in him a spring of water welling up to eternal life.

No, it was not possible, and he had almost escaped when another long finger of words reached out and held him. The hour is coming when neither on this mountain nor in Jerusalem will men worship the Father. The hour is coming—AND NOW IS—when the true worshippers will worship the Father in spirit and in truth. God is spirit, and those who worship him must worship him in spirit and in truth.

He was tiring now, but he came at last to the Temple. He would be safe inside, once past the warning sign placed on the threshold: No Gentile is to approach within this place, and whoever does so will be guilty of his own death. Behind the low curtain-wall, with its graven warning, the wall of the sanctuary rose heaven-high, many-gated but not for the Gentile Deep inside, within a dark and empty shrine, if anywhere on earth, dwelt the Shekhinah which is the Light of Lights, the Presence of the living God, but a voice said to Nicodemus before he could reach safety, beyond the warning of death to the Gentiles: what if the living God, whom neither the heavens nor the heavens that are above the heavens can contain should decide to come out to the Gentiles? Would not this Temple crumble, and all its stones dissolve to less than dust?

Again he read the words, but they were different. God will not come out of this place to the Gentiles, and anyone who says he can do so will be guilty of his own death. No, that was wrong, the letters were changing and the inscription was really facing inward: God has said that he will not go out of this place to the

Gentiles, and he is to be guarded within it even at the cost of our own death. Once more the letters dissolved, and the words were different: God is not to go out of this place to the Gentiles, and if he does so he will be guilty of his own death. Jesus was standing beside him, reading out the words.

Jesus was there again. I am the light of the world, he said, and left.

It is all nonsense, mad, impossible, said Nicodemus aloud, in the dark. The Word cannot have been made flesh and God cannot be rejected by his own people in obedience to his own commandments.

But there was no Temple to flee to, and no place of refuge. Everything had gone. Nicodemus was alone in the darkness, and his fantasy overtook him. God's people, trusting in God, would reject him. They would be ground to powder, because they trusted in God.

He did not seem to suffer, but in the morning when they found him they said that he was mad.

*   *   *

So from that day on the chief priests and the Pharisees took counsel together, how to put Jesus to death.

*   *   *

CHAPTER 34

John was dismayed but not daunted.

Their roles were reversed. The young man was the guide and protector. There was no-one else to whom the Rabbi would talk. Gorion and the rest of his family he recognised and sometimes greeted, and sometimes he spoke, a few words not always irrational, and he never had to be restrained.

It was not a dumb spirit which had taken possession of him, nor one which tore him, but one that caused him grief. He would sit quietly and listen to Samuel, but Samuel describing it afterwards could say only: 'He looked at me as if I was dead.' Over Samuel, Nicodemus wept bitterly, but with Annas he was merely withdrawn. Annas tried to comfort him: he installed in Nicodemus' library the first trial panes of window-glass from Sidon which he had intended to keep for himself. Nicodemus appeared grateful but distinguished little between light and darkness, turning his eyes inward upon his own thoughts.

To John, however, when they were alone, Nicodemus would talk, seated in his chair in the winter sunshine and sometimes even moving, almost normal, except for what he said—and that John never repeated.

John comforted him from the start. 'This kind of spirit,' he said authoritatively, 'is worse than usual but we have cast out many almost as bad. I will go and fetch Simon Peter, we generally work together in matters of this sort.'

Nicodemus appeared to understand him, for he simply said: 'Go in peace.' John was away for several days, for Rabbi Jesus was travelling and had to be followed, from secret place to place.

'This is the worst we have met,' said John to Simon, 'but I expect we can manage between us. Anyhow, we must try. It is dangerous for the Rabbi Jesus to come to Jerusalem, and he does not need us this week.'

Simon was shocked at the change in Nicodemus' appearance, and appalled at what he said.

'No, it is not the Rabbi Nakdemon who is blaspheming,' said John respectfully to his senior. 'You forget, the Rabbi is mad. It is an evil spirit who is speaking.'

'It is Satan himself!' said Simon Peter. 'Or worse, if that is possible. Why, Rabbi Jesus himself called *me* Satan, for saying much less than that!'

'He does not like to be called the Messiah,' said John, 'and you were needling him. Even if he really is. It causes misunderstanding.'

'It certainly would if he got arrested,' said Simon. 'I expect he was thinking of that.'

*

They tried what simple means they had, but they were defeated. The evil spirit remained.

Simon hit upon the answer, as usual. It was foolproof and simple. The Rabbi Nakdemon, and the evil spirit which possessed him, need only hear the truth from the lips of Rabbi Jesus, be assured by Jesus himself that Jesus was not—could not be, possibly—what the evil spirit said he was.

*

Nicodemus could not remember, later, where it had happened. He knew he had been transported, and it was not in Jerusalem, but he did not know if it had been in the dry hill country beyond Hebron or the wet rich uplands towards Samaria, or the table-land across Jordan, or the desolate shores of the Dead Sea. Wherever it was, there was Jesus, and there was Nicodemus, and there was nothing else.

At once he plunged into the abysses, head-first and down through a million worlds of darkness, seeking somewhere to hide, burying himself under all Creation, shielding the light from his eyes.

God of God.

Light of Light.

The least glow of the least particle of that infinite radiance was enough to burn Creation up, more than enough, for all Creation was nothing beside it. Yet Creation had nothing except the glow to sustain it; there was nowhere else it could turn.

Unable to face the Godhead—a nothing if it turned away.

There is nothing to be afraid of, my child, said Jesus to Esther, or to all the world.

Only death of one kind instead of another.

Death of oneself for a different reason, or death of another instead of oneself, death without justice or understanding.

The Word became flesh and dwelt among us, said Nicodemus, but did not tell us so.

Full of grace and truth, said another, for those who could behold it.

He came unto his own, said Nicodemus, and his own received him not.

There was an aeon of silence.

Nicodemus said: Because of the Law that he had given to Moses.

There was another pause.

Be silent, said another voice somewhere, for so it has come up before me in thought.

Jesus wept, and they rose on the flood of his sorrow above the whole of the world.

They who resist God shall vanish utterly, said Nicodemus. They shall be as if they had never been.

God so loved the world, all the world, said the other, that he sent of his own substance, as his Son, into the world, not to condemn the world but that the world might be saved by him.

Yet he came unto his own, said Nicodemus, and his own received him not.

None but his own would reject him. The rejection of the All-High by anything less than the highest would have no meaning. Even the best, alone, is not enough.

His own received him not, repeated Nicodemus, mourning, for this was a sorrow which nothing could take away.

But, said the other, to all those who received him he gave power to become children of God.

And those of his own who received him not? said Nicodemus, and was not consumed.

There was another silence, and heaven and earth had passed away and there was a new Jerusalem and a new Temple, without walls, and a voice said: God will dwell with all men and they shall be his people, and he will wipe away every tear from their eyes.

Part VIII
SPRING AD30

CHAPTER 35

After this, Nicodemus seemed better, though not restored. The evil spirit had not departed, but it was silent, no longer asserting, though refusing to retract. Nicodemus lay now unmoving, mourning something it seemed, but he mourned whatever it was in silence, within the circle of his mind. His wife, his daughters, even his son, rarely spoke to him and if he heard he answered. He gave no trouble at all.

John, on his errands to Jerusalem, came and visited him, but there was nothing more to be done, except to speak to him kindly. Perhaps the evil spirit would one day depart altogether, if unprovoked and left alone. John was downcast but loyal to his master. To all appearance, this was the first failure—though only partial—of his Rabbi's powers; they were so extraordinary that people had got in the habit of thinking they were unlimited, and this could lead to disappointment now and then.

The days lengthened, the rains were less abundant, and the sun grew warmer. The yellow-green of the young wheat dazzled, the silver-blue of the olives grew more intense, and the anemones opened, flecking the hills with blood.

The solemn preparation for another Passover was almost ended. Tomorrow would be the great Feast. Already the lambs were being slaughtered in the Temple, by thousands, and within a few hours, the same evening, the whole people of Israel would be celebrating its release. God had smitten the Egyptians and brought Israel out of Egypt, by the hand of his servant Moses, the greatest of all God's people, the mouthpiece of his Law.

Normally, at this time of day, Nicodemus could hear the buzz from the markets not far to the north of his house, near to the gate of the city by Golgotha, but it was now silent in that quarter for work had ceased some hours ago, at mid-day on the eve of the Feast.

He guessed the time, for his mind was stirring, awakened perhaps by the three trumpet blasts. Never before had he missed it, in Jerusalem, the Paschal sacrifice in the Temple, the lamb slain and the priests blowing their silver trumpets, but the sound carried and the scene was in front of him, the blood of the lamb in the golden bowl cast on the corners and the base of the Altar. Then the rows of priests lining the path to the Altar, with their gold and silver bowls, and the worshippers, all the sons of Israel bringing their lambs for the sacrifice, also for the feast.

The scene changed, and another sacrifice was in front of him, the sacrifice of Atonement, in his dream.

It was a dream, he said to himself. I have been dreaming a great deal, lately.

He raised his voice and shouted: 'Gorion!' It was the first time for many months.

After a little, Gorion was found, and entered. Nicodemus said to him, as if nothing had happened: 'I was not able to go to the Temple, for some reason. Have you taken our lamb?'

'No, father,' said Gorion, astonished. 'But now I will do it. I have only just come back.'

'What have you been doing?' asked Nicodemus. He was taking an interest once more.

Gorion said: 'I had something very important to attend to. Something that could not wait.'

'What can be more important than the lamb for Passover?' said Nicodemus. 'What is it that cannot wait?'

'Two of my friends,' said Gorion. 'They were dying. To-morrow would have been too late.'

His face did not change expression, but there were tears.

Nicodemus stretched out his hand and took Gorion's. 'Two at one time is uncommon. Were they both in the same house?'

'It was not in a house, father, and they were together because it is the way of the Romans. There were three altogether, and two of them were my friends.'

Nicodemus understood little, but enough. 'Pray God they did not suffer, more than they must.'

Gorion said: 'No. After all, they were dying for Israel, and they knew it.'

'The other one too, I hope,' said Nicodemus.

'Oh no, he had nothing like that to help him, poor fellow. He was not dying for anyone, not even for himself.'

'There must have been some reason. Why was he there?'

'There was no reason that anyone knew of. No good reason, that is. Some people talked as if he was a madman. But it all looked a dreadful mistake.'

'There must have been something behind it. The Romans do not often make mistakes.'

'Oh no, he was just a nobody.'

'He must have had a name.'

Gorion fidgeted with anger and said fiercely: 'Those Roman dogs mocked us when they wrote it over him. They shall pay, I swear! "The King of the Jews", they called him. A wretched creature like that!'

'But had he no other name?'

'His name was Jesus.'

'One Jew in every twenty is called Jesus. Which one was this? Who was his father?'

'Nobody knows his father.'

Gorion suddenly let the tears flow freely. 'The poor wretch!' he cried. 'He had done nothing to deserve it. The other two had fought against the Romans and been taken. But *he* . . . he had done nothing, only babble nonsense.'

'Nothing more than that?'

'Oh, there had been silly stories that he was one of us—*him*, a leader! Why, when they took him, he did not even resist!'

'Then why did he have to die?'

'He had enemies among our people who turned him in to the Romans. God knows why!' Gorion went on, passionately: 'For this, too, I swear it, the murderers shall pay. He was not one of ours, but he was an Israelite, and he was innocent.'

Nicodemus rose half-way out of his madness, beating the darkness into flakes of light. 'Son,' he said, 'vengeance is God's. By His Name I command you, it is not for you to repay.'

For many months now Gorion had missed the tone of command, and hearing it once more he quietened.

'Father,' he said gently, kneeling by the bedside, 'if you were young you would understand.'

'I was young once, my son, and I have seen innocent men murdered. But tell me, which Jesus was this? I have known many of that name.'

'You may have heard of him once, Father,' said Gorion, touched with compassion, for these old people sometimes had no sense of proportion and got upset by trifles. 'One of his followers used to come here.'

Holding the sleeve of his father's tunic Gorion once more fell to weeping, for no reason that he could understand. It had, after all, been a tiring day.

Nicodemus saw the flakes descending faster, settling in the bowl of darkness, filling it with light.

'Son,' he said, 'which Jesus was it? Much depends on that.'

Now Gorion remembered. His father had known the man. He might even have admired him: they both liked talking of things that were not much use. Perhaps the news of his death would hurt, would throw him back again into the madness from which, just now, he had seemed to be emerging.

'It is all over now, father,' he whispered, 'and nothing can bring him to life again. Jesus of Nazareth is dead.'

CHAPTER 36

'It is true,' said Joseph. 'They have done it, exactly as you feared.'

Nicodemus, rising from his bed, clothed and in his right mind again, had gone straight to see him, his ally in the affair.

'Then there was no trial?'

'Nothing within the Law. We were not told until it was all over. Azzai, Gamaliel and myself.'

'Who did it then?'

'Annas, his men and all the jackals. They held a meeting packed with their own mob, just to give colour to the business for the Romans.'

'And Samuel?' Nicodemus was sad. Annas had only behaved according to his nature, but Samuel was an angel.

'Samuel knew, but he did nothing. He let things take their course.'

'Oh Samuel! Samuel!'

'He said that Annas was protecting the Law by acting outside it.'

'Oh Samuel, my friend!' Nicodemus recognised the good doctrine, a weapon dexterously wielded in self-defence by the Rabbis: pray God it had not now been used to their own destruction.

'If you had been there,' said Joseph, 'they could not have done it. You would have been watching, and you would have found out.'

'But the Romans? They are just.'

'Not Pilate. Annas and the jackals threatened him. He held out for a little, but they wore him down. "You are no friend of Caesar!" Their usual line of attack.'

'He must have thought they spoke for all our people,' said Nicodemus. 'But they did not. I fell ill before I could tell

Festus.' He wished he had stayed mad, waking to a world of such horror, a horror that seemed to have happened only because he was mad.

'But now,' said Joseph, 'it is all over. Jesus of Nazareth is dead.'

There was safety for the mind only in action. 'There are only three hours left to bury him in,' said Nicodemus. At nightfall it would be Sabbath, and the Passover supper too. 'Where are his followers? They should see to it.'

'They are scattered. They are like chickens who have lost their mother,' said Joseph.

'The ones I know,' said Nicodemus, 'may turn out more than chickens, when they grow up.'

'But now they are absolutely useless.'

The two men looked at each other, patricians of the House of Israel, equal in spirit though not in guile to Annas, contemptuous of the jackals, fearing their fellows less than they feared another hazard, but this too they overcame.

'We shall not be able to eat the Passover because of corpse-defilement,' said Nicodemus. 'But for this body it is worth it. We could not save him living, but we can bury him now he is dead.'

*

A slave knocked the wedge away, and the stone rolled in its groove downward, closing the entrance to the cave.

The two men stood there for a moment, saluting in memory.

'Jesus is dead,' said Nicodemus, 'but he will live for ever. The men who killed him have made sure of that.'

Joseph of Arimathea looked at him curiously, in the fading evening light. His friend had not really returned to normal. 'You are as cheerful,' said Joseph, 'as if he was your greatest enemy, and you are mourning as if he was your greatest friend.'

'I am mourning,' said Nicodemus sadly, smiling. 'Israel has slain another Prophet, and he was also my friend.'

How impossible to say more, thought Nicodemus, to tell

Joseph how nearly he was right: that Nicodemus had come out of the valley of the shadow of death because of the death of Jesus. Jesus had turned out, after all, to be not more than a Prophet, for only men taste of death. The fancies of Nicodemus in his madness had been not more than fancies. The man whom sons of Israel had rejected they had wrongly rejected, but they had not rejected their God. The words of this man would live for ever, and Israel would suffer for not having listened, but Israel would only suffer and not be ground to powder. What had happened was only much as usual: another Prophet had been put to death.

'Is it not strange,' said Joseph, 'the way you were restored? It almost looks like the last and most extraordinary of the Rabbi's works. But of course it can't be, because he was already dead.'

They turned to go back to the city, past the group of women watching and the knoll with the three posts of wood. The eastern sky was not yet bright with the moon's rising but a single star was there. The wall cut off the view of the city and all but the topmost parts of the Temple, but northward in the open there were houses among the gardens, and then with the second and the third star appearing there was the sound of trumpets and the lights in the houses were kindled. The Sabbath had begun to shine.

It was less than ten minutes' walk to the house of Nicodemus. They shivered, for after nightfall it was cold. They were the only people abroad. Nicodemus felt excluded from the world which he inhabited: within the houses the Passover supper was going forward. Until this year, in all his life, he had never missed.

Joseph left in the direction of his own quarters, and Nicodemus entered the house alone. John was waiting: the porter knew him. Somewhere, also, there were two women. 'There is no Passover for us today,' said Nicodemus. He sent for a maid-servant to look after the women.

Nicodemus did not explain himself. John knew enough, even though not everything. He had listened to the evil spirit speaking when Nicodemus first went mad, though he knew nothing of what came after, for Nicodemus never spoke of what had passed when they took him to see Jesus, during his madness.

John saw that his master, having failed to convince Nicodemus in his lifetime that he was merely human, had now succeeded, by dying in the usual way. The recovery of Nicodemus was therefore not surprising. John took up their old relationship where it had left off, but now in greater dependence. His true master had vanished, and only Nicodemus was left.

'There is nothing to be afraid of, my son,' said Nicodemus briskly. 'Everything will come all right.'

'We had thought that he would be the one to redeem Israel,' said John miserably, weeping: for Jesus, or for himself? He was again a boy.

'So he may,' said Nicodemus comfortingly, with more assurance than he felt. 'Though not in the way you thought. He was a Prophet.'

'We looked for his kingdom on earth.'

'God has arranged things differently.'

'We do not understand.'

'You are not the only people. There are things which I too do not understand. He would not have died if I had not been stricken, and I was made well again only by his death.'

After a little, Nicodemus continued. He asked about John's plans. Already he saw the future: the life-interest of Rabbi Jesus in his followers having lapsed, John might be going free. A whole lifetime to recall the words of Jesus and to seek their meaning.

'We cannot stay with Azzai, he will be in danger. Tonight we are going to Bethany, we hope.'

'Who is "we"?'

'There is my mother and her sister, who are here already, and my brother and Simon Peter, and three other women.'

The first time that John had come to his house, Nicodemus

had detained him at the last moment as he was leaving. Nicodemus had felt then that it was a moment of decision, something tremendous for both John and himself. Now he again had this feeling, and he said at once: 'Bethany is beyond a Sabbath day's journey, and also it is dark and you might not get out of the city. You must stay here.'

'There are many of us,' said John, 'and you would be in danger.'

'My house is large,' said Nicodemus, 'and there is no danger, either to you or to me. Annas would not dare.'

John was too tired to thank properly. 'In a day or two,' he said, 'when everything is quiet we can go home and get back to our fishing.'

Nicodemus said: 'Tomorrow is the Sabbath and a time for resting. Stay here until the day after, and then we shall see.'

AUTHOR'S NOTE

This is a work of fiction about one person exposed to a breaking-strain. It is not intended as a reconstruction of Gospel events, but some assumptions have had to be made.

The book is written within an orthodox Christian framework. Even within the Christian churches, however, there is disagreement about the exact course and nature of many of these historical events (if not their significance), and in the wider world which may be termed Christoid the measure of agreement is even less. Adherents of the Jewish faith will differ in another sense: however, the author hopes that he has avoided cause for offence, and that he has fairly represented the resplendent features of Judaism and its inestimable achievements in a pagan world, things in no way to be measured by the trivial legalisms which any highly organised system based on law is liable to produce.

How then, among many different possible versions of events, can one know which version to adopt? Almost any choice may suggest overconfidence, but for the purpose of a narrative one is obliged to choose. There is a natural bias in favour of the 'probable', but this is less helpful than it seems, for the opinions of scholars on what is 'probable' vary, and have varied very greatly from time to time, and not least about the Fourth Gospel. And even if the 'most probable' can be arrived at, this is not necessarily the version to choose. In a story it is sometimes the less likely that imposes itself, just as, in life, the near-impossible is sometimes what occurs. It seems essential only that whatever version is chosen should fit in with the pattern, and should not be something clearly impossible in the light of other known facts.

Chronology

The chronology of the action is modelled closely on the order of the Fourth Gospel, with little assistance from the other three. The departures from the Gospel order are as follows:

The story of the woman taken in adultery, which does not form part of the original Gospel and could be fitted in almost anywhere, has been moved to the start.

The story of the cleansing of the Temple has been notionally moved to the end, as in the other three Gospels, instead of the start.

The order of Chapters 5 and 6 in the Gospel has been reversed, as many scholars prefer.

At a number of other points the chronology of the Fourth Gospel has been stretched. The raising of Lazarus has been moved as far as possible towards the preceding visit of Jesus to Jerusalem, instead of near the Passover feast. The healing of the blind man in Jerusalem has been placed earlier in the period of the Feast of Tabernacles than the order of the Gospel narrative suggests.

The chronology has also been filled out by bringing Jesus and the disciples to Jerusalem more often than is recorded, at the various feasts when attendance was likely in any event.

Characters

Nicodemus appears three times in St John's Gospel, and the book employs the whole of the material there, except that (as many people recommend) the last part of Chapter 3 is treated as not spoken by Jesus to Nicodemus, at least on that occasion. The accretions of legend about Nicodemus in apocryphal literature are not used at all, nor is the single and doubtful reference in the Talmud to a person of that name. His cast of mind owes something to his contemporary, the Hellenist Jewish philosopher Philo of Alexandria.

Annas' role in the book is not inconsistent with his appearances in the Gospels or with references to him or his family in Josephus and in Talmudic sources. It might be held that his overwhelming importance in relation to the titular High Priest, his son-in-law Joseph Caiaphas, is an exaggeration, but for narrative purposes one figure of the Sadducee faction is enough.

Samuel is an invention, but he simply must exist. He is a type not described but only hinted at in the Gospels. He may be considered a Gamaliel with a difference. *Gamaliel*, a well-known historical figure, does not appear personally in the book but is allotted a role consistent with his later behaviour in 'Acts'.

Gorion is an invention, but the Zealots played an important part in the Gospel scene.

The office of the Tribune *Festus* was real, but Festus himself is invented, and is identified here with the upright Porcius Festus who later came to Judaea as Governor and dealt with Paul. He is a necessary invention because the Romans played a leading part in these events, and Pilate was almost never on the spot. The interests of Festus, as depicted here, are probably less extraordinary than those of the elder Pliny, on whose well-documented behaviour that of Festus is partly modelled. The elder Pliny's works have been extensively plundered for the benefit of Festus, who may be imagined as one of the sources used by Pliny.

There is no evidence, except an ambiguous text in one of his Epistles, that *Saul*/Paul (a minor figure in this story) ever saw Jesus in the flesh. However, he was in Jerusalem shortly afterwards, and there is no obvious reason why he should not have been there also before Jesus' death.

There is no basis outside the Gospel for the story of the *'woman taken in adultery'*. Every detailed reconstruction of the incident is open to objections on historical or legal grounds, weighted more or less according to opinion about the most valuable of the later sources, the Mishnah, not compiled until after New Testament times. Nobody knows for certain the position in law at the time. The version used in this book was adopted less on grounds of probability than because of the moral problems which it threw up.

Details

A surprising amount of information, though with maddening gaps, is available about topography, daily life and ceremonies. Josephus and the Talmud are often very precise. The lay-out and dimensions of the Temple can be reconstructed with some confidence, though lacking many details. The location of the Antonia Fortress and Herod's great Palace are certain, though not the latter's full lay-out or extent. The High Priest's palace, in the book, has been placed in the traditional location, with the house of John Mark's mother therefore close by. There is no evidence, obviously, about the location of the house of Nicodemus, nor about the lay-out of patrician dwellings at that time, but if we imagine them on the Graeco-Roman model we are unlikely to be wrong.

The author has tried to be accurate in these matters, but cannot expect altogether to have escaped blunders, perhaps obvious to the more learned, and for these he can only ask indulgence, as also for a number of anachronisms which have been admitted for the sake of simplicity.

Inventions in the story

The teachings attributed to the two Rabbis, Jesus and Samuel, follow closely the Gospel and Talmudic texts. Many of the passages are verbatim quotations. Some are extrapolations, and two Talmudic-type passages (in Chapters 1 and 22) are only slightly fanciful conflations. Some passages of speech which may strike the reader as quotations though unfamiliar are precisely that: for instance, the saying of Jesus in Chapter 18 'Blessed is the man . . .' is based on an alternative MS reading in St Luke's Gospel,* and the saying in Chapter 34 'Be silent,

---

* The variant in the Gospel refers to Sabbath observance, not to the washing of hands as in the book. Luke's version of the hand-washing story is the only one which implicates Jesus personally in this breach of the Law, and it is possible to prefer Matthew and Mark.

for so it has come up before me in thought' is from a Talmudic text, put in the mouth of God when confronted with the appalling martyrdom of a very holy man.

The only substantial invention of teaching (or of incident with moral) is the offer by Jesus to heal Samuel's son (Chapter 14). The reason for this invention is that Jesus' teaching about the Sabbath was crucial for his relations with authority, and this variant of the Sabbath-cure story seems a missing link in a series, illustrating the point up to which Jesus could be accepted by the strictest Pharisee but beyond which he could not.

A different type of invention is the attribution to Jesus of a regular and advanced course of study in the Law, a thing not incompatible with continuing work as a craftsman (for very many of the Rabbis combined study or teaching with manual labour). This invention is not essential to the construction of the book, only useful: however, it has attractions, for it supplies the simplest and most natural answer to two questions—how did Jesus acquire his profound knowledge of the Law and his devastating skill in Rabbinic argument, and how did he come to remain unmarried for so long (Law study being the only generally accepted excuse)? The principal objection to the theory is probably not the views of his listeners in Jerusalem, who may have been ignorant—and ignorance was a favourite subject for the irony of John—but the surprise of those who knew him in his home country: even there, however, their wonder may have been not at the fact of his learning but at the brilliance and authority with which he expressed himself.

The 'trial' of Jesus, although of critical importance, is treated by foreshadowing rather than description because Nicodemus is affected by the foreshadow more than by the event. The suggestion that it was a 'non-trial' is open to objection, but the room for guesswork is large. The legal framework which existed at that time is not known for certain, and the Gospel accounts are not consistent or complete. If the trial was really a 'non-trial', this would at least explain why the procedure differed so outrageously from standard Jewish practice in later times.

On the part played by the Zealots, there is no evidence that the Zealot leaders deliberately implicated Jesus as a blind. However, Mark states that the arrest of Jesus was preceded by an 'insurrection', and it is difficult to understand why an intelligent man like Annas (or his party) could have taken seriously the story that Jesus was something—a national leader bent on opposing the Romans—which quite obviously he was not.

The theme

The story may be thought to lay unusual stress on two points usually left unstressed. The first is the degree of misunderstanding of Jesus' person and his mission in his lifetime, almost total even among his friends. The language of scholarly commentators on this point is very different from that of pious literature.

Readers who pay this book the compliment of looking below the surface may detect the assumption that, in the phrase of one commentator (Father Raymond E. Brown), there is 'a great deal of Christian post-Resurrectional insight' in the wording of certain passages in the Gospels, anticipating later understanding of the nature of Jesus Christ.

Since it took the Christian Church several hundred years to make up its mind, and then only at the cost of an almost mortal split, it would surely not be surprising if a truth of this awesome nature (or anything like it), utterly strange to the fierce monotheism of Israel, escaped those Jews—fisherman or Rabbi—who knew Jesus in his lifetime, a man among men like themselves.

For the purposes of this book, one Rabbi is allowed to perceive the truth, but he is given enormous and special advantages, and the consequences illuminate the situation both for him and for all the rest.

Some people may think that the treatment in this book diminishes the stature of the disciples. The truth however is surely that the other kind of treatment diminishes the Godhead (or our conception of it). The heights reached by Peter, John and—later—Paul after the Resurrection are surely best seen beside the stupendous gulf which separated them from Jesus before.

Least of all would the author wish to diminish the stature (if anyone could do so) of the sublime poet and literary artist, profound thinker and religious genius who generated the 'Gospel according to St John'. The next stage in the development of that figure will, if all goes well, be treated in a subsequent book.

The second point which may strike strangely touches the meaning and purpose of the 'rejection' of Jesus by 'the Jews'. The mystery of this matter devastates Nicodemus, as it later devastated St Paul. 'What shall we say, then? Is there injustice on God's part?' asks St Paul, and answers 'By no means'. He then explains why. His answer (Romans 9–11) may or may not be found convincing by the interested parties, but of the agonising nature of the question there can be no doubt. Nicodemus cannot improve on Paul, but at least he faces a question which it is easy, sometimes, to forget.

ACKNOWLEDGMENTS

The author's debts are innumerable and profound: how much so would be obvious if the pages were littered with footnotes more appropriate to a work of scholarship. Only the most notable can be mentioned here.

On the Judaic contemporary scene: especially G. F. Moore's *Judaism in the First Centuries of the Christian Era*; Emil Schürer's *The Jewish People in the Time of Jesus Christ*; works by A. Edersheim (for their erudition, not their judgment), *Life and Times of Jesus the Messiah*, and *The Temple; its Ministry and Services*; and J. Jeremias, *Jerusalem in the Time of Jesus*. Of works by Jews, first two of a luminous charity, by I. Abrahams, *Studies in Pharisaism and the Gospels*, and C. G. Montefiore, *Rabbinic Literature and Gospel Teachings*; also J. Klausner, *Jesus of Nazareth*; S. Zucrow, *Adjustment of Law to Life in Rabbinic Literature*; A. Cohen, *Everyman's Talmud*; and the *Jewish Encyclopaedia*.

On the interpretation of the Gospels: an inexpressible debt is owed to C. H. Dodd for two of his works among many others, *Interpretation of the Fourth Gospel*, and *Historical Tradition in the Fourth Gospel*; the *Anchor Bible Vol.* 29, text and commentary on St John's Gospel (I-XII), by Father Raymond E. Brown SS; O. Cullmann, *Christology of the New Testament*; Xavier Léon-Dufour SJ, *The Gospels and the Jesus of History* (tr. Father John McHugh); Dom Gregory Dix, *Jew and Greek*; J. Jeremias, *Unknown Sayings of Jesus*; Aileen Guilding, *The Fourth Gospel and Jewish Worship*; the *New Catholic Encyclopaedia*; and the *Jerome Biblical Commentary*.

On the Roman scene: above all, L. Friedländer, *Roman Life and Manners under the Early Empire*; M. Rostovtzeff, *Social and Economic History of the Roman Empire*; Jerome Carcopino, *Rome, its People, Life and Customs*; A. N. Sherwin-White, *Roman Society and Roman Law in the New Testament*.

On the topography of Jerusalem; especially charts in the *Palestine Exploration Quarterly*, July-Dec. 1966.

Without such aids as these, the vast mass of the primary sources would be indigestible, to say the least. The most important of these sources, obviously, are the *Old Testament* and *New Testament*, the *Mishnah* (tr. H. Danby), and the *Talmud* (the 'Babylonian', Soncino Press, 34 volumes with a superlative index). Some apocryphal writings of Old and inter-Testamental times are of use. *Josephus* is essential, sometimes the only source. Among Roman authors, the writings of the elder *Pliny* have been widely exploited. *Strabo* supplies a little. The works of *Philo* provide much material directly, and indirectly a good deal else.

*

The author would also like to record his gratitude to Marjorie Villiers and the late Manya Harari, who have supplied valued advice and encouragement for this and earlier books.